Alternate Take

Time Travel goes public.

by Hallie Baur

For those who miss a time they've never experienced.

Contents

Chapter I

Only minutes stood between Ellie Hayes and the news that would change her family's life. Rain was pounding against the side of the house. Ellie could no longer ignore the increasing volume of the storm outside.

"Jon!" Ellie shouted, "Will you help me close the windows? It's really starting to pour!"

Ellie heard the shower turn on. She rolled her eyes and closed the windows herself. Afterwards, she nestled back into her place on the sofa, pulled up a blanket to her chin, and flipped through channels.

Jon completed his shower and Ellie heard him beginning his nightly ritual.

"Are you going to be much longer?" Jon hollered from the bathroom.

Ellie swirled the wine in her glass.

"Go on to bed without me," she answered. "I'll be quiet when I come in."

"Alright," Jon said.

Over the last few years, Ellie had moved her bedtime later and later. She knew that when her head hit the pillow, her thoughts would race. She spent her days craving sleep, but her schedule didn't even allow a twenty-minute nap.

Ellie heard the buzz of Jon's toothbrush. She continued to click through the stations when a headline gripped her.

'Time Travel: Open to the Public.'

Ellie watched as bystanders on the TV cheered when the Time Traveler, who looked like a California surfer, emerged from his coffin-like shell. The Traveler went on to describe the vessel which kept him safe through his journey back in time.

"The Shell, it works man, look," he said, "not a scratch on me."

Ellie's mouth dropped open.

"They did it."

Jon finished brushing his teeth and wiped his mouth with a hand towel. His lips burned, still chapped from the long winter. Jon curled his fingers around the edge of the mirror and swung open the cabinet to retrieve lip balm. As he pressed on the salve, his reflection, replicated by the angled mirror, multiplied the wrinkles on his forehead. Jon sighed and reached back into the cabinet for his pill-bottle but as he fumbled for the prescription, he knocked one of Ellie's makeup compacts into the sink.

"Damnit!"

Jon scrambled to place the bits of powder back into their tins. Rather than erasing the mess, he streaked pigment across the recently cleaned sinks. Defeated, he stepped away and dropped his shoulders.

"Jon, it happened!" Ellie appeared from around the corner. She shook her head at the growing mess, then continued. "They Time Traveled! We'll worry about this later," she said. "Do we tell her now? She's in her room. I don't know if she's seen the news or not."

Jon hesitated, then nodded, "We might as well jump in right away. Before we go downstairs, remember, it's her future. She'll close off if we object."

They started toward their daughter's room in the basement. Ellie knocked and paused for a response. Seconds passed, then Ellie turned the knob. Mia's creaky bedroom door stuck, and Ellie shoved it open with her shoulder. Her entrance rippled the band posters on Mia's walls. Mia was startled by the unexpected motion and pulled the music from her ears.

"What's wrong?" Mia asked.

"Nothing this time," Ellie said, attempting to keep her cool. "Everyone's fine. There's… news."

Mia leapt from her bed. "It happened, didn't it?"

"Come, see for yourself," Jon said.

The three of them hurried to the living room. Ellie watched Mia read the headline. Jon's eyes widened as, for the first time, he saw the news for himself. A charged silence fell over the Hayes family.

Ellie's phone rang.

"It's Derek," Ellie said and answered the call.

"I'm coming home," Derek, her son, stated. "We've got to celebrate!"

Jon read Ellie's pained expression as she ended the call. Ellie had been increasingly on edge since the whispers of Time Travel started. Now that Travel was officially open to the public, Jon braced himself for the loss of their children to another era.

Mia was weeks away from her high school graduation. She brimmed with endearing innocence and had a wide, contagious smile which had gotten her both into and out of trouble. Mia beamed at the television screen as, for the first time in years, the news was good. Rather than provocation of debate and polarity, the world embraced the idea of Time Travel. The camera's shot widened, and the anchor was joined by a handsome, charismatic man.

"This isn't just for the wealthy," the handsome man stated.

"How can that be, Adrian? I can only imagine the fortune required to access this technology," the interviewer said, "and let's be honest, when the resource rations started, they said *those* would be fair to everyone too. What makes Travel different?"

Adrian Glass, a young, good-looking executive from the Time Regulatory Network, or TRN as it was abbreviated, smirked.

"Well, you see, the rate of exchange from now to then is a built-in safety net for those with limited means. Travel back twenty, thirty years and money goes much further than it does today. The process of getting to the past is also quite reasonable. The scientists who developed Travel…"

A knock at the door stole the Hayes' attention from the interview. Derek stepped inside the entryway. His dripping raincoat formed a puddle beneath him. He removed his hood and the family bore witness to one of Derek's rare, good moods. Derek soaked his family with embraces, but they didn't care; his overdue happiness was worth it.

"I smell the good stuff on your breath," Jon teased.

"Let's keep it going," Derek said. "Tonight has been a roller coaster."

"Do you want to talk about it?" Jon asked.

Derek shook his head no, "Not right now."

Jon stepped away and poured a glass of whisky for his son. He came back into the living room and the four of them settled in to watch the developing story. As the news continued, it remained untainted with discord.

"I've read some very positive articles on Time Travel," Derek said, hoping to diffuse the tension in the room. "It isn't fueled by fear. There's not the same reactive force which births most new

10

technology. It's not like one country came up with it because they were scared they'd be the last to advance."

"It's true," Mia stated.

Adrian Glass continued his onscreen promotion of Time Travel.

"Time Travel is a welcome option for those carrying on a lackluster existence in our society. Those who want to see the world in a different state yet maintain the progressive moral standards of our current era."

Ellie caught a glance between Derek and Mia. Seeing her children's barely-contained enthusiasm was all it took to know her time with them was running out.

Time Travel's potential was originally tapped as a long-awaited solution to a complex problem: depleted resources. The once green and blue Earth had been muddled into shades of brown and grey by the human hand. For decades, world leaders swept the problem under the rug while the complications built beyond their control.

Derek and Mia were members of the first generation to witness the inevitable crumble. The four seasons, which Jon and Ellie had described from their own childhoods, never materialized for Derek and Mia. They'd experienced very few snowy Christmases. April showers were scarce as the drought persisted. The events leading to the current society's state were challenging to reverse and people grew cynical as food and energy sources were strictly rationed.

Time Travel was launched privately, at first. Only the Time Regulatory Network and their daring test subjects were privy to the technology's potential. After a few months without a trial Traveler's death or disappearance, eccentric billionaires' attention was piqued, including Adrian Glass who bought his position as one of TRN's lead executives. The project was declassified, and word got out.

The government went all-in on accelerating Time Travel's development. Finally, their solution for redistributing the earth's population had arrived.

When Ellie watched the children's response to the news, her thoughts drifted back to her own life at their age. Ellie longed to return to her carefree college days; punk music blaring throughout house parties, the strip-version of every game, and the unapologetic wildness.

Then, she thought back to the dedication of time and monetary debt she accumulated in college. Though the memories were priceless, Ellie wasn't convinced that her education had been worth the investment. Ellie's generation hardly got to utilize their degrees. Though she daydreamed of going back to those days for the non-academic aspects, her time as an adolescent had expired.

'What was it all for?'

Her son had completed the college process and her daughter was about to start down the same path. While she struggled with the notion of her children departing for another era, she understood their desire to throw caution to the wind. The past year had shown the Hayes life's fragility.

"The ability to Time Travel presents us with an unanticipated new element to the human experience," Adrian Glass said. "The new technology will bring Travelers *into* history. It's like laying the needle on whatever track they want to hear versus spending their lives attempting to dance to a tune they despise."

"So, is Time Travel really open to the *entire* public? Not *everyone* is qualified for this type of journey, are they?" The interviewer asked. "Astronauts train for years to leave Earth. There's got to be some kind of psychological preparation to go to another era, right?"

Adrian Glass grinned.

"We have solutions to remedy our mental hurdles, but I can't elaborate on those at the moment. We have specialists to discuss those matters. Most communities have begun to prepare TRN hubs and, starting tonight, we are opening the books for Travel consultations. Though the volume of Travelers will be high to start, it will taper off once we get everyone where they want to go."

Ellie's mind whirred and she became restless. She walked to the window and saw the rain subsiding. Ellie selected a hoodie from the coat rack, opened the patio door, and stepped outside. The smell of wet earth flooded her nostrils. She walked onto the wooden deck with bare feet. A shiver of anticipation ran up her spine. Jon trailed her.

"You okay?" He asked.

He noticed Ellie shove her phone in her pocket.

"I'm fine," she said.

Ellie rested her forehead in her hands. Jon held Ellie in his arms, and, to his surprise, she leaned in. They watched through the window as their children exchanged unknown words about an uncharted frontier.

"Where would the two of you go?"

Jon and Ellie paused to consider Mia's question.

"We'd go back and pay more attention," Ellie answered, "though I don't know that we could change the outcome. Adrian Glass has yet to answer that question."

"I don't think that's what Mia was asking, dear," Jon said. "We can't afford to leave the business right now, but since I was young, I've fantasized about living in the past. Living through those times in history, that served as, I don't know," Jon shrugged, "a creative plethora. Explosive times, collision of the minds. I'd love to be alive at the same time as every foundational mover and shaker. The times when we still had a chance against the man."

"Once my generation gets out there," Mia began, "we'll stick it to the man."

The rest of them laughed, but Ellie zoned out.

"Stay present," Ellie could hear her therapist instruct, but Ellie couldn't help but wonder the direction her family's life would take.

Eventually, the drinks and magnitude of the day's news began to catch up with Jon and Ellie. They kissed their children goodnight and went to bed. Jon fell asleep, but Ellie lay awake on her phone. Laughter and excitement floated into their window from the patio. For the first time in their lives, Derek and Mia planned for the past rather than their future.

"It's open! The scheduling portal is open!" Derek said.

"Let's get those consultations booked!" Mia navigated the website.

After waiting in the queue for two hours, Derek and Mia were on TRN's schedule.

"God, I can't wait to get out of here," Derek stated. "But you, are you sure you want to do this? I thought you had college

14

nailed down this fall. Though, I read that they're allowing some fluidity with education."

"I'll ask their advice at my consultation. I get the feeling I'd better jump on Travel while I can. To be honest, I don't believe that Travel will remain open to *everyone* forever. You saw how things went with the rations. The elite threw their money at the rationing department to get an extra supply of food for their yacht or a boost of energy for their awards show. I'm hoping Adrian's different, but I'm not going to count on it. Plus, I'm just not sure I want to repeat the same life cycle as everyone else in this era," Mia said.

"How the norm played out for me must not have been very encouraging," Derek said, dreading the twenty-minute drive back to his empty bachelor pad, "but everything's about to change."

Mia lay awake, absently staring at her ceiling.

Every shred of certainty surrounding Mia's next step in life unraveled the moment she saw the headline. Earlier that night, as she watched the screen, she felt an enormous shift taking place. The world was about to separate and disperse through history.

Mia had a plan set in stone. She'd begin college in the fall. Mia would live in the dorms with a randomly assigned roommate. She was about to wade into the tributary of life's current. But no one had expected the reality of Time Travel to come so soon, or ever. Mia could still picture the crawler at the foot of the television screen.

'Time Travel: Open to the Public.'

She had taken a mental photo of her surroundings as she listened to the anchor; the rain, trickling down the window, the living room décor, the look on her parent's faces, aware they were about to suffer more loss, though this time, not through

15

death, but by their loved ones' free will. Mia's thoughts turned to the loss of her brother, Derek's twin. As she often did at night or during times of quiet, Mia wondered what her day would have been like if Cooper was still alive.

"Can we look at your old scrapbooks today?" Mia asked Ellie the morning after the news broke.

Ellie's inkling of Mia's intent to Travel was further validated, but she fulfilled Mia's request and pulled a bulky album from the top of the storage closet. In the photos, Ellie's hair was cut into a short, blunt bob, a version of which she still wore. Mia smiled at the tiny, butterfly hair clips used to fasten her mother's dark tendrils. Mia continued to turn the pages, touched by her mother's naivety.

"You should have saved your outfits," Mia said. "These looks are back."

"Why does it matter? You won't be here much longer anyway," Ellie quipped.

"You don't know that," Mia replied.

Jon kissed the top of both of their heads before leaving for work. Mia smiled but Ellie was expressionless.

"I'll be there in a couple of hours," Ellie said to Jon.

What started as a quick trip down memory lane bled into early afternoon. They looked through countless albums. The pages were decorated with Jon and Ellie's early dating years and Mia's grandparents' record store. None of the pictures on Mia's phone came close to administering the same emotional dosage as her mother's albums.

Ellie placed a step stool in front of the closet and put away one of their completed albums. She spotted one of her own parent's photo albums and grasped the binding. Ellie sat the keepsake on the kitchen table.

They cracked open the dusty album and their hearts warmed at the precious moments captured inside. Ellie knew many more heirlooms sat at her parent's vacant house, waiting to be sorted through. Though months had passed since their death, Ellie was not yet ready to begin the process of cleaning out Les and Valerie's home.

Mia and Ellie gazed at the photos of their family in its entirety. Mia, her brothers, parents, and grandparents. In one photo, Mia peered from the page with round eyes as she sat atop her grandpa Les' lap while he played guitar. Mia ran her finger along the glossy photo-sleeve. The same guitar which was frozen in the photo still stood in the corner of Mia's room. She longed to go back in time and play one last tune with her grandfather.

Despite Mia's introverted first impression, she loved to perform. The stage turned her into a different person, and she sang, played guitar, and behind closed doors, wrote songs. Mia and her friends formed a band early on in high school.

They played together for a couple of years, but Mia's initial excitement for the group waned with their desire to exclusively cover Top 20 popular hits. Mia's bandmates instructed her to loop a guitar riff and work the crowd. She resigned from the group and was replaced by another guitarist who had no problem fading into the background.

As she got older, Mia became fascinated by cultural figures of the past and their lack of inhibitions. Distracted by the lore of years gone by, Mia found it hard to be interested in the current, fast-paced pop culture. Mia feared that her time to create was dwindling with college on the horizon. She dreaded the impending trade of her creativity for the decent living and conformity demanded by adulthood.

After she and her mother put the albums away, Mia went to her room. She scanned her band posters. The legends seem to lure her away from the current era's compromises.

Mia was surprised as she pulled up to the TRN hub. Dense ivy climbed the structure's brick corners. The building was historic. Mia recalled reading that it was an old masonic temple. She stepped out of her car and made her way toward the entrance. Birds sang as she walked, and the ground's vivid green hurt her eyes.

She passed a quaint, bubbling koi pond on her way to the front door. The fleeting aroma of lilacs hung in the air. The institution was so beautiful that Mia questioned whether she was at the correct location.

A plaque on the entry-way door read, '*Time Regulatory Network-North Wing,*' quelling her doubt.

The appointment with TRN was a prerequisite to Time Travel, and Mia hoped to pass their test. Since the news broke, several TRN hubs popped up across the region, and Mia was thrilled that the hub closest to her had openings to Travel before her college registration. Mia paused before entering and scanned the majestic building. She had foreseen a no-frills institution. Something sterile, industrial. Mia took a deep breath, pushed open the door, and stepped inside.

Mia walked through the entryway to the lobby. Her footsteps rang across the marble floor. She approached the front desk and a woman with a squeaky-clean smile and perfect berry lips greeted Mia.

"Hi there, can I see your ID?" The receptionist asked.

Mia pulled out her wallet.

Before departing for the TRN facility that morning, Mia had double-checked that she had every required document with her. She slipped her ID from its pocket and handed it to the woman.

"Mia Hayes," the woman read Mia's name off the card. "You must be turned around. Travelers are supposed to enter through the South Wing."

"Sorry," Mia looked at the confirmation message again.

'Please enter through the South Wing. The North Wing is considered a secure area and you will not be allowed to pass through.'

"No need to apologize, we'll take the tunnel to the South Wing."

The receptionist guided Mia to the mouth of a corridor which hugged the perimeter of the building. The walkway reminded Mia of a secret passage, but it wasn't dark or ominous. Instead, the passage was lined with leafy plants and elegant up-lighting.

"This place really isn't what I expected," Mia said.

The woman looked back from her lead.

"We get that a lot," she giggled.

The passage opened to the South Wing's lobby. Mia gawked as they passed a salon. She was in awe of the finger waves, afros, and slick ponytails being sculpted behind the glass. They went down another hallway and the receptionist paused in front of a door that read *Consultation Suite 2.*

The receptionist lightly knocked.

Silence.

She opened the door anyway.

"Right this way," the receptionist directed Mia into the suite. "You can take a seat. They'll be in shortly. Just a reminder, when you leave, please exit from this wing."

"Thanks," Mia responded, and the woman began to close the door.

Mia melted into a smooth leather chair. An expensive smelling candle burned on the desk across from her. As the door closed, Mia came to her senses and realized that she didn't know who would be joining.

"Wait, who will be in soon?" Mia asked, but it was too late. She heard heels clicking away, echoing the woman's footsteps as she returned to her post.

Though the facility's ambiance was a welcome surprise, Mia had no idea what to expect next. She hoped that whoever arrived was as pleasant as the support staff. Minutes passed and her nerves were settled by the crackle of a fireplace in the corner of the room.

The door opened.

A tall woman with short, black hair entered the room first. She was followed by a slightly hunched man in a plaid shirt. He caught Mia's gaze and nodded to greet her. His eyes seemed to hold the emotion of the world. A weathered woman trailed in to complete the trio.

They took their seats. During her adoration of the facility, Mia hadn't noticed the three luxe chairs, identical to her own, forming a semi-circle around her. The kind-eyed man spoke first.

"Welcome Mia," he introduced himself. "I'm Dr. Lowell. I'll be walking you through the psychological piece of Travel. I'm here to help you fully adjust to your destination."

"I'll be walking you through the paperwork of your Travel process," the weathered woman said. She winked, "I'm Francis Platt," she extended her hand for Mia to shake. "You and I will be going through the legalities, you know, the fun stuff," Francis chuckled.

The TRN staff seated before Mia were speaking as if she was already committed to the journey.

"I'm not sure I want to go yet--" Mia began but was interrupted.

"Dr. Chandra," the dark-haired woman introduced herself. Her precise gaze met Mia's. "Physics is my field of expertise."

"Nice to meet you all," Mia offered.

Francis replied with a gravelly voice, "You too, honey."

"We reviewed your online application, and you checked all the right boxes. You absolutely qualify to Travel," Dr. Lowell told Mia. "There are just a few more things we need to learn about you."

"I'm not sure what else there is to know," Mia said. "The questionnaire was longer than my college application."

Mia recalled the relief she felt upon reaching the last page. The document had required her to include every shred of demographic information, past physician's notes, family medical history, and complete an assessment detailing her current living dynamics.

"I approach this with compassion for you and your family," Dr. Lowell started, "but we must consider the aftermath of your brother's accident. We have something to help you overcome the residual pain his death must have caused you," Dr. Lowell said. "And we can tailor this experience to suit your needs. I believe, on the news, Adrian Glass mentioned that we have something to soothe Traveler's fear of the unknown."

"He did, yes," Mia stated.

Mia's attention turned to Francis. Francis snickered at Dr. Lowell and his gentle expression turned sharp at Francis' distracting response. Francis ignored his annoyance and busied herself by flipping through a large binder.

Dr. Lowell continued.

"I'm going to ask you a few more questions, just to be sure you have the best journey possible," he said and referred to his notes.

Mia peeked at his tablet and saw the words underlined.

'Family Medical History'

When filling out the assessment, Mia's scribbling had come to a halt upon seeing that heading. Cooper's death was the ultimate, unexpected blow to the Hayes family. Mia wasn't sure Derek would ever recover from finding his deceased twin on the floor that night.

Cooper's road to demise began with minuscule changes in behavior; ignoring phone calls, sleeping for long periods of time, but he was a young adult figuring out his place in the world. Establishing a post-college life was a hump most of his generation had struggled to surpass, so the Hayes didn't think much of Cooper's gloomy spells.

When he was around others, Cooper remained the life of the party. He made the Hayes laugh like no one else could. Cooper created an outward illusion of lightheartedness, however when he was alone, he was suffocated by the heaviness of his existence.

"Your life doesn't have to be defined by your job," Derek told his struggling twin.

"Easy for you to say," Cooper would respond. "You're shaping the modern world. What am I doing?"

"I know discussing that trauma is *very* hard," Dr. Lowell said, pulling Mia back to her consultation, "and I don't intend on counseling you. The good news is, mental illness, or in your case, family history of such disease, isn't a red flag for Time Travel. We just have to get an understanding of the ways in which you may react to the Adjustment period when you arrive at your destination."

Dr. Lowell placed a handout in front of Mia.

'*Travel Processing,*' was written at the top of the page.

"I want to introduce you to the chronology of Time Travel," Dr. Lowell stated. "There are three general phases. I know you'll have many questions, but I would like to start with a broad orientation before we get to the details," he locked eyes with Mia. "The details cause Travelers to fret more than necessary."

Mia nodded. The reality surrounding the newness of Time Travel began to set in and she couldn't decipher if the feeling in her stomach was excitement or nerves.

"Phase one," Dr. Lowell began, "Journey in the Shell," Mia followed along on her handout. "More on that later. Dr. Chandra will explain that phase in more depth than my expertise allows. Phase two," he said before Mia could spill her questions, "Acclimation. You will have someone waiting for you at your destination. Your acclimator. They'll accompany you for a time frame ranging from a few hours to a few weeks. Your acclimator is a trusted TRN employee whose sole purpose is to introduce you to your new time and ensure your initial safety."

Mia's nerves began to diminish with Dr. Lowell's confidence.

"Phase three, you're *there*. Allow me to hand the reins to Dr. Chandra," Dr. Lowell gestured to his colleague.

"Yes," Dr. Chandra said, "as previously stated, I oversee the physical science of Time Travel."

"How does this *work?*" Mia asked, leaning in to absorb Dr. Chandra's genius.

Dr. Chandra sighed. The condensed version of quantum physics rarely satisfied Time Travelers.

"Well, that's a complicated question. Your phone works and your car radio works," Dr. Chandra said. "Think of Time Travel in the same way. It was once a theory, just like many other aspects of modern technology. Now, after much review, the theory of Time Travel has been proven. We have derived our conclusions. Now, we're observing our successful method."

"I *do* know that phones involve satellites, radios involve towers, and so on," Mia probed for more information. "What about Time Travel? Does it involve black holes?"

Mia's curiosity cracked Dr. Chandra's tough façade.

"Space and time both exist, right?" Dr. Chandra asked rhetorically. "The landscape of Time Travel is 'space-time.' And as for black holes," she shrugged, "there's still a lot to learn."

The physicist stood. She made her way toward a shelf and pulled a diagram from its place. Dr. Chandra referred to a visual model which depicted two surfaces and connected by an hourglass-shaped vortex.

"A wormhole," Mia said. "I saw something like it in physics."

"Ah, so you know more than some of our other Travelers," Dr. Chandra stated, hoping the validation would spare her from another lengthy attempt to explain the technology.

"My teacher wouldn't go there. He said it would be more useful to focus on *real* principles," Mia said.

Dr. Chandra further softened, empathizing with Mia over her dismissive educator.

"We've found a way to manipulate the linear landscape. We removed the limitations of our 'beginning to end' timeline which we've occupied for all of history," Dr. Chandra explained.

Though Mia's questioning began as an attempt to comprehend the intricate journey on which she was about to embark, the explanation of the science made Mia more apprehensive. As Dr. Chandra went on, Mia wondered if Travel was even real. Mia couldn't help but suspect a ruse in TRN's over-manicured facility as experts sat before her. She wondered if Travel was an elaborate conspiracy or psychological experiment. Mia became fearful of falling into a trap from which she couldn't escape.

"We will get you from here to there," Mia tuned back into Dr. Chandra's words, "and that all begins with creating your Shell," she explained. "Because you've 'checked all the boxes' as Dr. Lowell stated, we can schedule a time to create your body's Travel mold. Your Shell will act as your vessel."

"My Shell?" Mia bristled.

"Yes," Dr. Chandra clarified, "it will serve as armor for this journey. Have you not seen the vessel's unveiling on the news?"

Mia shook her head no and wondered how she'd missed that bit of information about Time Travel. Dr. Chandra paused to let Mia process. During consultations, the notion of the Shell was often the point when fear entered the conversation.

The physicist continued.

"In order to transport you safely, we must enclose you in a very durable piece of material. Because of the required speed, extreme temperature, the frequency of the lasers—"

"Let's pause there," Dr. Lowell interjected. "Mia, I see your expression has changed."

Mia had forgotten he was in the room.

"I understand it sounds frightening," Dr. Lowell took out his tablet and swiped through Mia's Travel application. "I see on your *Fear Exploration* page that you are a bit claustrophobic. You are very safe in this Shell that Dr. Chandra is talking about."

"Safer than you can imagine," Dr. Chandra confirmed. "The material we selected to construct the Shell is fortified with a new element," the excitement in her voice was audible.

Dr. Lowell went on. "Not only are you safe, but you won't be scared."

"How is that possible?" Mia asked.

"Psilopram," Dr. Lowell said with a smile.

He spoke the unfamiliar word with the same enthusiasm as Dr. Chandra displayed for quantum physics.

"*Sil-o-pram?*" Mia repeated the foreign term.

She was no stranger to the suffix; a drug ending in 'pram' had taken her brother's life. Dr. Lowell pursed his lips. Dr. Chandra and Mrs. Platt shot him warning gazes.

"I don't usually share this with Travelers, but with your brother's situation, I feel it's appropriate," Dr. Lowell stated. "I started in trauma therapy. I heard ugly things," he paused with a faraway expression, "things that haunted me when I went home at night. Worse yet, I had to record the things my patients endured and review the horrors every time they returned to my practice. Over time, it became too much. I did something a doctor should never do," Dr. Lowell wrung his hands.

"Dr. Lowell," Francis attempted to interrupt.

"No, I want to tell her. I've made peace with my past," Dr. Lowell retorted. "I used my own medicine to dull the pain. Soon, I was hooked. I thought I had found the perfect solution. By numbing myself, I could still help my patients. But then, the board found out. My license was nearly revoked. I had a decision to make. It was a challenge only an addict could understand."

"I'm sorry you went through that," Mia offered, unsure how to respond.

"It's okay," Dr. Lowell said. "It led to *this*. It led to Psilopram. I had a colleague, an eccentric, holistic doctor. He diverted me from my opiate addiction with hallucinogens."

"What?" Mia asked. She pictured two, middle aged doctors tripping out and held back a laugh.

"I think that's more than Mia needs to know, Dr. Lowell," Dr. Chandra said.

Dr. Lowell shot her a defiant look.

"I disagree," he replied. "If I didn't trust the medication, how could Travelers trust it? How could she?" He gestured to Mia. "God knows the drug companies haven't exuded a consistently trustworthy image."

Mia nodded.

"For your journey in the Shell, for everyone's Travel through time, myself and my colleague's team created Psilopram. It's going to sedate you. It will move you *through* your fears so when you come out on the other side, the human capability of Time Travel will no longer perplex you," Dr. Lowell said. "We've even started using it on astronauts. It's the secret behind the last five years' refined understanding of Earth's solar system."

"Incredible," Mia responded. "But is the journey rough? Moving through fears and everything?"

"Frankly, yes," Dr. Lowell admitted. "But you'll be in a near anesthetic state. You will remember very little of the journey endured by your mind and body. Though, once you get there, we strongly discourage the use of synthetic drugs." He and Dr. Chandra exchanged a glance. "Unnatural compounds can... stir up old fears depending on the societal state of your chosen era."

"Why don't you use Psilopram on people here in this era? It sounds like you could knock out the drugs that... hook people," Mia said.

"Adrian Glass has bought the patent. He limited the drug to be indicated exclusively for Time Travelers. He wants to incentivize going to the past for, well," Dr. Lowell hesitated, "obvious reasons if you look around at the world."

Mia shook her head.

"There is so much to take in," she said. "How bad have things gotten for us to get here? So much has been created. All the experiments, the risks, is it really worth it?"

"That's for you to decide. And don't let Dr. Lowell's doom and gloom attitude about the world make you think things haven't always been this way," Francis said. "We've always been on 'the brink of the end.' Yes, things have gotten a bit dire now, but, in a way, it's what drives us forward."

"As we spoke about earlier, we will coordinate a TRN acclimator to care for you upon your arrival. Remember, the term 'acclimator' is the title given to your temporary live-in nurse. They will give you the care needed for your mental and physical recovery," Dr. Lowell said.

"I'm impressed," Mia stated. "It seems there is no stone left unturned."

The trio of experts exchanged a look of satisfaction.

"That's where I come in," Francis began. "I'll make sure *every* detail is covered. I know you'll have more questions for these geniuses," Francis gestured to Dr. Chandra and Dr. Lowell, "but it's their time to scoot. You'll have the opportunity to speak with their assistants before your departure to the past."

"Wait, I'm not going today, am I?" Mia panicked.

"Of course not, you'll have two weeks to decide. In the meantime, think of more questions and write them down," Francis instructed.

"Wonderful to meet you, Mia. Enjoy your time," Dr. Lowell said and shook her hand.

He stood and exited the Consultation Suite.

"You can trust the technology dear," Dr. Chandra assured. "I've Traveled myself, and look at me," she shrugged, "still in one piece."

Dr. Chandra left and Mia sat alone with Francis.

"These documents we're about to go through are tedious, but important," Francis said. "I'm here as your advocate. The next few hours might be a little boring, but we must ensure that you understand the parameters surrounding Travel. TRN has created non-negotiable requirements by which Travelers must abide," Francis paused, "There are certain legal agreements you must adhere to."

Francis laid out the three main Travel agreements as specified by TRN and Mia read along on a consent form.

1. *Do not reveal your origins to your destination's natives.*
2. *Avoid world-renowned fame.*
3. *Do not kill or intentionally injure another human.*

"Inability to follow any of these agreements will result in instant retrieval from your destination and it won't be pretty," Francis stated. "No Psilopram, and immediate trial upon your return to OT."

Mia's blood ran cold. Though she was naïve to Psilopram, she couldn't imagine the Shell without the drug.

"What if any of those things happen by accident?" Mia asked. "And what's OT?"

"OT is what we call our current era. It's short for Original Time. And frankly dear," Francis started, "there are too many people Traveling for TRN to nitpick. If you tell people from the past that you're from the future, they'll probably just think you're crazy. Just don't do something that makes them believe it. Don't do anything stupid, nothing that could go down in the history books, and you'll be fine."

Mia's TRN consultation continued for another two hours. They went on to discuss the agreements by scenario. Mia's concerns began to ease when she saw the leniency built into the guidelines. As Mia's appointment ended, Francis shifted the direction of their conversation.

"Now, I know I've bored you for hours on this beautiful day," Francis pulled a pamphlet from her binder, "however I do have some fun information for you."

She handed the pamphlet to Mia.

'TRN Styling Sessions,' the cover read.

Mia grinned.

"The South Wing Salon receptionist can get you set up. Our TRN stylists have repeatedly Traveled to their specialty time and will really teach you how to look the part," Francis explained. "I'd ask for Rae; she'll take special care of you."

Their session concluded and Mia walked to the salon. She peered in the window and noticed a stylist, seated in her own chair, waiting for a client.

"I was told to ask for Rae," Mia told the salon receptionist.

"She happens to be free right now," the receptionist said, "you're lucky."

Mia spent just fifteen minutes seated in Rae's chair and emerged from the salon with a playful updo.

"This is nothing," Rae said before Mia left. "I've got so much more I can teach you. Book a longer session sometime before you Travel."

Before Mia left the TRN hub, she was reminded that she had two weeks to confirm if she would indeed take the journey. If the window lapsed, another application and consultation were required.

"The volume is high right now," the South Wing receptionist advised. "Let them know your decision as soon as possible."

Mia drove home in silence and returned to an empty house. She was relieved for the time alone. Mia thought of her parents. *'They're always at work, they won't miss me anyway.'*

Something Rae, the stylist, had said about changing the outcome, not just for Mia's life, but for the society of Original Time, left Mia feeling dutiful in her desire to Time Travel. Mia understood that her absence would grant resources to the current era and her decision became influenced by more than her own desire to Travel.

She heard her brother pull into the driveway. Derek parked and walked to the front door. He stepped inside with an unreadable expression.

"We've got a lot to talk about."

Jon and Ellie watched Mia exit the TRN hub. They held their breath and sunk down into their seats.

"She told me she was going to a friend's house for the afternoon," Ellie said.

Jon replied, "Ells, I know you don't want to hear this, but she's scared to bring up anything Travel-related with you."

Ellie nodded. She understood why.

31

They watched Mia get in her car, admire her hair, and drive away. Once the coast was clear, Jon and Ellie stepped outside and walked toward the TRN hub.

Ellie examined their Consultation Suite. The room was flawless, eerily posh. She heard footsteps approaching the door. Three of TRN's employees walked in. They introduced themselves as Dr. Lowell, Dr. Chandra, and Francis Platt.

"This place is lovely," Ellie said.

"A little too lovely," Jon mumbled.

Ellie shot him a surprised look. He'd played the good cop with the kids since the news broke. The trio went on to share the intricacies regarding the technology of Time Travel including a brief on physics and a surprising new medication developed by Dr. Lowell. Francis assured she would go through all of Travel's legalities in detail at the end of their session.

"As I was going through your forms, I noticed that you have suffered great loss over the last couple of years," Dr. Lowell said.

"We have," Ellie agreed. "We just saw our daughter leave this place. She and her brother will likely Time Travel, so we're trying to prepare ourselves for that loss as well."

"I'm sorry," Dr. Lowell said.

"Is there anything we can do to keep them here? As their parents, can we override this decision? Especially Mia. She's so young," Ellie pleaded.

"She's eighteen," Francis said, "she can do whatever she wants."

"We really can't discuss other Traveler's plans without their written permission," Dr. Lowell stated. "What era are the two of you considering for your destination?"

Ellie took a deep breath.

"Well, you know what happened to our son. We know it's a long shot, but we had to be certain of our options. Can we go back to change the course of events? Maybe pay more attention to him, give him some of that drug you talked about."

Dr. Lowell sighed.

"TRN cannot stand by that," he said. "I'm so sorry. Francis will go through the guidelines with you later but going back to save lives is prohibited. We know too little about the ways that may influence our current era."

Ellie's eyes brimmed with tears. Jon rested his hand on hers.

"We best be going," Jon said.

"You have no idea what this is doing to us, to the world, do you?" Ellie said.

She stood and Jon followed suit. The Hayes stepped over the threshold of the doorway when Francis stopped them.

"Come back in," Francis requested.

Ellie turned to face her, "Why? So that you can validate *why* this hasty business of Time Travel is taking away our children? So you can turn down our chance to save Cooper because it wouldn't serve the 'greater good' concept that you all pat yourself on the back for?"

"We can't discuss other Travelers' plans, but we can offer you some peace of mind. There's no harm in that. Yes, there's a fee, but I can see the pain this is causing you. As a mother myself, I want to ease your worries," Francis said.

Dr. Lowell and Dr. Chandra took Francis' cue and left the room before the situation could escalate. They'd learned that it was best to keep their hands clean and let Francis work out the kinks.

"First, you can visit the kids, with their permission that is. And second, we have a security program launched by our

33

generous TRN monitors. The monitors' job is to give certain Travelers a little extra attention. They act as a shadow and maintain constant safety. I can tell you the associated costs if you're interested."

Jon and Ellie looked at each other and took their seats.

"We're listening."

Chapter II

Mia emerged from her apartment and stepped into 1997.

The balmy evening air welcomed her outside. The day was beginning to dim, and she lifted her sunglasses. Mia breathed another sigh of relief that she made it safely.

Mia took the full two weeks allotted by TRN to make her decision. The only factor that delayed her verdict was the look in her parent's eyes when she suggested her intention to depart.

"Mom, if I don't do it now, I may never have the chance again. I could meet someone at college, get married, have kids, then I'll look back and wonder," Mia stated.

Ellie bit her lip and nodded her head. She knew her daughter's rationale was sound, but it didn't make losing Mia easier.

"It's just so new, I worry about the reliability," Ellie had said.

Jon came up behind his wife and put his arms around her. He whispered into Ellie's ear, reminding her of their agreement with TRN, and she began to soften.

"What about Derek?" Mia responded. "You both mentioned that you *knew* he'd Travel, and you didn't even put up a fight."

"I can hear you," Derek said from the other room.

'They probably want me to go.'

"It was just," Jon paused, "different back in the day. Especially for girls your age. It was different for a lot of people.

Not that it's perfect now…" he trailed off. "But we're working on trusting TRN."

"I suppose we don't have a choice," Ellie said, defeated.

Mia pictured the look on her mother's face as they secured Mia's custom Shell. Just as the latch was fastened, Mia felt her chest tighten with overwhelming anxiety; then the Psilopram kicked in. The next moment Mia could recall was the hum of fluorescent lights in the all-white room where she was transitioned into her acclimator's care.

After her journey in the Shell, Mia spent just two days adjusting to her new era. Her TRN acclimator was a sweet, elderly woman from Original Time who resided in 1997. The acclimator was a retired nurse, roused from retirement by the opportunity to go back to an era she remembered fondly.

The nurse ushered Mia into the gentle routine of acclimation. She evaluated Mia's mental state daily with a series of questions to ensure Time Travelers' cognitive stability. The acclimator also showed Mia to the nearest transport hub.

"You can make your return when you're ready. Just be aware, the volume of Travelers is going up, so make your plans plenty far out."

The acclimator also gave Mia the geographical layout of Birchmont, her new home: a college town near the Great Lakes.

Dr. Lowell suggested that Mia pose as a student in Birchmont. After Francis' call advising Mia to discuss her plans with her parents, Mia took the leap and spilled her plans to Jon and Ellie. She signed a release form which allowed her parents access to her location. She also gave TRN permission to notify Jon and Ellie if Mia's plans changed. When Jon and Ellie accompanied Mia to her final consultation, Mia watched their worries dissipate as they learned about Birchmont and TRN's system for Travelers getting an education in another era.

TRN supplied academic Time Travelers with valid identification documents for their destination. Mia had charmed her way into a nineteen-year-old ID so she could get into the college town bars.

"How will I make new friends if I can't go out?" Mia had argued.

"I'll see what I can do," Francis said with a wink.

Though they were still reluctant at best, Jon and Ellie were relieved that Mia could pursue a college education while Traveling.

"I'm surprised you're warming up to this," Mia told her parents.

Before Jon and Ellie could respond, Dr. Lowell interjected.

"We leave no stone unturned, Mia. Jon, Ellie, you should visit Mia in the nineties. We can plan a trip today. We recommend getting a visit on the books before the anticipated holiday rush," he advised.

Jon sighed and looked to Ellie for an answer.

"Let's do it," Ellie said.

"It will be good to check in on her, to see the life she's created for herself," Dr. Lowell stated. "Come to my desk, just in this next room and we can solidify the dates."

While Mia's parents stepped away, Francis outlined a four-year contract to supply Mia with the necessary paperwork to complete her education.

"Take a seat," Dr. Lowell gestured to the chairs across from his desk. "I think we've made it clear; you are to visit Mia this fall to see her new life, not to try to change certain... outcomes. Remember, only so much can be done through Travel. We will assign someone to keep an eye on her and Derek, but at any moment, our monitor can shift their focus to," he paused, "non-compliant Travelers."

Mia popped in the doorway.

"Are we all set?" She asked.

Dr. Lowell smiled and provided Jon and Ellie with pens.

"Just sign above the line and confirm your payment method. That should do it."

It was August when Mia arrived. Life flooded into Birchmont with the return of the students. Mia tried not to gawk at the era's natives, but she remembered the stylist, Rae's, recommendation.

"If you're not sure you fit in, look around," Rae had said.

Mia smiled as she looked down at the slip dress selected by Rae. The garment was identical to a dress Mia had seen in an old picture of her mother. A late-summer breeze ruffled the hemline. Mia took a deep breath.

She recalled Dr. Lowell's assurance that Psilopram would remove her underlying fears. Though Mia recalled nothing from the Shell, she was certain she'd experienced an ongoing shift in perspective. Mia was oddly comfortable with the strangeness of being in the past. She was no longer plagued with remorse for leaving her parents. The petty things she fussed over in Original Time felt as far away as they were.

Music wafted out of a bar across the street. A neon sign titled the establishment from where it played, '*the Loop*.' Mia made her way to the crosswalk.

A sector of TRN known as the Accurate Generational Etiquette team, or AGE, oversaw technology standards for Travelers. They only allowed those going to the late nineties a beeper and landline. No cell phone, no social media, no GPS. It was a completely new concept for Mia. Despite the challenge, she was interested to see what life was like without the technology to which she had grown accustomed.

Before Mia Traveled, her parents offered a rundown on life without modern conveniences.

"When you meet up with people, you have to stick to a place and time," Ellie had said.

"If you're going somewhere new, you must know your directions; north, south, east, west. You need to write instructions down with a pen and paper. You won't have your mobile notes," Jon advised.

Their warnings were stern but held an heir of nostalgia.

Mia walked into the Loop and scoped out the scene.

High-top tables were surrounded by vinyl barstools. Multi-colored lights twinkled above the bar. A beer-stained pool table stood in the back. The joint resembled bars Mia had observed in divey, time capsule bars of Original Time.

Something was missing, some oppressive force Mia was used to had vanished. Then it struck her; there were no phones. Everyone was present. The option *not* to be present didn't exist.

Though she was excited to be in public and out of acclimation, Mia was mildly intimidated to be on her own. The lack of society's blue light distraction didn't allow Mia to pass through unnoticed. Mia wanted to reach out but was uncertain how to begin.

'*Do I just walk up and introduce myself?*'

She gazed around the bar in search of a friendly face. A blonde girl wearing a bucket hat caught Mia's eye. They exchanged a smile. Though the blonde girl's face was shaded by her hat, Mia couldn't help but notice the stranger's beauty. She accidentally stared too long, and the blonde turned away.

Mia reached into her pocket and felt for her phone. She realized how much of a crutch the device had been. Mia scanned the room for an open table where she could collect her thoughts, then, Mia felt a tap on her shoulder.

"Need a light?"

Mia turned to see the blonde girl, face to face. The girl, around Mia's age, outstretched her hand. In her palm was an orange lighter.

"Ah, thanks!"

Mia caught onto the stranger's assumption that she was reaching for a cigarette, not for her phone. Any social interaction was worth engaging, but Mia didn't have anything to light. She patted the pockets of her dress in hopes that the stranger would offer a cigarette.

"All out?" The blonde asked and rustled through her purse. "No lighter or cigarettes. You are in need of help, woman!"

"Excuse Macy," a redhead with damp hair inserted herself into the conversation. The redhead placed her hand on the blonde's back. "Making new friends?" she laughed.

Macy ignored her.

The redhead gestured to Mia, "Macy, who is this?"

The blonde extended her hand to Mia, this time with no lighter. Rather than answer the redhead, the blonde introduced herself.

"Macy, how d'ya do," she mumbled with an unlit cigarette hanging from the side of her mouth.

"Mia Hayes. What's your name?" Mia asked the redhead.

"Tiffany," she replied and gave Mia a once-over.

Macy lit her cigarette and tossed the pack to Mia. Mia vaped a handful of times but had never smoked a cigarette. All forms of smoking were uncommon in Original Time, especially once people could eat their dope.

After several attempts to get the paper burning, Mia realized she was in trouble.

"I can't get it lit," Mia admitted.

"Here, you take this one," Macy said.

Macy handed her own lit cigarette to Mia, holding it between her thumb and index finger. Mia accepted and placed the damp filter between her lips.

"Now to inhale, breathe in, then breathe in a little bit more," Macy instructed.

Mia did as she was told, perhaps too well. She fought to restrain the cough building in her throat.

"Where are we going next, Mace? Do you wanna go to the Lakehouse? I guess the guys playing there tonight are *killer*," Tiffany stated. "And we've gotta make some connections. That place is crawling with people who could book us."

A male member of the group chimed in.

"If you wanna book more gigs, you need a guitarist," he said. "And Macy, you don't count. The axe gets in your way."

Mia's ears perked up. Before she could ask the guy more about their need for a guitarist, she burst into a coughing fit. The man raised an eyebrow and walked toward the back of the bar. Macy and Tiffany laughed.

"I play guitar," Mia wheezed.

Tiffany turned to face Mia, her copper waves whipping through the air. She continued to chuckle at Mia's inability to tolerate the cigarette.

"Ha," Tiffany said, "*you* play? Besides in high school jazz band?"

Mia's cough began to ease and was replaced with a pleasant nicotine buzz. Rather than take offense to Tiffany's teasing, Mia chuckled at the truth of Tiffany's assumption. Macy came to Mia's rescue.

"Hang with us tonight, girl," Macy said. "If we hit it off, who knows, maybe we can jam sometime."

Macy put her arm around Mia's shoulders and directed her to the group's table at the back of the Loop. Tiffany trailed sourly. The man who had mentioned a guitar-player, along with another friend, held a table for the girls.

"Hey guys, we're going to the Lakehouse next! This is Mia," Macy pulled Mia in for a half-embrace. "She's coming with!"

Mia looked at the second man who wore yellow-lensed glasses and had shoulder length hair. He smiled at Mia. Every one of his teeth were visible as he grinned, and his eyes crinkled. With a casual two-fingered wave, he introduced himself.

"EJ."

Next to EJ, the man who mentioned the need for a guitarist remained stoic. He went to the bar without introducing himself. Mia's heart sank as he walked away, and she was further ashamed by her coughing fit.

Mia watched the mystery man take a seat at the bar top. He struck up a conversation with someone who seemed important, then turned and acknowledged Mia with a nod. As Tiffany, Macy, and EJ spoke amongst themselves, Mia eavesdropped on the mystery man's conversation.

"We're gonna head to the Lakehouse," he said. "Guess there's a good band there tonight. I'll let you know if they're worth booking here, though this is a smaller venue. If they're as good as I heard, I don't know if they'll backtrack."

Mia furrowed her brow at the mystery man's backhanded offer.

"Maybe you could finesse them to do a short set here" the manager said. "Feel it out and let me know, will ya? It's been a while since we've had a strong act."

"I'll ask Gene if he can get me backstage to feel out their vibe. He's bartending tonight," the mystery man said. "You know, you'll owe me one if I'm onto something with them."

"A couple of drinks on the house should do it, right? Help yourself in the back tonight for your good word with the band."

He shook the manager's hand and turned back to join the group. Mia looked off in another direction and smoothed her hair.

The rest of the group closed their tabs and they all stepped outside. They began their trek along Birchmont's row of college bars in the direction of the Lakehouse. Though Mia was with strangers, she was relieved for the company.

One minute, she was in a bar, by herself, in another era, the next, she was walking to see a band with potential new friends. The mystery man pulled a cheap bottle of wine from his jacket. Mia chuckled to herself at his disregard for their public surroundings.

"From the Loop's backroom," he explained. "Gotta get our buzz on before the show."

They walked along the edge of the road and rotated the current drinker away from the view of passing traffic.

"Who are we seeing tonight?" EJ asked Tiffany.

"A band from Kansas City. They've got some blues flair with this crazy harmonica player and --"

"Ugh, a harmonica? Blues?" The mystery man interrupted. "No wonder Gene's got them playing on a Tuesday and not a weekend. Are you taking us to see a country band?"

"Excuse me," Tiffany began, "just because they have a harmonica doesn't mean they're country-western. Some of the greatest bands have a harmonica player." Tiffany shook her head, "How is it that you are considered the ear for music in this town, and you don't know that?"

"I think they sound like a great band," Mia said.

"You're not a pop fiend like this guy?" Tiffany gestured to the mystery man.

Mia shook her head no.

In Original Time, Mia tried to introduce all kinds of music to her friends, but they had no interest in anything besides what was on the radio. If it hadn't been for Les, Mia's grandfather, she knew that she would have been none-the-wiser to music played before the new millennium.

Every time Mia went to her family's record store, Les introduced her to another one of his favorites. Mia was reluctant to listen at first, but the more of Les' music that she heard, the more she acquired a taste for the sound. Eventually, she didn't put up a fight when he suggested an artist or album she'd never heard.

Les' music was divine, poetic. It was dynamic. There were real instruments, and not one piece was overproduced. Though Mia appreciated the convenience of OT's music devices, there was something anticipatory about a needle dropping on vinyl. The crackle signaled the beginning of an expedition.

Macy brought Mia back into the conversation. "So, Mia, what's your story? What kind of music do you play?" Macy asked. "Where are you from?"

Mia paused at the irony of the question.

"I moved here from Maine. And I was just in a cover band. I wanted to put together some originals, but I had different taste than the rest of the group so the music we played didn't really reflect what I liked."

"Bummer it didn't work out, Tiffany stated, "but we could use some of our own material. We'd be open if what you've got is good."

Mia changed the subject, not wanting to come off as a stickler of music.

"What's the Lakehouse like?"

"The Lakehouse is a place to hear who's up-and-coming. There aren't a lot of big names, not at first, but most of the bands who play there get big in a year or two. We hope to play there sometime," Tiffany explained.

"Excuse me?" The mystery man said. "Not a lot of big names?"

Tiffany ignored him.

"I'm glad to hear we're in good company as far as music goes. Do you like punk?" Tiffany asked.

"Yeah! Especially the loose, garage band stuff. My grandpa listened to it sometimes," Mia said.

"Hold the phone," Macy laughed, "your grandpa listens to punk?"

"Wanna hang around after the show, Mia?" The mystery man asked, commanding her attention. "I bet we can meet the band. I'm Lars by the way."

An introduction. He had more gel in his hair than Mia cared for, but Lars was handsome and smooth-talking. Mia felt her cheeks redden.

"I'd stay for a drink after the show," Mia answered.

Macy put her arm around Tiffany and two of them walked ahead. Mia hoped she hadn't said something to offend Tiffany. She held back to give the established girlfriends their space.

"How do you all know each other?" Mia asked the boys. "And what does EJ stand for?"

"Well," Lars began, "our friend Eduardo Jaquez here could barely speak English when I met him in the dorms."

"Hey! My English was fine. Your Spanish though…" EJ made a lighthearted grimace.

"Why would I learn Spanish? You people are the ones who moved to this country. You learn English."

Mia cringed at Lars' comment.

"You sound like the kids in the first American middle school I moved to," EJ remarked.

"Anyway, I passed by EJ's dorm, and he's drumming away on a three-ring binder. I talk to him and find out he's played since he was just a little kid in Mexico, so invited him to an open jam night to see what he could do. His English may have been shaky, but what he did on stage *translated*. The chicks went berserk."

EJ blushed and scratched his head.

"Macy and Tiffany approached me, and we started practicing," EJ said.

"Maybe you can help these knuckleheads out. They need a solid guitarist," Lars winked at Mia. "You must be a freshman. I would have remembered seeing you around campus last year."

"I'm technically a freshman, yes," Mia had rehearsed her backstory to perfection. "I was able to enroll as a sophomore though. I earned some credits during high school."

"Impressive," Lars responded.

Mia's cheeks grew hot.

They continued toward the Lakehouse and Mia admired the edge of the college campus. The smell of cut grass hung in the air. Birchmont's campus was freshly landscaped for the student's upcoming arrival with bright crimson and yellow blooms and trimmed hedges.

A spell of silence fell over the group as they trudged on. Mia thought back to the Loop when she reached for her phone, an instinctive action. People wanted to look busy in Original Time, like they had better things to do. Many of Mia's closest friendships involved an illusion of closeness narrated by content.

Macy, Tiffany, EJ and Lars had chosen to include Mia based on five minutes of casual bar-talk. Had her gaze been on a screen, they may have passed her by. Mia was invigorated by the connection. The guys resumed their conversation and Mia realized it had been blocks since she'd contributed, so she walked ahead to join Macy and Tiffany.

"I didn't ask, where are you from Macy and Tiffany?" Mia asked.

"Did either of you play in high school?"

"I grew up two hours south of Birchmont," Macy said.

"And she was practically born singing," Tiffany added.

Macy grinned, "When I was young, my parents took me along to karaoke night at their favorite bar. I begged for months before they finally let me go onstage with my little sister."

Tiffany chuckled, "She was a goner after that first taste of the spotlight."

Mia understood. She had felt the same way during the applause after her first solo in middle school jazz band.

"How about you, Tiffany?" Mia asked.

"I grew up less than an hour away," Tiffany said. "I started taking bass lessons in middle school. I played with a band in high school, but we all went to different colleges, so it fizzled out."

They quieted as the Lakehouse came into view. The rest of the walk was downhill. Lights outlined the venue's giant, crowded dock and music blared through the front doors.

"I'm glad you came with us," Macy said.

Mia smiled. The five of them took their place in line outside the entrance.

"Five-dollar cover," the doorman grumbled.

Lars ignored the doorman and wove through the line into the Lakehouse.

Mia slipped her wallet from her wrist. She reached into the pouch for cash which was the form of currency required by TRN for Travel. TRN regulated the flow of cash to circulate back to Original Time. They created the system to avoid unanticipated inflation for other times in history.

"We've made too many footprints already," Adrian Glass had said. "We must leave the past unscathed."

Aside from Lars, the rest of the group paid the bouncer and stepped into the Lakehouse. The colossal wooden A-frame created a comfortable atmosphere. The concert floor was packed. Mia thought back to her family's venue. Two of the Hayes' band halls could have fit inside the Lakehouse.

"Fifteen minutes 'til they start," Lars said with a glance at his watch. "I'll get us some drinks."

Lars went to the bar and Mia watched him connect with the man she suspected would grant him backstage access. Mia felt Macy's hands cup around her ear.

"You're gonna love this band. If Tiff says they're good, then you know they're freakin' fly! Lars acts like he finds all these bands, but really, it's Tiff. That's why she can't stand him."

They swayed to the opening band. After two songs, Lars rejoined the group. He doled out a round of beers and they closed in on the stage. Macy offered Mia another cigarette.

"No thanks," Mia declined. The Lakehouse's smoky haze was making her queasy.

The opening band played their final song then, after a short intermission, the overhead lights dimmed, and the crowd cheered. Lars squeezed Mia's shoulders from behind. For her view's sake, Mia was glad to be in front of him. The band opened with their newest hit which had yet to be overplayed.

Macy's hair grazed her bare shoulders. Her face was lit by the stage lights and Mia was in awestruck. Mia sang along with the band's cues and moved with the crowd. She remembered asking Dr. Lowell if all the fuss of Time Travel was worth it. As she watched Macy's presence draw the lead singer to their side of the stage, Mia had her answer.

"So, was your band as good as these guys?" Lars asked Mia as the crowd began to thin.

"I can't speak for the rest of the group, but I think I play alright," Mia smirked. "I'd love to do what these guys are doing. I've been dying to play a few gigs and see where it goes, ya know?"

Lars raised his eyebrows, walked up a set of stairs, and disappeared backstage.

Mia tapped Macy's arm.

"Is he famous here?" Mia asked in response to Lars' cool disappearance behind the curtain. She thought back to Lars' conversation with the manager at the Loop. Mia also recalled Lars' waived cover charge.

"Textbook Lars," Macy responded and rolled her eyes, "probably got the hookup from Gene at the bar. He's the assistant manager of the Lakehouse. Gene and Marty from the Loop are frenemies. Sometimes they're promoting each other, sometimes they're at each other's throats. Lars seems to smooth things out between them." Macy's expression changed as she looked at Mia. "It was cool of you to come tonight," Macy said and fixed Mia's post-concert hair.

Lars appeared in Mia's peripheral vision, and she turned to see what he was up to now.

"Come on back ladies," Lars said with a gesture backstage.

Mia's mouth dropped open, "For real?"

"Wait," Tiffany narrowed her eyes at Lars, "Let's pump the brakes. No strings attached, right? Like, no," she cocked her head, "expectations?"

"Yeah, it's fine," Lars dismissed Tiffany's concern. "Hey Mia, you ready for your tryout?" Lars put his arm around Mia's neck and messed up her hair.

Mia laughed. Lars' playfulness reminded Mia of her brothers.

"Let's go."

They headed toward the backstage hallway, but Tiffany remained glued in place.

"C'mon, Tiff," EJ said. "We've got to go together!"

Tiffany sighed and followed the rest of the group. Lars led the pack. He reached the dressing room door and knocked.

A voice on the other side shouted, "Come in!"

"Hey man," the lead singer said as Lars led the group inside. "Loved the crowd tonight. Gene sent you back, right?"

"Yeah, I help him with recruiting acts sometimes, but you guys must have slipped under my radar. I would have booked you on the spot had I heard you before! These are some of my friends. They're big fans."

The harmonica player and lead singer introduced themselves. The guitarist perched on a speaker across the room, beer in hand. The drummer lounged in a chair; his wiry arms hung over the armrests. The headliner's roadies were scattered around the room, along with the members of the opening band, and other lucky, backstage guests.

"Love playing these college towns," the singer said.

The ring of a phone cut through the backstage area. Lars sauntered to the wall mount to answer the call.

"Hello?"

Mia still couldn't believe that there was not a cell phone in sight. The backstage fans with their disposable cameras in hand caused Mia to chuckle. Weeks would likely pass before they saw their photos and after that, they'd end up in an album much like the ones in Ellie's closet.

"Oh shit," Lars said and turned his back to the rest of the room. "Uh huh," he continued. "Find someone to help him… you want me to go get him?"

Lars groaned and snapped his fingers to get the lead singer's attention.

"You owe me big time for this," Lars gestured at the phone and hung up.

"I don't know if I *owe* you," the lead singer scoffed. "I just *met* you. What's goin' on? Who called?"

51

One of the roadies faced the ceiling in anguish. He placed his palms on his temples.

"Not again! How does the driver, the one person who's not supposed to be drunk get blitzed every time we go to a college town?"

The guitar player chuckled, "Cheap beer."

"I've been summoned to pick him up," Lars stated. "I'll borrow Gene's car. Your driver's just down the road at the Loop. That was the manager, Marty, another friend of mine. You guys load up while I'm gone and maybe your driver will be sobered up by the time I get him back here."

The roadie sighed, "You're a lifesaver. I can start the drive, but I'm not driving all night for him again." The roadie looked at the lead singer. "Hate to admit it, but we might owe this kid."

The lead singer nodded, "Thanks for taking care of this."

"Hey, I hear you can play this thing?" The guitarist addressed Mia and pointed to his guitar which was leaned against a wall across the room. "Let's hear it, little sister!"

"Are you sure?" Mia ogled the instrument. Light beamed across the guitar's golden wood grain. "Don't you guys need to pack up?"

"The way Marty was talking, it may take a lot of coercing to get the driver out of the Loop," Lars said. "Plus, I still need to get Gene's keys. I'll be a little bit. Go ahead, Mia. Take your time."

Mia's self-consciousness would have shielded her from the opportunity in OT, but something within her had changed and she picked up the guitar with no further apprehension. She closed her eyes and strummed a few bars. Mia hit a rhythm and went into one of her grandfather's favorite songs. Her blood pulsed with the thrill of the night.

"Woo!" Lars exclaimed on his way out the door. "I'll hurry back!"

When Mia opened her eyes, the guitarist was nodding along with her.

"Keep going!"

He retrieved an acoustic guitar and, after a brief tuning, weaved with Mia. She drove their tempo. The drummer added a tambourine beat. Mia laughed blissfully as the room was filled with music. They hit the next verse and the singer recited the lyrics to Les' old favorite.

Mia and the guitarist continued to challenge each other's speed and everyone in the room was enlivened by their reciprocity. EJ, Macy and Tiffany fell in love with Mia.

The group looked at each other and knew they'd found their missing piece.

Chapter III

Derek released a smoke-thickened laugh.

It was 1967 and he was in the epicenter of it all— Carnaby Street, London.

Mini skirts. Freedom. Colour.

The sun warmed his back as he strolled down the street with ease. In Derek's state, tension couldn't survive. Derek had abandoned the late-summer wind-down of Original Time and ventured far enough back in time for the season to retrograde.

"The further we go back, the earlier the season," Dr. Chandra had explained.

He left during late summer and arrived at his destination in early spring. Derek was released from acclimation just as 1967's residual winter chill vanished, and he welcomed the lengthened summer. Derek removed his sunglasses. The colors were even more vivid without his ochre lenses. He acquainted himself with the city and found eye-catching spectacles in every direction.

Storefronts were doused in an array of hues. An occasional dark, brick building contrasted the era's splashy colors, a reminder of the city's age amidst the dominant youth. Derek felt as though he was floating through a rainbow.

He pulled a handkerchief from his pocket and patted beads of sweat from his face then rolled up his sleeves and nodded to the groovy women as they passed. He wondered where they were headed.

Though Derek recalled none of his journey, he was told that his time in the Shell had been grueling. Derek had no doubt that, over the previous year, he had accumulated an abundance of buried fears and layers upon layers of grief. In the Shell, many of his issues had unearthed themselves and his acclimator was put to the test.

"Was there someone else here right after you pulled me from the Shell?" Derek had asked his acclimator. "Maybe I imagined it, but I was envisioning another person."

"I had to call for another TRN employee's assistance," his acclimator stated.

"I'm so sorry. It's been quite a year," Derek replied, embarrassed.

Though Derek had endured a rocky landing into the sixties, he was ready to make up for the turbulence with a smooth day out.

"Am I good to go then?" He asked his Acclimator earlier that morning.

"You're good. I'll pop in tomorrow. As long as you're stable these next couple of weeks, you're free to be. Remember, I'll be in Europe for summer if you need anything," the acclimator said. "And I left you a little something to help you chill out," she winked.

Derek left his apartment feeling lighter than he had in months. His thought patterns were uncharacteristically harmonious. His natural inclination toward cascades of worry had completely subsided.

One by one, his potent tragedies dissolved. First to go was Derek's twin's overdose, then his beloved Grandpa Les' death, and finally Derek's break-up with his almost-fiancé, Anna.

Derek was twenty-four. He graduated from college and landed a job in Artificial Intelligence research. Like his classmates, Derek paid a four-year penance for a stable nine-to-five with good benefits and comfortable wages. He excelled at his job and received a generous, consistent paycheck. Derek's life was materializing in the exact way society coveted, until Derek's work required more and more ethical compromise. The demand for Artificial Intelligence was shaping society. Though Derek was on the benefiting side, his self-convictions became harder to ignore.

One of his first sickening projects was to replace an entire company's need for accountants by engineering a new, state-of-the-art calculating program. Next, Derek was assigned to work on a home-cleaning device putting hundreds of housekeeping companies out of business.

"The unemployment rate just keeps going up," Derek's friend Vaughn had said. "Ever think about doing something to fix it?"

Throughout college, Vaughn and Derek kept each other in check and Vaughn's comment stung Derek.

"Of course I think about how the world's situation could be improved, but maybe, for some people, AI closed one door and opened another. Maybe they wouldn't have taken the leap to follow their passions. Maybe this is the push people need to start their own business or study their interests rather than make a living doing something they hate," Derek reasoned.

But, deep down, Derek knew the truth. There was no plan to support the unemployed mass's pursuit of happiness. Derek lay awake at night, riddled with guilt. Vaughn's lack of compassion for Derek's situation didn't help.

"I don't know why you're doing this, man," Vaughn would say. "You should apply that brain of yours to a technology that's going to help humanity, not cripple it."

Derek's bitterness toward Vaughn grew with the harsh, persistent criticism. The one person Derek could always call was Cooper. Cooper answered Derek's calls at any hour. Derek's twin always checked in at the right time, as though he could sense Derek's need for support.

But Cooper was going through his own struggles. Bouts of debilitating depression. Multiple jobs within one year of college graduation. Leaning into a cycle of toxic relationships.

Then, Cooper discovered a poison, disguised as an antidote. And he was gone.

Derek was paralyzed. Following Cooper's death, Derek flipped to autopilot for his own survival. Derek showed up for his job but was unable to feign care for the mundane, daily tasks. He began to call in sick, only to spend the day in bed.

He didn't know how he could have missed his brother's muffled cries for help. After weeks of spotty attendance, little focus, and no motivation, Derek was fired from his stable job. At first Anna, Derek's long-term girlfriend, sympathized with his situation.

"Take all the time you need," she said.

Eventually, Anna encouraged Derek to update his resume and get back into a routine. She came over and cooked for Derek. She even bought Derek new clothes to fit his narrowing frame. As months passed with no spark from Derek, Anna began to distance herself from his dark world.

The Hayes struggled to fish Derek from the depths into which he'd fallen.

"You need human connection, Derek," Ellie said. "Go help your grandpa at the store."

Derek's grandpa Les welcomed the extra help along with his grandson's company. Less than a year before, Les' wife, Derek's grandmother Valerie, had died.

Derek was lifted by his grandfather's sound wisdom. No matter how bad things got, Les always said the right thing. For every step of grief, glimpse of bliss, and phase of moodiness, Grandpa Les had a song on cue. Derek was revived by their family record store, 'King's Music Lounge,' or 'King's' as they called it.

'The Court,' their family's small concert venue, was located just below King's. Derek began to spend his evenings there. The job was a breath of fresh air after spending countless nights buried in a pile of blankets. Purpose found its way back into Derek's life.

Anna started to accompany Derek to the venue. She was thrilled to see the light return to his eyes. The man she fell in love with was slowly returning.

Then one night, as a show revved up, Derek searched for Les.

"You haven't seen him since before the show?" Derek asked the stage crew.

They shook their heads no. A jolt of dread shot through Derek. He dismissed himself from the floor.

"I need to run to the restroom quick," Derek told Anna and pushed his way through the crowd.

Derek ran up the stairs to King's and into the secluded room where customers could sample records before buying. The light was off, and as Derek rounded the corner, his eerie feeling was validated.

Les lay on the couch in eternal peace. His favorite record came to a halt, leaving Derek alone with the silence. Derek's fragmented heart shattered further.

Following Les' stroke, maintaining the business required all hands-on deck from the Hayes. The long working hours minimized Derek and Anna's time together. Then, the remaining shards of Derek's heart dissolved to nothingness when he saw *them* seated at the bar.

Derek watched from the entrance, soaked from the rain, as they smiled and drank. He knew it was over when he heard Anna's laugh. She lit up for Vaughn and the sight was the final nail in the coffin for Derek and Anna's relationship.

That night, Derek left the bar where Anna betrayed him and walked the streets. He stopped into another lounge where he sipped the nicest cognac he could afford. There, Derek watched the news of public Time Travel break and he made plans to leave it all behind.

Derek evaluated the area's heavy foot traffic and slipped into an alleyway. He slid the tiny joint, left by his acclimator, from his shirt pocket and chuckled to himself.

"Let's say you break one of your destination's laws," Francis Platt had said. "First line of defense? Don't get caught. Second? You will pay for it. Literally." Derek could still picture the lawyer's smile, "We've got you covered. You've heard of settlements, right? The rate of exchange is so good for Travelers that unless you kill someone, TRN's lawyers will represent you and get you off the hook. We want to support your longevity in your chosen destination. Otherwise, Time Travel's initial motives to build up our current era's resources have been for nothing."

The explanation comforted Derek and he took the risk of doping in public.

Derek lit the end of the paper and took a sweet inhale. He held the plume of smoke in his mouth, then dropped his head back as he exhaled, facing the blue sky.

'Grandpa would have loved this.'

Once the spliff burned down to his fingers, Derek dropped it on the pavement and squashed the delicate skin. He put on his sunglasses and reclaimed his place in the flow. After passing a few more storefronts, Derek came upon a boutique.

Giant daisies were painted on the front window. Two mannequins, one dressed in a vibrant mini-dress and the other in baroque menswear, stood behind the glass. Derek was drawn inside the boutique.

As he entered, a bell chimed, and he heard an upbeat piano melody spinning off a record. The delightful sound drifted through the bright little space. All shades of the visible spectrum emanated from the display floor. Not only did color begin to paint the televisions of the time, but it seemed to disperse across society. Derek was overwhelmed with the boutique's selection. His eyes darted from one ensemble to the next.

He ran his fingers across the satin lining of a sport jacket. The fabric was sturdy. Derek was reminded of being a child, burying his face in Les' well-loved, yet quality attire.

Derek's eyes landed across the room on a stunning, dark-haired woman. He watched as she put the finishing touches on a mannequin's outfit, oblivious to Derek's gaze. Derek feigned interest in a pair of trousers which hung near the woman. He watched as she struggled with the decision between two hats for her display. She held one hat in each hand placing one on the mannequin, then the other. She pursed her lips and cocked her head to the side as she considered each option.

The raven-haired beauty continued to alternate between two newsboy hats, the first was blue, the second, green, to accessorize her dashing mannequin's ensemble.

"I like the blue," Derek offered.

She turned to face Derek.

He wasn't prepared for her exquisiteness. Derek was frozen by her emerald eyes and perfectly full lips. He was thankful for the herbal assistance to maintain his relaxed state. Normally, a face like hers would send him reeling into nonsensical conversation, instead, his nerves stayed in check.

She walked closer to Derek and placed the green hat atop his head.

"Actually, I fancy the green."

She tipped the hat to shadow one of Derek's eyes.

"You're a long way from home, aren't you?" She asked.

Derek wondered how he'd given himself away as a Traveler, then he remembered his American accent.

"This is home now," he answered.

"Happy to hear it," she replied with a smile.

Her lined eyes resembled those of Cleopatra. Derek was certain that the queen standing before him could get what she wanted from anyone.

"Now," she gestured to the mannequin, "which scarf?"

She pulled the green hat from Derek's head. While her back was to Derek, he fixed his hair in a nearby mirror. He watched as she placed the hat atop a mannequin's head and gave it a tilt, just as she had done on Derek.

'Lucky mannequin.'

She draped two silk scarves across the mannequin's plastic chest and adjusted them until they lay perfect. One was paisley and the other was striped.

"That one," Derek pointed to the striped scarf.

She nodded and tied the square of fabric above the mannequin's high-collared shirt.

"Last," she reached for a rack of sport jackets, "the final touch."

"I'm on the payroll now, am I?" Derek joked, "Or you could at least give me the hat that you don't display," Derek winked. "You know, for the expertise."

"Well, I need to see that you fit the personality of someone that I *want* to dress," she teased.

Derek imagined being dressed by her. He stopped himself before the fantasy got too sweet.

"Are you a writer?" She asked. "Or a photographer? Please tell me you're not a musician."

Derek hesitated, almost forgetting his story.

"I just finished college in America. I'm taking some time to figure out where I want to be," he shrugged and went on to introduce himself. "Derek Hayes."

"Far out," she said, extending her elegant hand. "Renee Blum," she stated with Parisian élan.

A devious smile crept onto Renee's face as she placed the hat on Derek.

"I'll take it," Derek said.

Derek followed Renee to the counter, eyes fixed on the snug parts of her wiggle-dress, and set the hat by Renee's tarnished, metal cash register. Renee calculated his total and Derek handed over the payment.

"This is quite a place," Derek said.

63

"Thank you," Renee replied. "This boutique of mine is my pride and joy. I turn everyone into a star."

"You're the owner?"

Renee nodded, "Yes."

Derek took a deep breath and asked the question on his mind.

"Do you have plans tonight? Now that this is home," Derek gestured to the bustling street beyond her storefront, "I'd like to get to know the city. What better eyes to see this neighborhood through than those of a local business owner? Plus," Derek put on his new hat, "I've got to wear this out on the town."

Renee paused for a moment, scanning Derek from head to toe.

"We can meet up later," she responded. "Some friends and I plan to see a band at the Ace. You can join us."

"Right on," Derek replied. "I'll be there. What time?"

"The band is on at nine, let's meet at eight."

Derek felt someone bump him and turned to see a growing line of customers behind him.

"Sorry to hold up the line. Looks like you could use some help around here. Eight it is. Until then," Derek tipped his hat to Renee.

"Pleasure to meet you Mr. Hayes. And if you find good help, please send them my way."

Derek returned to a busying sidewalk. He discarded his sales receipt in a trash bin and contemplated working for Renee. While the rate of exchange strongly favored Travelers from Original Time, Derek knew how quickly he'd blow through the cash in his dream era. His stomach rumbled and demanded his attention. Derek couldn't recall the last time he'd eaten and searched for a restaurant.

The sound of beat poetry traveled down the street and into his ears. Derek located the source, a cafe just a few storefronts down. Derek heard a bongo drum and words amplified by a microphone. Derek walked through the open entryway, sat at a table, and ordered tea, a scone, and jam. Derek's acclimator had introduced him to the ritual of afternoon tea for his first post-acclimation meal. He resolved to make the custom a part of his routine.

Derek ate and allowed himself to be sucked in by the dramatic prose. Warm sips of tea soothed his scratchy throat. Derek's high began to wane, and he became intrigued by the poet standing on the cafe's insignificant platform.

She was very thin and wore matchstick pants and a turtleneck. She exuded depth and complication. Her head was crowned with fuzzy blonde ringlets which bounced in front of her glasses as she articulated her words. The poet's pale blue eyes met Derek's, then quickly fleeted. The intensity of the bongos picked up; it seemed the poet was coming to a close.

"And there they were.

They stood together, but their minds diverted.

Wrapped in fur, she yearns to go back to where she came from, from classes below.

The broadcaster tells her it's something new, another way to be,

"It's no longer for you," she's told. "You're far too old."

'But could it be for me?' She thinks. 'Could it make me free?'

Guess we'll wait, we'll wait and see."

The drums rapped. Nods of approval bobbed throughout the cafe. The audience was *with* her. The poet's message captured the time's insurgent energy. She bowed at the waist and exited the stage.

To be *in* the sixties, not just reading about them, or seeing the decade through the snapshots of an old camera was incredibly surreal. Just one day about in the city was enough to show Derek the wedge between the young and the old. He heard comments as he passed the newspaper stands.

"In our war, we really fought for something."

"This ain't about you, your generation created the war machine! Peace, now!"

"Don't you realize there's a war here? On the side streets where people are fighting for food and shelter?"

Despite the growing upheaval, Derek was glad to be in England and off the radar where he wouldn't have to succumb to the draft.

Derek left his payment on the table and stepped outside. The city's pulse escalated with each passing moment. Derek allowed himself to be distracted with the excitement of the era and to set aside his uneasiness surrounding the distant war.

'*Am I selfish to detach? To have the advantage of knowing how it ends?*'

Derek's churning mind quieted as he spotted the poet. She stood at the corner, waiting to step onto the crosswalk. He decided to engage with the real-life beatnik of the time. Derek approached the poet with the same confidence he had approached Renee.

"Excuse me miss," he said.

She stopped and locked eyes with Derek. They made the connection just as another wave of Derek's high set in. The words to compliment her poetry vanished along with any chance of charming her.

"I, uh, liked what you had to say in there," Derek muttered.

"Thanks, glad to know I'm in good company," her mouth formed a hint of a smile. "I'm in this area every week, usually around this time."

They crossed the intersection and Derek remained a stride behind the poet. Once they reached the opposite side of the street, she turned to face him.

"Anything else?" She asked with a furrowed brow.

A warm breeze wove through the poet's golden spirals. She pushed them away revealing her soft, ethereal face. Derek tried to come up with a reasonable explanation as to why he followed her and searched his mind for a question worthy of her time.

"What's your name?" Derek blurted.

The poet answered, "What's it to you?"

Derek received her message and softened his pursuit.

"I need to know so I can look up the dates of your readings," he explained. "Sorry, this must happen to you all the time, I apologize if I'm coming off too forward," Derek said, his self-assurance hanging by a thread.

"You know, I think if we're meant to run across one another again, we will," she said. "And this doesn't happen to me all the time, so thank you for your compliment. I've just got somewhere to be."

"Before you leave, I want to introduce myself. I'm Derek."

With one last tuck of a tendril behind her ear, she said, "See you around, Derek," and the poet disappeared into the crowd.

The streets filled as the city concluded its workday. Derek resolved to go back to his flat and take a rest. He needed a reset and hoped that the night out with Renee would not end like his encounter with the poet.

Derek flowed with the crowd's current. He forked at the turn to his flat. Once he had distanced himself from the mass, he pulled another joint from his shirt pocket. He ignited the end and the paper burned down with his inhale. Derek's eyelids relaxed.

He pulled the spring air deep into his lungs and an old, familiar song floated from a shop nearby. Derek's mind emptied. Through his sunglasses, the world presented itself in shades of amber. He took one last moment to soak up the day and Derek's cracks from past damage were filled with sunlight.

Derek woke from his nap just a few minutes before seven o'clock. Refreshed from his snooze, he poured himself a glass of water. Derek showered and as he dried off with a large towel, he noticed that droplets of condensation had accumulated on his water glass. He smiled as the water streamed across his fingers. Throughout the day, Derek had become increasingly aware of sensory moments, and he grew more impressed with Psilopram's effects.

Derek opened the bathroom door and steam rolled into the hallway.

He moved onto the task of selecting an outfit worthy for his first night out on the town. Derek's immersion into his chosen era had been delayed due to his long recovery, but during the time between his arrival and full acclimation, Derek often looked down from his balcony, envious of those below. He longed to be a part of the scene. Life radiated from the streets.

Derek realized his flat was too quiet and he needed a boost. He pulled a record from the small collection acquired for him by his acclimator. The rotation started and he dropped the needle. Derek closed his eyes and drifted off with the harmonious voices.

The song which played was one of Anna's favorites, but Derek didn't listen with a sense of melancholy, instead, it dawned on Derek that he hadn't thought of Anna for days. The fact that he was going to give her *the* ring, the hurt of Vaughn's betrayal, and the shame he felt for not giving her enough, were gone.

Rather than attempt to revive the sadness, Derek selected his clothing for the evening. He chose a pair of tan trousers and a jersey turtleneck. He pulled a bottle of cognac from his top cupboard and poured it into a tulip glass.

Derek was thankful for the time's excellent rate of exchange as he sipped the high-end spirit. Even after the cost of Travel, Derek still had enough funds remaining to rent a flat and fill it with simple luxuries which he could barely afford in Original Time.

Derek walked to his balcony and slid open the door. He rested his forearms on the patio rail and listened to cars roll through his new neighborhood. Derek sighed with adoration as he took in the rhythm of the city.

He couldn't stop checking his watch. When he saw it was finally time to go, Derek downed the rest of his drink. Derek put on his hat, hand-selected by Renee, gave himself one last look in the mirror, then stepped out into the night.

A light mist began to fall as Derek approached the Ace. The venue stood proudly in the drizzle and Derek's eyes followed the brick and mortar to an upstairs patio. Lively voices descended from above.

Derek looked around and realized his attire was incredibly drab in the array of ruffled shirts and psychedelic prints. All walks of swinging London congregated at the club's entrance.

Derek tried to recall if they had set a meeting place as he searched the crowd for Renee.

He began to block the club's inward traffic flow and was directed away from the entrance. Derek posted up along the Ace's sidewall. A sense of vulnerability set in while he waited. He wondered how on-lookers perceived his standing alone.

To Derek's relief, he peered around and saw others in the same predicament. A difference in time presented itself. Before Traveling, to bide time, Derek would have pulled out his phone. He would have wanted to look occupied.

Derek's comprehension of presence deepened without a screen to dictate his thoughts and actions. The world around him diffused into his being. The damp aroma of springtime was more potent. Delicate petals of flowering trees glowed beneath the streetlamps. Everything around him felt new.

The sounds of spring were interrupted when Derek heard the band inside, beginning their set. Opening riffs sounded from the guitar. Drums started in and led the groove. Derek was tempted to go in but didn't want to miss Renee's arrival.

"Hopefully she gets here soon," a man said to Derek. "You won't want to miss these guys."

The stranger patted Derek's shoulder and sauntered into the club.

From around the corner of the Ace, whoops and laughter chimed through the dusk. Derek turned to face the commotion. An animated group became visible beneath the Ace's illuminated sign. Textures and colors adorned their bodies. Derek's eyes darted from indigo velvet to pink feathers, then finally, to Renee's pristine face. She was linked arm in arm with another member of the flamboyance.

"Hey baby!" Renee shouted as she caught sight of Derek.

Derek summoned his bravery as Renee presented him to her accompanying group.

"This is Derek," she began the introductions. "He's," she smoldered him with her gaze, "quite a bit of alright."

"So nice to meet you all," Derek nodded to her friends. "Do you know each other from the boutique?"

Renee sighed and answered for the eccentric crew.

"We've got a rather extensive history", she stated, "but we'll save that for another time. Derek, this is Germain, Grant, Lorraine and Carole."

Renee took Derek's hand and melded him into the group.

"Sounds like the band's got quite a *do* going, let's get inside."

Grant approached Derek and held up a peace sign.

"Nice to meet you, mate," Grant said. "American, yeah? Well, I'm sure glad you're here and not swept off to the jungle. What a mess it's all become."

"You and me both," Derek replied, guilt hanging on his words.

Grant placed his hand on Derek's shoulder.

"Sorry to bring up the matter. Tonight, we carry on with no heaviness, only good vibrations. That's all we've got is *right now,*" Grant said. "It's all love."

Grant exuded kindness. He was on the tall side of average with globular eyes and wavy, sand-colored hair. Grant wore a white, airy-sleeved shirt under a suede vest with matching trousers. He was the original hippie Derek had hoped to meet.

Renee directed the group into the club but stalled back to hang with Derek. She locked her arm in his. Renee knocked his hat off-center.

"Tonight's one of those nights," she said with a grin.

Renee squeezed Derek's arm and they followed her friends inside.

A keyboard solo began as they entered the Ace. Trippy and intricate, the ditty tumbled across the club's vast dance floor. Women walked by wearing skin-tight boots. They took their places and began to dance at the sides of the stage. The staff wore bikini-like uniforms, barely covering their lean, painted bodies. Spotlights flashed off their golden jewelry.

Derek looked at Renee and gestured to the bar.

"Shall I get us a round?" He asked, but the crew was migrating toward the dance floor.

Derek shrugged and followed suit. The club was lit with no overhead lights. Instead, spotlights waved throughout the venue and the clubbers were lit in vibrant flashes turning each movement into a moment.

"You've got some moves," Renee said.

"Thanks," Derek replied.

Derek had studied online go-go videos before his journey to the era and to his surprise, he moved with ease to the music of the time. As he looked around, he saw that at the Ace, there was no illusion of moral standard to uphold. Every hint of insecurity evaded the club. Everyone gave in to the spirit of the music as the singer's low voice sang of utopian dreams.

The silver chain of Lorraine's purse caught Derek's eye as she slipped her bag from her shoulder. Lorraine surveyed the floor, ensuring no hint of authority-figures, and pulled a handful of cubes from her purse. She placed a cube on Grant's tongue. He nodded and continued to dance.

Derek had a decision to make—partake or abstain.

During the psychological screening phase of Derek's Travel consultation, Dr. Lowell had warned Derek about the effect drugs may have on his psyche.

"Sometimes, we see people react beautifully to Psilopram. They wake up in a euphoric state, so euphoric that their acclimator is simply present to aid their physical recovery. Other times, Psilopram facilitates an unloading of Traveler's toxic conformities to the world they've experienced. Let's be realistic," Dr. Lowell had said, "you've had a bit of a rough go the last couple of years and you're going to the sixties. You should know, Psilopram has no negative interaction with natural substances, but the Time Regulatory Network has too little data to determine how Psilopram mixes with synthetic substances. I'd be cautious with anything created in a lab, so you don't blow your cover and get carted back to OT for breaking the guidelines."

Derek was leery of LSD after his long acclimation period. Not only was he fearful for what his mind would conjure should he partake, but as Dr. Lowell had warned, Derek was uncertain of his ability to keep his origins a secret if he had a bad trip.

TRN threatened a Psilopram-restricted return to Original Time if Travelers gave away their identity, and Derek wasn't about to take the risk lightly. Travelers received no refunds, and civil penalties ensued upon their return.

Though he knew he couldn't partake, Derek didn't want to appear square to his new friends. He wracked his mind for an out. He pretended not to see Lorraine's sunshine candy and excused himself from the circle.

"I'm off for a drink," Derek shouted over the music, "anyone else?"

"No, but I'll be waiting for another dance with you. Hurry back!" Renee yelled.

Derek squeezed his way to the bar and placed his order. He leaned his body weight on the sticky counter. The break from dancing was a welcome cool-down. Derek noticed two narrow-framed men seated on barstools just feet away. They faced one another and Derek listened in on their conversation.

"Listen man, their drummer is just what we need!"

Meanwhile, a jaw-dropping woman walked into the Ace, flanked by two shaggy-haired men. Derek studied their faces and recognized the artists from one of his grandfather's old album covers. Derek held back a grin and began to understand that Renee had invited him to an assembly of the stars.

Another TRN guideline echoed in his mind.

"Avoid fame," Derek heard Francis Platt's voice inside his head. "Don't end up in the history books."

The bartender presented Derek with his cocktail. Derek peeled the sturdy glass from the bar top, paid, and made his way back to Renee.

When Derek returned, the group had retreated into their own worlds. He reached for his phone only to find its absence and laughed at himself. Renee caught Derek's laughter and joined in, unaware of the source of his amusement.

Pink light from the ceiling flared across Derek's eyes. Grant pulsed with the beat. Lorraine's eyes were half-closed as she serpentined to a lengthy guitar solo. Germain mingled with many circles throughout the club. It seemed he was well-known. Carole cut through the bodies to face Grant and they danced as if the club were vacant.

Renee devoured Derek with her stare. Derek was pulled closer and closer until there was no space between them. Derek traced Renee's silhouette with his fingers and his senses electrified.

The Ace's crowd met the night with sweaty bodies, damp hair, and makeup-streaked faces. A breeze swept by, cooler than the one Derek remembered from his afternoon about.

"Ahh," Renee sighed.

"That keyboard was outta sight," Germain shook his head. "Took me to another place."

Derek nodded in agreement.

Renee nestled in at Derek's side and he wrapped his fingers just beneath her rib cage. Derek was envious of the enhanced lens through which the rest of the group experienced the evening. He wondered if it was a mistake to decline the trip.

Derek accidentally grazed Renee's backside. Rather than pull away, Renee rose to her tiptoes. Her lips touched Derek's ear as she spoke.

"Walk me home?"

"Really?" He asked.

"Wouldn't it be dangerous for me to go alone?" Renee asked. "Plus, everything looks a little," she giggled, "different right now. I might get lost," she smirked.

"I don't know where we're going either," Derek replied, "but I'll walk with you. I'll keep you safe."

They said their goodbyes and Derek and Renee started toward her flat. Derek repressed the urge to find a soft patch of grass or empty alleyway to tumble into with Renee. Along the way, Renee spotted a patch of flowers. They were tiny and pink, their petals heavy from the evening's mist. Derek plucked one of the blooms and placed it behind Renee's ear.

"*En Blum*," Renee said. "My favorite time of year and the name of my boutique."

Five minutes into their walk, Derek and Renee reached her doorstep.

"Here we are," she said.

"You didn't even need my help," Derek stated.

Renee's skin glowed in the moonlight. A velvety strand of hair clung to the drying sweat of her décolleté. Derek knew what he *should* do, she was high, and he was not, but his instincts stirred.

Just when Derek began to reel in his lust, Renee pressed her lips against his. He roamed his hands across Renee's round hips. Derek and Renee stuck to one another, unable to get close enough.

Renee pulled away to catch her breath and reached into the front pocket of her dress for her flat key. Her hand brushed against Derek's thigh.

"Renee," Derek tucked a lock of hair behind her ear, "I- um, I didn't take any of the cubes Lorraine had. I want to make sure you really want to do this."

"Baby," Renee replied, "you know what I want."

She wove her fingers into the nape of Derek's hair.

He didn't have the discipline to ask twice.

Renee unlocked the door to her building. They caressed each other up two flights of stairs. By the time they reached the top floor, Renee struggled to get the key into the lock of her flat.

Finally, the key slid into place. Renee flung her door open, knocking a frame from the wall. The crash heightened their already elevated heart rates. Derek kicked the door closed behind them.

Renee went for his belt buckle, her breasts spilling from her dress. She unfastened Derek's buckle and unzipped his pants with expertise and shoved him onto her leather couch. The cold fabric took Derek's breath away then Renee's lips sent a surge of ecstasy through his system.

Derek curled his fingers around the bottom of her dress and pulled the soft material up over her head. With only her knee highs on, Renee straddled Derek. She reached down and pulled a feather boa from the floor, tickled Derek's chest, then lay the boa across Derek's eyes. As Renee slid onto Derek, he became hooked on the drug known as Renee Blum.

A mid-day sun shone through Renee's bedroom window.

Derek awoke, uncertain of his whereabouts, with Renee fast asleep next to him. The night before came back to him in clips, inducing an unapologetic lust he hadn't felt since his first encounter with pornography.

Renee's eyes remained shut. Derek gazed around her room. The universe in which Renee resided looked like something from a fantasy book. Textiles were draped over doors, lamps, any furniture that would support them. Derek's eyes landed on a green, floral scarf made of silk. It fell perfectly across the headboard above where they lay. He reached out and ran his fingers across the luxurious material.

Derek yawned and stole a glance at the goddess' body, lit by the fresh morning light. A flash of bright pink caught Derek's eye as he scanned the floor. On the carpet lay the flower he placed behind Renee's ear just hours before. He pulled it from the heap of material. To Derek's surprise, it was intact, the petals a flawless display of nature's symmetry.

Renee's nightstand was just the place to rest their walk's souvenir. Derek kissed Renee's dark hair and hoped the flower would bring a smile to her face. She roused and smiled at Derek.

"What's the time?" Renee asked.

Derek pulled his watch from a nearby desk.

"Twelve-thirty."

Renee groaned.

"I don't want to kick you out, but I need to freshen up and get into the boutique. We're due for a shipment today."

Derek stroked her hair.

"Sure," he said. "Last night—"

Renee nodded, "I know. We'll be seeing more of each other Mr. Hayes."

Derek dressed and began the walk to his flat. As he passed the pink flowers, Derek plucked another bloom to adorn his table.

He returned to his new home and, as he hung his hat from *En Blum,* he caught the scent of the fabric. Rose, Renee's perfume. The smell Derek would forever associate with his freefall into the Summer of Love.

Chapter IV

Mia heard a knock at the door. She set her textbook aside and went to look through the peephole with the hope that Macy had arrived to offer refuge from homework. Instead, an unfamiliar man stood outside.

"Hello?" Mia said.

The stranger held a padded envelope.

"I need a signature," he stated.

"Oh. Usually, people leave deliveries at the front office."

He replied, "Not this one. Are you Mia Hayes?"

"Yes," Mia answered.

"Do you have any guests right now? The sender wants this package to stay confidential."

Mia hesitated.

"Not right now, but I'm expecting someone soon," she bluffed.

"Can you step out here? I need to see your ID."

Mia had signed for many packages at King's Records, but she'd never been asked for an ID. She put her trust in the nearby apartment neighbors who were within earshot and opened the door. Mia pulled her ID from her wallet and presented it to the man.

The stranger took her ID and held it beside her face.

"Here you go," he said and handed over Mia's package.

He scanned the hallway again, then flashed his own ID card to Mia. Mia saw TRN's emblem in the corner.

"I'm supposed to remind you that delivery is confidential, open it in private, we will know if you don't."

"Okay," Mia agreed.

"Take care," the courier said, and left Mia alone in the hallway.

Mia rushed back into her apartment. She locked her door and ripped open the envelope's seal. Inside the package was a tri-folded letter which Mia opened. Aside from the Time Regulatory Network's emblem, the paper appeared to be blank. Mia turned the envelope upside down. Two objects spilled onto her kitchen island: a round, iridescent piece of glass and a button-like gadget.

She held the piece of glass between her thumb and index finger. The purpose of the glass was a mystery. Mia set it on top of the TRN letterhead and was shocked by what she saw next. Text was revealed beneath the glass. She grinned and wondered what TRN had up their sleeve. Mia moved the literary tool across the letter.

'To our Time Traveler,

This parcel's contents are meant to keep you connected with Original Time. It is important that you notify TRN if you change residence so we can continue to have our courier deliver this quarterly newsletter. Keep your decryption glass safe along with the device enclosed.

The device is known as 'the Aid.' If emergency strikes, you will not be left to fend for yourself in your chosen era. Instead, you can signal for help with this new piece of technology.'

Mia reached the bottom of the letter and flipped it over. Printed on the back were directions for the Aid.

80

'Green: Default setting, Time Traveler is safe.

Yellow: Minor threat to Time Traveler. TRN is notified of location. Standby coordinates will be communicated within 24 hours by undercover TRN monitoring staff. Yellow setting may also be used to notify the legal department of convictions.

Red: Immediate departure required. To be used only in EMERGENCIES.
*Flex-Shell used, Psilopram administration based on supply.

Transport to accommodate Code Red requires a new, universal type of Shell. The Flex-Shell molds to ninety percent of bodies, however the new Shell requires a longer acclimation period upon return to Original Time.
We recommend that you always keep the Aid on you. It may be buttoned to clothing or disguised as jewelry. Despite the gadget's role in your safety, do not use the Aid as a crutch. Please turn to the authorities of your time and use this device as a last resort.
Best,
Adrian Glass
TRN Chief Operations Officer'

Mia was both comforted and unsettled by the device's arrival. The need for the Aid underlined Time Travel's fragility. Mia's stomach dropped when imagining the scenarios that required TRN's intervention. Then, she remembered the courier's warning to open the package in private.
"We will know if you don't."
Mia tucked the letter and the Aid into her underwear drawer. She debated whether to comply with TRN's

recommendations and keep the device with her at all times; the implication of TRN's ever-watching eye caused a chill to run up Mia's spine.

Later that night, Mia's phone rang.

Macy always called before heading over to Mia's apartment between eight and nine o'clock. Mia awaited the company every night.

Mia and Macy's typical evening at Mia's apartment began with the latest reality show episode. Homework inevitably entered the nightly routine, and it wasn't so bad as they scribbled away and listened to CDs together. When they completed a satisfactory amount of work, they rewarded themselves with magazines and music videos. Macy had also begun to come over on the weekends before house parties and Lakehouse shows. Whether out with people or by themselves, Macy recharged Mia.

The only days when Mia and Macy weren't together were the days when Macy had band practice with EJ and Tiffany. Though Mia's jam session with the Lakehouse headliners had won the group's approval, they had yet to extend the invitation to join their band. Every time she was with the group, Mia worked toward integrating herself into their dynamic.

Macy was a natural frontwoman. Her voice was extraordinary and was only outdone by her outrageous stage presence. Tiffany played bass, EJ was on drums, and Lars played the unofficial manager. As Mia had seen at the Lakehouse, Lars had the hook-ups.

A smile crept onto Mia's face as she pressed the talk button.

"Shall I start the popcorn?" Mia answered.

"Is that how you greet all your callers?" A familiar male voice laughed. "If you're offering, then yes!"

Mia tried to place the voice.

"It's Lars!"

Mia laughed, "Oh!"

"I got your number from Macy. Not to be picky, but if you have the popcorn with extra butter, that's my preference."

"Sorry, Macy always comes over around this time. I thought you'd be her," Mia smacked her forehead.

"Sorry to disappoint. Sounds like you two have a cute thing going on," Lars teased. "So, as much as I would love to come over to your place, I called because I'm in charge of booking an opener for a pretty decent band at the Lakehouse. It's a weekend show and you'd open for the band that played at the end of summer. It was the night, you know," Lars paused, "the first night you came out with us."

"I'm surprised you remember that," Mia said. Lars' personality was hot and cold, and Mia never knew which setting she would get.

"How could I forget? I'm calling to give you a heads up," Lars continued, "that I might have planted a seed for you to start practicing with Macy's band. That night we met you, you knocked those headliners' socks off. If that's what you can do in a casual setting, it'd be pretty dope to see what you could do onstage."

"That's so rad Lars! Thank you!" Mia said. "Should I call Macy? Do you know when they're practicing next? When's the show?"

"Easy tiger," Lars advised. "I'd let her ask you. She'll invite you to play soon. I'm pretty sure she loves you," Lars laughed. "Like she actually might. Anyways, just wanted to let you know what I've got in the works."

The call waiting beeped on Mia's phone.

"Sorry, I have someone on the other line," Mia stated, pausing Lars' stream of good news.

"Well sleep tight, I'm pretty stoked to see how this all works out. Peace," Lars said and hung up.

"Hello?" Mia answered.

After the previous conversation, she realized that she shouldn't assume who was on the other end of the receiver. Mia looked at the clock and wondered if Macy would still come over.

"Hey girl, got that popcorn ready for me?"

Macy. Mia let out a sigh of relief.

"You know I do!"

"Right on, be there soon," Macy said.

Mia was left with a dial tone.

She looked down at her frumpy grey sweatpants and t-shirt. With a band invitation on the line, Mia was determined to look the part. She kept the sweatpants but exchanged her worn shirt for a spaghetti strap tank top. Mia selected a black choker from her jewelry box and strapped it around her neck. She let down her hair and looked at herself in the mirror.

'Good enough.'

Mia cleared the accumulation of junk from her coffee table then strolled into her kitchen and plucked a bag of popcorn from the cupboard. She removed the cellophane and placed the bag in the microwave. As the seconds counted down, Mia leaned her guitar against the living room wall where Macy could see the instrument upon her entrance.

Mia slid on her favorite cherry lip gloss while the popcorn sizzled. Just as she screwed on the gloss's lid, a knock sounded at the front door. Mia unlocked the entrance.

"Come in!"

Macy sniffed loudly, "Ooh, smells good! Take a seat, host," Macy gestured Mia to the living room, "I know where the bowls are. Find something good on the tube!"

Mia flipped through the channels and settled on a lighthearted dating show. She heard Macy empty the popcorn into a large metal bowl. Macy made her way into the living room, her pajama shorts inching up her thighs. She paused and smirked at the guitar then plopped down next to Mia, leaving no space between them.

They watched as things got ridiculous on the dating game show.

"Where do they find these people?" Macy asked.

Mia did her best to fake interest in the show, but the band offer was at the forefront of her mind. She saw Macy notice the guitar and was both annoyed and enticed by Macy's coolness. A commercial break offered Mia the chance to delve into the prospect.

"So, how has band practice been going?" Mia asked. "You guys sounded great at that house party last weekend!"

Macy sighed.

"You're too sweet. It really wasn't our best. We seem to be, I don't know," Macy hinted, "missing something. Or maybe someone."

Mia took the bait.

"I think I could help you with that."

"Since that very first night at the Lakehouse, EJ, Tiffany and I haven't gotten over your playing backstage," Macy stated. "I know it's short notice, but Lars got us a gig as openers in a couple weeks. Would you want to play with us?"

"Yes!" Mia replied without thinking.

"Well alright," Macy laughed. "Did you know this was coming?"

"Guilty," Mia admitted.

"Lars?" Macy guessed.

Mia nodded.

"I wondered why he asked me for your number. We've considered inviting you to join for a long time, but we had to get to know you first," Macy explained. "We had drama in the band before, and we obviously want to avoid that."

"No drama here," Mia said.

Macy turned to face Mia on the couch.

"This is gonna be so bitchin'!"

She held Mia's hands. Mia got butterflies in her stomach. She was pulled in by Macy's virility. Before Macy noticed Mia's cheeks reddening, Mia pulled away from Macy's gaze and resumed the conversation.

"When is the next practice?" Mia asked.

"Tuesday," Macy said, "at EJ's brother's place. We usually practice on Tuesdays. It's early enough in the week to rework any kinks before the weekend."

"Tuesdays it is," Mia stated.

She could already see the mid-week jam cutting into her studying but didn't care.

"We have a really good set-up in EJ's brother's shed," Macy continued. "And I see you come equipped with a guitar. Do you have an amp too?"

"Yes, I do," Mia said.

Shortly after her acclimation period, Mia had sprung for a guitar to fill the silence of her empty apartment. She selected a cheap Telecaster from a used-instrument shop in downtown Birchmont. The owner, an old, rock-n-roll cowboy, even cut Mia a deal on a small amplifier. The guitar was beat up, but Mia loved to imagine the story that came with each dent.

"I am so psyched about this," Macy said with a wide grin. "You know, we don't have a name for our band yet. We've tried a few names, but they all left with our former members. You'll have to think about it. We need something that sticks!" Macy clapped her hands together.

Macy leaned in for an embrace and the fabric of Macy's fuzzy bandana tickled Mia's cheek.

"That first night when you played, I knew..." Macy trailed off.

"I did too," Mia replied.

Macy released Mia from her arms. Mia scooted away and her knee landed on the remote control. The volume climbed and Macy shrieked at the startling noise.

Her reaction sent them both into a fit of uncontrollable laughter. Tears rolled down Macy's cheeks and Mia let out a snort, furthering the hilarity. Mia's apartment was filled with an heir of celebration and the hours flew by without Mia and Macy's awareness.

"Oh shit, it's almost two?" Macy hung her head. "There's no way I'll make my eight o'clock class tomorrow if I don't leave now. I might not make it as it is," Macy paused and rested her hand on Mia's shoulder. "Welcome to the band, Mia. We'll make it official at our next practice."

After Macy left, Mia went to lay in her bed. She closed her eyes but was too giddy to sleep. Mia finally had a friend for the spaces between the frames. To make matters even more perfect, the band was a dream that could only come true in Mia's new era of residence.

The music industry of OT had a few gems however, most music was overproduced. Songs were boiled down to a reduction of the artist's original vision. What was once a musician's fervent piece of poetry was often stripped of its timbre and sold to the masses. Even if a musician had the right ingredients for emotional evocation, the road to recognition was merciless.

In the nineties, Mia was finally presented with the opportunity to satisfy her overdue urge for expression. The wait for her first practice was unbearable. Mia looked to the corner of her room and was beckoned by her guitar.

'I'll sleep when I'm dead,' she thought and gave into the strings' invitation.

EJ hit the final crash.

The crowd erupted.

The Lakehouse's crew ushered them back to their dressing room, away from the bright lights. Music from the venue's stereo system filled the intermittent gap between the openers and headliners.

"So worth the practices, right?" EJ shouted.

A stage crew member opened the dressing room door and turned on the overhead lights. The fluorescence was far less romantic than the blaring lights of the stage. The girls continued to buzz and EJ beelined to a cooler. He tossed waters to the girls and flicked them with the melting ice.

"Ahh," Macy said, "that feels amazing."

EJ beamed, *"Dios mio,* we knocked it out of the park!"

While Mia wasn't looking, Lars had entered the room and joined the band's celebratory moment. Lars approached Mia and swept her off her feet.

"Babe, you pulled this all together!" He exclaimed. "You were exactly what was missing."

Lars' flashy grin grew. He set Mia down, held both sides of her face, and kissed her on the forehead. From there, he went on to congratulate the rest of the band. Mia took a long drink of water. Uncertain what to do next, she wandered to retrieve her guitar from its lean on the wall and placed the instrument back into its case.

Earlier in the evening, Mia had debated whether she should tuck the Aid into her guitar case but decided against bringing the device. She didn't want to risk losing the new piece of technology in the shuffle of their debut performance. Plus, she was skirting the edge of TRN's fame avoidance rule and was suspicious of the device's tracking capability.

"Ready to see the headliners?" Lars asked. "EJ, I've got the keys to the room. I'll lock up and you can keep everything stored 'til tomorrow morning. That way, your brother doesn't have to bring the van tonight and you guys can wait to load up."

"Sounds good," EJ said, "I'll call him and tell him not to come tonight."

EJ grabbed the mounted phone.

"Alright, I gotta go see if the stage crew needs orchestrating. Headliner's on soon! Get out there and enjoy it," Lars paused and locked eyes with Mia, "you deserve to celebrate. Catch you dudes after the show. I'll lock up here after I check with the crew."

EJ called his brother. Though Mia could only understand select words as the siblings spoke, EJ beamed the entire time. EJ hung up and skipped over to his bag. He pulled out a cheap bottle of champagne.

"This has been a long time coming," EJ said and popped the cork.

The Tuesdaze cheered and began to pass the bottle, adrenaline still pumping through Mia's system.

"Mia," EJ said, his eyes crinkling, "thank you for showing up at the right time."

Mia chuckled in response to the unbeknownst accuracy of EJ's sentiment.

"And thank you for being right here, waiting for me," she responded.

"Oh, alright you saps," Tiffany joked, "let's get out there and see if these guys can follow us!"

They polished off the champagne and exited the Lakehouse's backstage. The Tuesdaze were adulated by the crowd as they permeated into the mass. Throughout the night, despite their missing wristbands, the underage Tuesdaze were supplied with any drink they fancied. They even received a shout-out from the headliner's lead singer.

"Hopefully Lars can get us more gigs," Macy said. "I could get used to this."

The show ended and the crowd began to thin. Lars came into Mia's view from across the floor. He appeared to be wrapping things up with the Lakehouse stage crew. Mia yawned. The rush was wearing off and exhaustion replaced her high.

"I think I'm best to drive," Macy said. "If anyone's gonna put the Cav out of its misery, it's going to be me."

"If you say so," EJ replied. He cupped his hands around Mia's ear. "Better than Tiff. Look at her."

Mia chuckled as Tiffany struggled to stand up straight.

"What time is it?" Mia asked EJ, not yet accustomed to her phone's absence. Mia looked around the Lakehouse, but all the clocks were set at different times.

"We're on 'lake time' as Gene would say," EJ explained then looked at his watch. "It's 1:45."

"Guys, I gotta go home soon," Tiffany mumbled.

Mia could think of nothing more luxurious than the notion of closing her eyes.

"While we're conscious, may I suggest breakfast tomorrow at the Diner?" EJ asked.

Macy replied, "You know it." She paused and looked toward the stage, "How long did Lars want us to stick around? Does he need a ride downtown?"

They observed their friends' demeanor from afar.

"Wow. Someone hit the bottle hard tonight," Tiffany observed.

Lars stumbled and barked nonsensical orders at the crew. He wandered to the edge of the stage and waved at the Tuesdaze.

"He looks pretty smashed," EJ said through clenched teeth as he waved back at Lars. "We should probably hang around."

They waited for Lars near the venue's entrance. As the audience trickled out from the Lakehouse, they paid their respects to the Tuesdaze.

"Do you have a CD?" They asked.

"You've gotta play more shows, I'll be looking for flyers!"

EJ laughed when a departing fan yelled, "Girl power!"

Time passed and the audience cleared completely. Delirium set in.

"You girls," EJ began, "you make me look so good! No joke, we've gotta do a photo shoot," EJ posed on the floor with one leg propped up, his hand supporting his head. The girls laughed at EJ.

Gene walked around from behind the bar. In his hand, he held a disposable camera.

"Say cheese!" Gene said and snapped a photo. He spun the camera's thumbwheel.

"We weren't ready!" Macy said.

EJ pulled Macy down to a squat in front of him.

"Hold on Gene, we need you to take another picture. Here, you're like this," EJ gestured. He pulled Tiffany down to crouch behind him. Tiffany lost her balance and slapped her hands down on the drenched floor to catch herself.

"Nasty!" Tiffany made a disgusted expression. "I don't feel so good."

"And Mia!" EJ reached for her arm, "You lay right in front of me and rest your face in your hands," EJ patted the area in front of him.

They tug-of-war'ed Mia onto the filthy floor until they were a pile of laughing, beer-soaked wannabes.

"Now this," EJ said through the laughter, "this is a proper band poster. Let's sell it at the next gig!"

Gene laughed and took two more photos.

"I'll give you copies! We can have them blown up! The Tuesdaze have merch, people!" Gene announced to the empty venue. "I'm cashed for the night; Lars can show you out of here. If you can find him, that is. I haven't seen him for a few minutes. Love the kid, but he's pushed some buttons tonight."

With that, Gene gathered his jacket and left the Lakehouse.

Mia pressed herself up from the floor and picked a skinny black stir stick off her leg. She continued laughing but came to a standstill when she saw Tiffany's face. Tiffany was pale. She swallowed hard. Macy and Mia exchanged a concerned look.

"Let's get you outside," Macy said and rushed Tiffany out the front door.

EJ and Mia remained inside.

"Poor Tiff," Mia said.

"She'll feel better than the rest of us tomorrow," EJ reasoned. "Should we go back and check on Lars?"

"I guess," Mia replied, dreading the state in which she anticipated Lars to be.

The two of them headed backstage and passed the dressing room. The dressing room door was wide open; Lars hadn't locked up. As they turned down the back corridor, they saw that the skeleton stage crew was struggling to haul the headliner's instruments through the exit door to their trailer out back. A crew member caught EJ's attention.

"Can you give us a hand with the keyboard?" They pleaded. EJ sighed.

"Yeah, I guess. Mia, just go up front if you don't find him in a few minutes. Our instruments should be alright with the building locked."

"Okay," Mia said and meandered down the hall.

Just as she was about to exit backstage to check on Macy and Tiffany, Mia heard a familiar voice behind her.

"There she is," he slurred, "I hoped you hadn't left me here!"

Lars walked around the corner to meet Mia. He had a bottle of whisky in one hand and a cigarette in the other. He took a drag and left the cigarette hanging from the side of his mouth. Lars reached for his pack of smokes and offered a cigarette to Mia. She accepted and Lars lit the end.

'Why not? It's a celebratory night.'

Mia's shoulders relaxed with the nicotine.

"Did you come back here to find me?" Lars asked. "You were such a stunner up there; the headliners wouldn't shut up about the Tuesdaze."

"Thanks. And yeah, EJ and I were trying to find you. I think we're ready to go. Tiff got sick," Mia explained. Lars leaned in close, and she smelled whisky on his breath.

"She never could handle her booze," Lars stated.

Mia soured, "Doesn't look like you're doing much better."

"I think there's a way I could do better…" Lars traced down Mia's arm and rested his hand on her waist. He beamed his bright white smile, looking carnivorous.

"I'm just glad I could hook you up with this gig. You looked so sexy playing," Lars bit his lip. He scanned Mia from head to toe. "From the sound of it, everyone enjoyed it almost as much as I did."

Lars hooked his index finger around her front belt loop.

"Thanks," Mia said, unsure how to take the arrogantly tinged compliment.

Lars breached Mia's line of comfort, and this wasn't his first offense. During the Tuesdaze's practices, Lars had pulled Mia onto his lap a few times and gave her plenty of casual spanks, but she chalked it up to being in a different time. Mia stood isolated in the backstage hallway and became hyperaware of her surroundings.

"Lars, we just came back to check on you. EJ will be here any minute."

"I don't know how to take you," Lars said. "You're a tease is what you are. A tease. What's in all this for me?"

Mia's mouth dropped open. Her cigarette fell to the floor. Mia smudged it out with her stage platforms. Her rosy, post-Psilopram world began to darken.

"We better be on our way, don't wanna cause any band disputes this early on in our career," Mia said.

She yearned to be in a well-lit area.

Lars grabbed her other belt loop and pulled Mia's hips toward his pelvis. He pressed his lips against hers and thrust his tongue to the back of her mouth. Lars used his body weight and stumbled himself and Mia against the cold cement wall. Mia gasped, shocked by the frigid surface, and wondered where EJ was at.

"Lars!" She barely yelled before his tongue was back in her mouth.

He grabbed the seam where her pants came together and lowered Mia's zipper.

"Lars," Mia shouted, "Lars, stop it! Stop right now! Please!"

"Honey, you've been asking for this," he said. "Don't worry, I won't tell anyone."

Mia activated the remainder of her adrenaline. She mustered the strength to push Lars far enough away to catch her breath. Then, the back door opened.

Down the hallway from Mia and Lars, the guitarist of the headlining band stepped into the back entrance. His eyes were bloodshot. He spotted Lars and was about to ask him a question but paused instead. The back door closed behind the musician and looked back and forth between Lars and Mia. Mia heard the crew outside, yelling for him to open the door.

"Am I interrupting?" He asked.

Mia was humiliated. She imagined how it looked to the well-known artist, like she was sleeping with the manager. Tears streaked down her cheeks. Mia attempted to articulate an explanation to the artist.

"I'm…" she started, "thank you," was all she could stammer.

Free from Lars' confinement, Mia sprinted away.

She hurried down the hallway toward the main floor of the Lakehouse. Her shoes clacked on the floor beneath her, inhibiting a quiet escape. The noise upset Mia. She wanted to meet her friends outside as if nothing had happened and wanted to convince herself of the same story.

As she distanced herself from the back hallway, the venue's isolated corners transformed back into the familiar Lakehouse. Mia slowed down to a fast-paced walk. She was livid, but her shame was even stronger.

The Tuesdaze were gathered by the entrance. Tiffany and Macy were laughing about something, but EJ saw Mia and his expression sobered.

"Mia?" EJ blurted. His eyes grew round. EJ ran to Mia. He rested his hands on her shoulders. "Mia," EJ repeated, trying to reach her, "are you okay? What's wrong?"

"Holy shit," Macy said as she saw Mia's tears.

Macy placed her hand on Mia's back, her expression wild with concern.

"Talk to us, Mia," Tiffany said.

"I- I- I..." Mia struggled. "Where did you *go*, EJ?"

"Me and the crew got locked out," EJ explained, "so I walked around to the front entrance. Macy had it propped open to get Tiffany and herself back inside

"I found Lars...one of the headliners stopped him..."

Mia didn't know how much to say. She was hit with emotion. She hid her face in her hands and began to sob.

"I found Lars and he --"

Mia watched as Tiffany's nostrils flared. Tiffany's expression turned grave, and she clenched her hands into fists. She looked as though she'd gone mad.

EJ's eyes went blank as he processed what happened backstage.

"I should have stayed with you," EJ said.

Tiffany beelined toward the dressing room, but EJ stopped her by locking his forearm around her abdomen.

"Not now Tiff, not now," EJ said. "You know how he is when he's like this. Plus, you're sick. You can't fight him like this."

Tiffany writhed to escape his grip, but EJ persisted.

"Tiff," he said with a lowered voice. "Listen, I hate the vice he's got us into, but if the headliners are still here, if we want to play this venue again, the last thing we can do is make a scene."

"How can you keep dismissing his behavior?" Tiffany asked.

Meanwhile, Macy locked arms with Mia and stroked her head. She guided Mia toward the exit of the Lakehouse while Tiffany and EJ argued.

"You want to play more, right?" EJ asked, disgusted by his own acquittal of Lars' actions. "This is hard for me too, but we *have* to be cool right now."

EJ's words no longer registered as Tiffany remembered what Lars had done to her on that late summer night.

"Someone's gotta bring him down, EJ," Tiffany's eyes welled with tears. "I know, you're right; this isn't the place for a scene. No one would believe me anyway, and I refuse to be just another girl with a story, but I've got to tell you, EJ, he's got everyone fooled."

EJ dropped his head, "I should have stayed with Mia."

"Let's go check on her," Tiffany said and scanned the Lakehouse's open concert floor. "Macy must have taken her outside."

EJ replied, "Yeah, let's head out, Lars will figure out his own ride."

"Damn right he will," Tiffany muttered.

They heaved open the Lakehouse's front entrance doors and hurried across the gravel parking lot to Macy's car. When EJ and Tiffany opened the back doors of Macy's Cavalier, they found Mia curled up in the center of the backseat. Macy stroked Mia's back.

"Let's sit you up, Mia," Macy said. "Should we get out of here?"

Mia nodded and Macy got in the driver's seat. Tiffany and EJ sat on either side of Mia. They were at a loss for what to do or say. The silence was heavy, so Macy switched on the radio.

An artist sang with a low, steady voice. The song's organ created a shrillness, perfectly matching the mood. Mia trembled like the last few leaves hanging onto a tree at the end of autumn. EJ sang along. Mia lay her head down on his shoulder, comforted by the vibration of his soft voice. EJ stroked Mia's hair back from her face and Tiffany wiped Mia's tears with cold fingers.

"We've got you," Macy said from the driver's seat. "We'll stick together. That show was amazing, and he *will not* take that away from us," Macy stated.

Mia's thoughts drifted back to their performance.

"*Nothing* can take that show away," Macy reiterated, determined not to ruin the accomplishment of their debut. "Once this town sees what we've got, how we turn that audience on, scouts will be all over us."

Macy's words brought life back into Mia.

"Did Lars have something to do with the drama you talked about before?" Mia asked.

"He had everything to do with it," Tiffany said.

"But if we play our cards right, if we don't let him get us down, if we have each other's backs, eventually, he'll have nothing to do with us. Mia, we'll stay at your place with you tonight if you'd like," Macy offered.

Tiffany and EJ nodded in agreement.

"Sure," Mia accepted.

Macy pulled up to Mia's apartment and parked then climbed the stairs to her unit. Mia went to take a shower as soon as they got inside. Laying on Mia's bed when she dried off were her favorite band t-shirt and grey sweatpants. The smell of popcorn wafted from the kitchen.

Mia stepped into the living room.

"Thank you for being here," Mia said with a weak smile.

Exhaustion took over and the time had come to rest. They collected pillows and blankets from the living room. Macy lay down in bed next to Mia while EJ and Tiffany slept in the living room.

The emotional swing had finally caught up with them, and they fell asleep.

Mia woke in the night with a busy mind. She couldn't wrap her head around an evening, so phenomenal, taking such an ugly turn within minutes. Mia felt like a fool.

Macy had specifically said that the band wanted to avoid drama, and Mia fretted that the evening's events would jeopardize the Tuesdaze' newfound success.

'I gave Lars the wrong idea.'

Mia had the urge to get up and pace, but with Macy at her side, Mia was confined to the bed. She wished the sun would rise sooner, but daylight savings time was still weeks away. Mia closed her eyes and went back to her family's record store. She could still smell the musk of the attics from which King's Records' stacks were derived. Mia wondered what tune Les would play to remedy a night like the one she'd just had. She thought back to the look on her grandpa's face when he played his favorites for her.

"I've got just the tunes for the mood," Les would say.

And he always did. Mia smiled to herself in the darkness.

When Les first selected albums from his personal collection, Mia was a skeptical, resistant teen. Mia had assumed that he would lay the needle on a twangy, irrelevant artist of the past's dying manifesto. Instead, Mia was swept away by hypnotic melodies. The artists bestowed an indescribable sense of knowing upon their listeners. A universal understanding of human intricacies which they publicly denied.

At last, Mia settled into her body's craving for rest.

Mia awoke with the morning sun in her window.

The acceptable hour to rise had arrived, but Mia didn't want to get out of bed. She heard her friends begin to rouse but couldn't muster the effort to join. Macy bounced Mia's bed as she took a seat on the mattress' edge. The rest of the group joined her, and pried Mia from her cocoon. Before departing Mia excused herself while the Tuesdaze remained in the kitchen. She hurried to her bedroom and slid the Aid in her pocket with the resolve to follow TRN's rules and keep the device nearby.

The waitress placed four mugs and a thermos in the middle of the table. One by one, Tiffany filled their cups. Steam spiraled upward from the dense mugs.

Mia was reluctant to leave her bed, but once they had squeezed into their usual booth, Mia was glad her friends drug her to the Diner. Although Mia's outlook had dramatically shifted the night before, the Diner's crowd served as evidence that the world carried on.

The Diner was reminiscent of the place Mia's grandparents went every Sunday after church. As a child, Mia didn't absorb much of the mundane recitations when she tagged along to feign worship, but she loved the ritualistic aspect. The smell of incense at Easter. The light as it gleamed through the stained glass. Sunday breakfast with her grandparents (church optional) was something Mia cherished. It was the beginning of a new week, and everything was fresh. Unscathed.

Mia warmed her hands on her coffee cup.

"Mia, I am so sorry for what happened to you last night," Tiffany took a deep, shaky breath. "We wouldn't have had to leave you and EJ if I hadn't gone overboard."

"Hey, this isn't your apology to make," Mia said. "I probably let him get away with too much before. He's been flirty at practice. I guess I didn't know he would take it so far."

"Last summer, there was a night," Tiffany struggled, "a night that Lars pulled the same thing with me. I woke up in bed with him. I didn't remember anything."

Mia shook her head in disbelief.

EJ and Macy's mouths dropped open.

"I knew you two hooked up," EJ started, "he bragged to me, but I had no idea that's how it went down. That is what you were trying to tell me about last night, wasn't it?"

"Yeah, though I couldn't articulate it very well," Tiffany stated. "I know bringing it up is long overdue, maybe I'm just exhausted and hungry, but I had to tell you guys before he gets away with it again."

The color drained from EJ's face.

Macy took Tiffany's hand.

"I wish we would have known sooner," Macy said. "We may be in deep with Lars, but we can't let him win. He can't drive us away from this, especially now that we have Mia."

Silence fell upon them.

They watched an employee walk up from a discreet downstairs area of the Diner. She balanced the weight of a box on her torso. Once she was at the top, she dropped the container with a thud.

'Halloween,' was written on the box's side. The Tuesdaze watched her, but it didn't seem right to move on from such a heavy conversation. After a few more minutes, Macy took the leap.

"Costume ideas anyone?" Macy said, changing the subject.

Before anyone could answer, the Diner's entryway bell rang. EJ was seated next to Mia, and he turned to face the door where Lars stood. The group exchanged a look of concern.

EJ walked toward the entrance before anyone could react. Macy and Tiffany spun their heads to watch EJ approach Lars. Mia rested her head in her hands. Tiffany began to slide out of the booth, but Macy stopped her.

"Let EJ handle this," Macy said. "Don't give Lars the reaction he's looking for."

The doorbell chimed as the boys walked around the corner and out of sight. Tiffany, Macy, and Mia sat in anticipatory silence. Mia stirred her coffee. Time passed.

"It's been a while, should we go check on them?" Tiffany asked.

"It's only been five minutes," Macy responded.

Tiffany sighed, "It feels like it's been much longer. I just don't know how Lars will react if EJ calls him out. EJ might need backup."

Just then, the boys re-entered the Diner. EJ walked in first with Lars trailing him.

EJ gestured to Lars, "Lars has something he wants to say."

EJ slid in the booth, next to Mia, and Lars stood at the end of the table. Navy bags had formed under Lars' eyes, and he was pale. EJ, on the other hand, sat tall.

"I- uh, I was pretty messed up last night," Lars said.

Tiffany rolled her eyes, "You can say that again."

"I'm sorry for making you uncomfortable Mia," Lars said as he pulled up a chair. "I just thought we hit it off before and I don't know, I thought you wanted me to make a move."

"Because I was nice to you, you thought I wanted... that?" Mia said.

Lars scoffed.

"You came back. We had a cigarette. Alone. What was I supposed to think?" He asked. "I made a move. That's it."

Mia lowered her voice and hunched forward.

"Pushing someone up against a cement wall is considered a *move?*" She asked.

A waitress arrived at their table.

"I can't talk about this here," Mia said, trembling with anger.

The *extent* of the era's differences caught up with Mia and she saw what her parents had worried about.

"Can I get you anything to drink?" The waitress asked.

Lars answered, "Yeah, can I get an orange juice?"

"One orange juice," the waitress scribbled. "Is everyone ready to order?" She gazed around at the group. "Or maybe a few more minutes?"

They nodded and focused on the menu. Mia read the same menu items over and over, but she couldn't comprehend the words. The waitress returned after a few minutes, and Mia blurted an order which she forgot as soon as the waitress left. Mia wasn't even sure if she would be able to stomach her food.

"All this aside," Lars began, "we have to get another Tuesdaze show on the books. Halloween's coming up. I can try & find a venue for y'all around the holiday. I bet Gene would be happy to have you back onstage at the Lakehouse."

Tiffany shook her head, "God, I can't believe you."

Lars pursed his lips.

"Go on, Lars," Macy prompted. "You owe us this time."

Lars turned to face Mia.

"Look, I'm sorry," he said. "I guess I was out of line. Mia, I'm sorry I hurt you. I read the situation wrong."

Mia avoided his persistent eye contact.

"Do you guys wanna play again or not? It won't happen again. I promise," Lars said and looked to Mia for a response.

She said nothing.

Lars turned to EJ.

"Man, I know you've wanted to play in a group like this since you joined band in junior high," Lars elbowed EJ. "I remember you telling me in the dorms how, onstage, you didn't feel like a nerd. How playing with a *real* band made you feel cool."

"That was between you and me," EJ said as his cheeks flushed.

"Let me hook you guys up. It's the least I can do to make it right," Lars continued.

"You just tell us when and where," Macy chimed. "In the meantime, have a little respect. You can't keep scaring away our talent."

Macy punched Lars' arm.

"Ouch," Lars held the site of her hit. "I guess I deserve that." Macy smirked at his guilty plea.

The waitress returned and sat their plates on the table. As they ate, the five of them discussed prospective Halloween plans.

"My brother has a party in the works," EJ said. "It's the night after Halloween. That's when we grew up celebrating." EJ crunched his bacon. "No getting in without a costume."

They continued to scheme and devoured their meals. Mia caught only fragments of the conversation, lost in thought.

When they walked to the check-out podium, Mia fumbled with her wallet. She felt the outline of her safety device and wondered what would have happened if she'd signaled TRN on the Aid backstage. Lars pulled out a twenty-dollar bill.

"I can be decent you know," he said.

Macy cut in and snatched the bill from Lars, crumpled it into a ball, and dropped it on the floor.

"Buy our friendship in gigs," she said.

After the group paid, they left the Diner. A sharp, early October gust of wind chilled Mia to the bone. They began to walk toward Mia's apartment where Macy's car was parked.

"It got cold overnight," EJ stated.

Macy and Tiffany walked ahead, but Mia remained at EJ's side.

"Ugh," EJ continued, "why do I play drums again? I'm already dreading loading them."

"Gene will meet you there at 11:00. We'll be in touch about Halloween," Lars said. With that, he diverted from the group toward his car which appeared to have been terribly parallel parked the night before. Mia wondered how many more people he upset before leaving the Lakehouse. She chuckled at the parking ticket tucked beneath Lars' windshield wipers. The rest of the crew continued to Mia's parking lot and piled into Macy's Cav.

Macy fired up the old vehicle's engine and they started toward the Lakehouse. As the Tuesdaze drove, Mia was relieved by Lars' shrinking in the rear-view mirror.

Chapter V

Summer came and the streets were wrapped in every hue. The air itself was electric as societal limitations were dismantled. Revolution steadily hummed throughout the city streets. People simultaneously tuned in and tripped out. The collective solidified their independence from all outdated confinements.

Renee rounded the corner to her shop, adding more color to the scene. She was filled with pride every time she faced her storefront. Renee inherited the boutique, *En Blum*, from her grandmother, Sylvia.

The space was not just a clothing store, but a creative medium, a source of inspiration under constant evolution. Renee gazed in the front window before stepping inside; before daily operations stole her presence. She could still picture her grandmother pacing about. Renee stepped inside and breathed in the familiar aroma of rose. Though Sylvia was gone physically, Renee kept her memory alive by filling the boutique with plumes of rose-scented incense, Sylvia's favorite smell. When Renee was a child, Sylvia would always have a chair pulled up to the sewing machine for Renee to observe.

Sylvia's lessons began with replacing a button and over time, progressed to threading a bobbin. She taught Renee how to assess the quality of fabric and what materials were best suited for each type of garment. Sylvia shared the art of tailoring and finally, patternmaking. In her younger years, Renee often suppressed her desire to go play and stayed inside to absorb every piece of advice offered by her grandmother.

Sylvia' hands grew achy with age. The boutique had gained local popularity and Sylvia could no longer keep up with the growing demand. Though Renee tried help throughout her teenage years, her earnestness didn't make up for Sylvia's years of expertise.

Sylvia began to have clothing shipped to the boutique to supplement her handmade garments. Though Sylvia had only resorted to ordering clothing out of desperation, she made the most of the necessary change. Sylvia made tea and cakes for herself and Renee, and they sang Sylvia's favorite French tunes while selecting the next season's inventory. As an adult, Renee continued to observe their tradition when selecting the boutique's seasonal apparel.

Renee achieved her first styling triumph in her late teenage years. Sylvia nodded with approval at Renee's "teddy boy" window display and finally acknowledged her granddaughter's good taste. Renee still remembered the houndstooth sport jacket with black lapels. The slim fit trousers. The silk pocket square.

The joy Renee brought to her grandmother was a stark contrast to the hardships Sylvia had endured. Renee knew only a fraction of what Sylvia had seen and held high reverence for her grandmother's durability. Sylvia and Renee's grandfather Oliver, who Renee only knew for a short time, epitomized a life fully lived.

Sylvia grew up in a small Bohemian village in France. After years of roaming, Sylvia's nomadic parents settled in the community which was known for its rich supply of wool. The people were skeptical of Sylvia's family.

At the market, people avoided being near her family for extended periods, but the town couldn't deny that Sylvia's mother created the most beautiful creations. Despite her family's limited means, Sylvia followed her mother's footsteps and crafted clothing from a very early age.

Sylvia's father was a musician. He was a tinkerer and repaired many instruments throughout his youth which gave him the ability to play nearly any instrument. He played accordion and sang at their market booth, making even more of a spectacle of Sylvia's family. They leaned into the village's conditional acceptance, ignoring the fact that they earned their keep by serving as a source of gossip and fascination.

At the edge of the village stood an ornate theatre. The building was a staple of the region and served as the perfect outlet for the family's trades. Sylvia's mother created exquisite costumes for shows and her father joined the theatre's house orchestra. Their dedication to music and apparel provided food and shelter for Sylvia and her four siblings.

Then, the First Great War hit.

"The war to end all wars," rang in Sylvia's ears as she tried to fall asleep at night.

An abrupt halt in theatrical productions eliminated the need for stage costumes leaving too much time for Sylvia's mother to look out the window and fret. The stall in shows also put Sylvia's father out of work and he was too elderly to join the service, so he joined his wife in her state of constant anxiety. They watched the hill which oversaw the city, anticipating the day when enemy troops breached the peak.

"We're sitting ducks," Sylvia heard her older siblings say. "I heard on the streets that there's been an invasion just north of us."

"We've got to run. At least we'd have some control," Sylvia told her parents.

Sylvia's mother dropped her head back and sighed.

"Sylvie, baby, we don't know where the next frontline will be. We must stay. To uproot will only cause more trouble."

The family scraped by and helped the war effort in any way they could. To keep their hands and minds occupied, Sylvia, her sister, and mother lent their skills to uniform production by dressing the French soldiers. Sylvia's two brothers joined the service, and her eldest sister volunteered as a medic.

After what seemed like an eternity, victory was finally celebrated. Sylvia's siblings returned home. Her parents anticipated word for the show to go on, for their employment to resume. But, just as the celebration commenced, another battle took center stage.

The Influenza outbreak hit Europe. Their small village stalled trade with the neighboring city. The theatre remained dark and vacant.

The family waited.

They dreamed of the day when Sylvia's father's music filled the theatre and her mother's costumes danced across the stage. It seemed Sylvia's days of assisting her mother with final fittings had come to an end.

In the meantime, to keep her worry at bay, Sylvia perfected her tailoring skills. As their family grew rail-thin, Sylvia altered her family's waistlines. Sylvia also bided time by assembling gowns from old scraps of fabric. She donned her custom eveningwear with pride when the family gathered for sparse dinners.

One night after their meal, Sylvia stepped out of the house to dispose of the little waste they had. Before she left the door, she wrapped a leftover cut of fabric around her nose and mouth.

Sylvia hoisted her family's trash into the bin. She noticed another person outside; a handsome young man nodded hello from across the street. Like Sylvia, he carried a small heap to dispose. The young man's eyes crinkled with the smile beneath his scarf.

The opportunity to socialize was too rare for Sylvia to shy away.

"*Bonjour,*" Sylvia greeted him.

"Bonjour," he replied. "I've got to be honest; my French is rubbish. Do you speak English?"

Sylvia nodded.

"My name is Oliver Blum," he said.

"Sylvia Wood," she responded. "I like your accent. What brought you here? The war, I assume?"

"Yes, it did. Though, how I arrived in this village has proven to be quite a long story," Oliver said. "Do you have the time?"

Sylvia nodded, "It seems that's all we have."

"I came here after being released from the service. I fell ill, see. Since recovering, I've spent time wandering through the French countryside. I live with my brother-in-arms, Leon. We're renting from the kindest elder-woman."

"Why did you choose to stay here when you could have returned home?"

Oliver's gaze turned downward.

"So, the story lengthens. Should I ever return home, my father would expect me to join the line as a factory worker. He's a loyal laborer and has made a good life for me, but I'm not cut out to do the same thing all day. There's no romance in the

111

house where I was born. I heard this village was once alive with music and I'm waiting for its return."

"I wish you could have seen this town years ago. It seems everything will remain dormant forever. At least you have company. I'm stuck with my family," Sylvia hung her head. "Is your friend also an Englishman?"

"Leon was brought up in the American south," Oliver explained. "Like my mum, Leon's mother also passed on too early. Leon's father was a music man and had exhausted his options in New Orleans, so the two of them jumped a northbound train with hopes of a fresh start in the Big Apple. They made their home in Harlem, New York City. Before they could get settled, Leon received his orders. He would go on to become a 'Man of Bronze,'" Oliver paused. "We wouldn't have won without them, the 'Harlem Hellfighters.'"

"A Hellfighter," Sylvia repeated. She'd heard of the troupe who largely contributed to the war's favorable outcome.

"Yes, and not just a hell of a fighter, but a hell of a musician," Oliver stated. "The night I met Leon was one of the troupe's performances. Amidst the world of trenches and horrors, their music shed a precious beam of light into the bleakness. For the first time in months, I felt something worth feeling," Oliver shuddered.

"After the show, before Leon was pulled away, I made it a point to compliment his remarkable horn solos. On the nights when camp was too quiet, when the encroaching explosions prohibited sleep, I hoped to, once again, hear the tunes in a more peaceful world. My God, it seemed the war would never end," Oliver continued, "when at last, sweet victory."

"What a day that was," Sylvia recalled the festive spirit of the occasion.

"Shortly after the war ended, I became horribly ill, as I mentioned. I barely got to celebrate before I was quarantined. One day in the infirmary, I looked over and there he was. Leon pulled that scratchy wool blanket up to his chin and turned to face me. We met eyes, and he recognized me from the show."

"Fate," Sylvia said.

"Long story short," Oliver continued, "well, too late for that I suppose, we became mates. By some miracle we survived that awful illness. Leon missed the last ship home, but he wasn't broken up about it. He shared with me what awaited him in America. Their Civil War may be over, but not in all aspects."

"So, you plan to remain here?" Sylvia asked. "I hope to see you in the light one day."

"I would like that," Oliver responded. "And you'll stay as well?"

"This is my home," Sylvia said. "Bombs thundered to the north, but we endured."

Her multicolored dress of rags rippled with the breeze, enchanting Oliver. The days grew longer, and the illness slowly began to vanish. After months of getting to know each other from across the cobblestone, Oliver asked Sylvia to be his wife. They went on to birth one daughter, Vivienne, Renee's mother.

Sylvia and Oliver fled from France to England due to the circumstances of World War II. Leon fled along with them, and their once idyllic village was mercilessly overrun by the Gestapo.

Leon and the Blums landed in an artistic region of London. Oliver and Leon, no longer young soldiers, contributed to the British World War II efforts by lending their skills to the Essential Work Order. Sylvia worked in a clothing factory while her daughter, Vivienne, went to school. While Vivienne slept, Sylvia often took the time to create beautiful dresses for her little girl. The ruffles and pastels lent sunshine to her grey, green, and camel-colored days.

World War II ended and Leon and the Blums remained in their corner of the city. Their new settlement served as a hideaway for the upper class who were on the hunt for meaning and authenticity in their buttoned-up lives.

With a refreshed gratitude for normal, post-war life, Sylvia and Oliver took a risk and opened a boutique. Sylvia named the shop, '*En Blum.*' Oliver took care of the books while Sylvia created ballgowns, outerwear, and suits. She was grateful for any piece of fabric she could get her hands on and spared none of her talent.

"I may not be an artist or musician," Oliver said, "but I will support you in any way I can. To be surrounded by inspiration is all I need to sustain myself."

En Blum gained traction and became a destination in the growing hot spot of the city. Sylvia crafted ensembles until fingers would no longer allow. Then, she worked through her only grandchild, Renee.

Renee paused her playtime with Leon's grandson, Germain, to watch Sylvia create. Sylvia passed her knowledge on to Renee by wrapping her mastery in the special love between a grandparent and grandchild. Renee's interest in the craft was a welcome contrast to Vivienne's complete lack of interest in apparel.

Vivienne, Oliver and Sylvia's only child, was often gone with no explanation. Renee never met her own father. The few memories Renee conjured of her mother involved late arrivals, gifts of expensive jewelry, and eventually, unfulfilled letters promising Vivienne's return.

Renee was often overwhelmed with emotion when she stopped to think about how *En Blum* came to be. The boutique had endured so much, but a fork in Renee's life was beginning to present itself. Renee's determination to make Sylvia proud was ever-present, however Renee's social status left her with little tinder to fuel the boutique's daily operations. Her life was propelling forward with no brakes.

On busy days, her new employee, Derek, offered much needed relief. Renee was intrigued by Derek, though she found it odd that he committed to the boutique so hastily. His prompt devotion led Renee to stall their physical relationship. She couldn't put her finger on what exactly, but something about Derek was different than anyone she had met. He spoke of years to come with a mysterious wisdom. It was as though he saw the future.

Derek was satisfied with the part-time gig. He enjoyed the pace of the boutique and it felt more like a hangout than a rigid workplace.

In Original Time, Derek's job was focused on efficiency and metrics. Derek's quarterly work assessments included a manager's review based on productivity and "innovation." Derek had been playing a part in Original Time, the script written by those in charge.

Being with Renee offered more than a role in the production of perceived success. Renee was teaching Derek how to live as himself rather than a job title. Derek watched as, with the right look, Renee turned many imitators back to themselves.

Men were the primary clothing designers of the era, but Renee served as an exception to the bias. Derek saw the power of Renee's selections. She was magnetic with just the right amount of madness, and London was noticing.

Grant, Germain, Lorraine, and Carole spent their summer afternoons lounging in the boutique. They played music from a turntable behind the register and smoked weed between customers. Grant could always be counted upon to bring the newest psychedelic tunes and Derek reveled in the moment. *En Blum* was quickly becoming a hub where musicians, it-girls, and artists frequented.

One quiet weekday afternoon, the crew lazed around *En Blum* while Renee layered Carole in pieces from her newest shipment. Carole transformed into a live mannequin, stratified in luxe fabrics near the front window. After Renee evaluated the fit of each new garment, she gave Carole permission to undress.

Carole removed a floor length coat.

"Too hot for June," Carole stated. "Don't you think?"

"You forget, I'm planning for next season," Renee replied.

Next, Carole slipped her fingers, one at a time, from a pair of silk gloves. A small group began to gather outside the window and gawk at the exhibition. Carole untied the scarf from her neck. She floated the square piece of fabric across the air, matching the ups and downs of the spinning record.

Carole unbuttoned the collared blouse, exposing her black lingerie beneath. The crowd grew exponentially. The six friends were at a loss for words as they watched from inside the boutique.

"Carole love, keep going," Renee encouraged, "look at this crowd!"

Carole faced away from the window and unfastened the buttons down to her navel. She shrugged the fabric off her shoulders and turned to face the onlookers. Carole blew a kiss to her gaping fans.

116

"Do I dare continue?"

"Without question," Renee answered.

Carole let her blouse slip onto the floor. She began to unzip the first inch of her mini skirt when two cops blazed a path through the audience.

Bang, bang, bang!

They knocked on the windows.

"Stop this indecency at once!" They waved the crowd on. "Break it up, break it up!"

Renee laughed at the authorities' efforts.

"I'll settle this," Renee said and stepped outside. She approached the officers. "What's the problem here?" She asked.

Derek couldn't hear the officers' response over Carole and Lorraine's laughter.

"Oh, she's going to pull out all the stops," Carole cupped her hands around her mouth and yelled toward Renee. "Tell them to pull the stick out their arses! They were watching too!".

Derek watched the cops' bristly fronts begin to soften. After a few minutes, they shook Renee's hand and were on with their day. Renee walked inside, suppressing a smile.

"Next order," Renee stated as the entryway bell rang, "*En Blum* is selling lingerie."

The temperature continued to rise.

One day, as Derek assisted *En Blum's* customers, commotion arose outside the boutique. Young girls shrieked and teenage boys whooped.

"They're free!" The adolescents proclaimed.

"Do you know what's going on?" Derek asked a shopper.

Before the shopper could answer, Grant burst through the front door.

117

"Rock and roll will never die, baby!" Grant stated. "They've been released!"

When Grant said the artists' names, Derek couldn't help but chuckle. The band was far from the end of the line. The youth's relief was tangible, and by seeing the event unfold, Derek was woven further into the era.

During the weeks that followed, Derek and Grant wandered the streets together. They smoked marijuana in secluded areas over Derek's lunch break, and when they grew tired of walking, they often found a park bench to support their lazy bones. No subject, other than Derek's origin, was off limits with Grant.

Closing time arrived and Derek balanced the cash drawer. Grant had been in the boutique all day, keeping Derek company during the lulls. Derek and Grant stepped outside, and Derek fumbled through his keys to lock up when Renee popped her head out the front door.

"Derek love, can I trouble you for just a few more minutes?" Renee asked. "Some hefty boxes need pulled from storage."

"Sure!" Derek responded.

Grant patted Derek's back, "I'll catch up with you tomorrow man," he said. "I've still got a few days before I fly west. You sure you don't want to join me?"

Derek sighed, "I'm sure. I've got a lot to do here."

"That's cool," Grant responded. "See you tomorrow," he said and walked down the street toward his flat.

Derek realized how much he would miss Grant's company through the summer's end. Though Derek looked forward to hearing about the Bay upon Grant's return, Grant's upcoming adventure-tinged Derek with envy. Derek had contemplated making the 1960s United States' west coast his home when considering Travel destinations, but he was deterred by getting mixed up in the Vietnam draft. Still, Derek could only imagine the groovy stories Grant would share when he came back in the fall.

Derek walked across the showroom floor and back to the storage room where Renee had fashioned a lounge. What could have been a cold, cement inventory room was transformed into Renee's mystical work haven.

A bottle of Burgundy sat on the sewing machine desk. Various articles of clothing, hats, and dresses were strewn about the area, reminding Derek of Renee's bedroom. In the back corner was an afghan-draped chaise. Derek wondered how often Renee slept in the boutique.

"You know Grant leaves soon," Derek teased, "this must be an important shipment to keep me from him."

A lamp draped with scarves stood in the corner of the room. The translucent piece of fabric further enriched the old bulb's incandescent light, painting the walls in shades of amber.

"Relax, you're together all day. That one," Renee pointed to a box on the top shelf, "can you get it down?"

Renee stood at the top of a step ladder and raised onto her tiptoes. She extended her fingertips to show Derek that the box was beyond her reach. As she descended the ladder, Derek's eyes were drawn to the cinch of her waist. He shook off his growing sensations and offered a hand to assist Renee to the floor. Renee playfully swatted his hand away and smirked as she stepped down to the cement with grace.

She stepped aside and Derek climbed the ladder. He began to coerce the box from the top shelf. The weight of its contents shifted, and Derek nearly lost his balance.

"Careful! It's very heavy," Renee advised from below.

Derek heaved down the box with a grunt.

"What's *in* here?" He asked as the box crashed onto the cement floor.

Renee laughed and opened the box.

"Go-go boots," Derek said, "an important shipment, indeed."

He clapped the residual dust from his hands.

"Any others you need help with?" He offered.

"That takes care of the boxes," Renee walked to the record player.

She opened the cover and set a record into rotation.

Derek couldn't understand the French lyrics of Renee's chosen album, but the evening's mood shifted with the sound. The artist's smooth, clear voice sat at the center of the tune's bright melody. Renee sang along.

"I've been putting off the next order," she said. "It's been so busy. I don't know how *Grandmere* did it all those years."

Derek moved the box of boots from the walkway. Renee had not dismissed him, and he was in no hurry to go. The room was charged as silence fell between the tracks.

"What are you up to tonight?" Renee asked.

"No plans," Derek shrugged. He pinched the scarf that lay across the lamp. "This is going to start a fire though."

'*Old halogen bulbs.*'

"Leave it there," Renee exclaimed. "Look at what it does to this shabby old room."

They gazed around the space. Direct eye contact would set something in motion from which neither of them couldn't back away. Renee knew she needed to buckle down on her work, but she couldn't shake off the tension.

"I know how you're feeling. I feel it too. Where do we go from here?"

Renee flipped the record and the unknown words bewitched Derek. He had two choices; dismiss himself or give in to what they both desired. Renee took Derek's hand and led him to the chaise. Derek sat and put his hands on her hips.

"You're the boss around here," he said, "tell me what you want."

Their lips met, and the anticipation finally broke. Derek sculpted Renee's body. Her form brought Derek a potent, familiar sensation. He'd missed the indulgence. Derek traced his fingers from her collarbone to the peak of her breasts.

Renee rubbed one hand against his sideburns. She used the other to unbutton his pants and pull down his zipper. Derek sighed. He slipped Renee's dress straps down. Derek moved his fingers beyond the seam of her silk underwear when *En Blum's* front doorbell chimed.

Renee gasped and pulled up the top of her dress. She hurried to a full-length mirror and smoothed her hair.

"Ugh," Renee groaned, "I didn't think he'd wait til the last bloody minute. I'm sorry love, wait here for me."

Renee pulled herself together and rushed out to the floor. Derek was left alone. He was dizzy and his heart raced.

"Sorry to drop in last minute," a voice said from the floor. "I'm here to pick up the red trousers."

"Yes," Renee said, short of breath. Derek could hear her scramble for the right words. "Sorry I was sorting some orders. I-I'll be right back."

Renee returned to the storage room. She grabbed a pair of poppy-colored slacks from the rack, winked at Derek, and returned to the counter. Enough time passed for Derek to come down. He heard Renee ringing up the customer and Derek walked out to the floor to see who had interrupted.

Derek could see the customer's mass of curly brown hair as he grew closer. The customer heard Derek's approach and turned to face him. Derek repressed the urge to react. He recognized the legend.

Renee introduced them.

"Ah yes, this is Derek, he's been helping out," Renee smirked.

Derek shook the prodigy's hand.

"Derek, would you care to join us tonight? It's a real groovy scene," the musician assured. "Everyone's gonna be there."

"Yes! Are you kidding?" Derek blurted. "I mean yeah, I'm down."

"See you there, mate," he grinned at Derek, "and Renee, thank you."

The doorbell jingled and the customer made his exit.

"Listen," Renee coached Derek, "if you want to be a part of the scene tonight you're going to have to work on those starry eyes. Where we're going, there will be quite a few people you recognize." She cradled Derek's face with one hand. "They're just people. You'll keep up with them."

The A-List scene of 1967 was uncharted territory for Derek. Despite Derek's progress, facilitated by Psilopram, the prospect of going to a club occupied by legends ripped open his bag of insecurities.

Renee locked the cash register.

"Come with me," she said.

Derek followed Renee back, wondering if their romance would resume.

Renee poured two glasses of wine.

"Let's get you dressed!" Renee said,

"I am dressed," Derek looked down at his outfit.

"Derek my dear," Renee said as she started a new record, "I don't know what it is like in America, but the club tonight is far out. You can be as wild as you please with no judgment. Kick those Puritan values! Tonight, you are my handsome date. Here," she fumbled through a desk drawer and pulled out a camera bag, "you're *le photographe*. This camera will serve as your admission ticket."

Derek unzipped the black camera bag. Though his photography knowledge was limited to dabbling online, Derek was familiar with the piece of equipment Renee handed him. The camera was a quality classic.

"This was my grandad Ollie's, he never used it. He received it as a gift right before he passed away," Renee explained. "Inside is nearly an entire roll of film. I'm dying to see what's developed. Finish it tonight"

"Are you sure you want me to take this out? To carry it around a club?" Derek asked.

"Of course. I trust you. Plus, you've got a good eye, that's why I like having you around here, you've got *perspective d'artistes,*" Renee encouraged.

Derek fiddled with the camera. The Leica had a great lens, one which was hard to find in Original Time. He pointed the camera at Renee and snapped a photo.

"I wasn't ready!"

Renee went on to fix her hair in the mirror. She faced Derek and posed. Derek was locked into her presence. He captured one more shot, then set the camera on Renee's desk. Renee directed Derek to a mirror, stood behind him, and studied his face.

"I've got it!" Renee said and disappeared to the boutique floor.

Derek finished his glass of wine then took the bottle from her sewing table and refilled his glass. His hands trembled.

Renee returned with a heap of clothing over her arm. Green trousers, a striped shirt, and a black sport coat. She handed the pieces to Derek.

"Here, put these on," Renee directed before rushing back to the boutique floor.

Derek layered the pieces and was surprised at his reflection. He no longer saw Derek, former AI specialist, he wasn't a title. He was himself. Renee returned and tied a scarf around his neck.

"There," she praised her work, "better!"

Derek held back a smile as he processed his new image. He realized how much his hair had grown since his arrival. Renee pulled Derek's hair forward and tousled his overgrown cut. She fussed over small details; the placement of Derek's scarf, the fold of his sleeves, then, she finally settled. Renee's eyes glimmered.

"My turn now." Renee said.

She sat at a small vanity which was tucked in the corner of the storage room. Renee went on to perfect her hair with a red-and-black brush. She gestured Derek to where she was seated.

"Here, bring your face to me," she said.

Derek squatted to her eye level.

"Look up," Renee said.

She pulled an inky pot and small makeup brush from her vanity and applied eyeliner to Derek's inner rims. He relaxed into the hand holding his face. Renee traced his jawline with her fingers. When she was done, he approached the mirror.

"You're sure this isn't too much?" Derek asked.

Renee rolled her eyes and shook her head no. After touching up her pastel lipstick, she locked her arm in Derek's.

"Ready?"

Derek strapped the camera bag over his shoulder. "Ready."

Derek gained an instant heir of mystique upon their arrival. The camera provoked curious reactions. Some individuals turned on for the camera, displaying photogenic laughter. Others adopted moody pouts and strategically varied their gaze. A few of the clubbers positioned themselves further away from Derek, misreading his intentions, actively avoiding any party photos plastered in the news.

"Keep that thing away from me," one man said.

Despite the mixed reactions, the camera gave Derek something to focus on in the presence of stars and served as his security blanket when Renee separated herself to socialize. Renee became the evening's center of attention. Once her surrounding frenzy died down, Derek approached Renee as she was comfortably seated at the bar. He felt a hand squeeze his shoulder.

Derek turned to see Germain standing behind him with another man. Derek was star struck. Standing next to Germain was the boutique's late-afternoon customer. Derek hoped his jaw-drop went unnoticed as the icon left Germain's side and mingled into the crowd.

Germain wrapped his fingers around the back of Derek's neck, "Be cool brother," Germain said with a laugh, "I know he smashed Barbeque '67 and all, but he's here to have a good time, just like us. This joint's happening tonight," Germain stated. "Hey, I got a mate over at that corner booth, I just met him a couple days ago," Germain gestured across the dance floor. "You cats should meet. He's American too."

"Sure, lead the way," Derek replied.

Germain patted Derek's back and they started toward the corner booth. The closer they drew to Germain's booth; the more Derek recognized the man seated. Derek's heart dropped.

It was Vaughn, Derek's former friend, the thief of Anna's heart. They hadn't spoken since the night of the dramatic encounter. Derek stalled his stride.

"You... know one another?" Germain asked as he and Derek stood facing the booth.

"Yeah!" Vaughn answered before Derek had a chance to reply. "We're from the same town!"

"Good to see you man!" Derek played along.

Vaughn stood to shake Derek's hand. Derek grimaced.

"What a trip, I did not expect this," Germain narrowed his eyes.

"It's a surprise for us too!" Derek said and patted Vaughn's shoulder.

Germain attempted to start multiple conversations, each of them stifled with awkwardness. Germain grew fidgety and searched for an out. He was relieved when a waitress appeared to get their drink orders.

"Sidecar please," Vaughn ordered.

"Make that two," Derek said. "Three, Germain?"

"Nah man, I'm going to check in on Renee," Germain stated. "I'll let you two catch up."

Germain maneuvered his way through the growing crowd, leaving Vaughn and Derek alone.

"Why are you here, Vaughn? I am having the time of my life," Derek stated, "are you going to come in and ruin everything like you did before?"

"I know what I did that night was wrong," Vaughn said and hung his head. "I really thought I'd be able to-"

"Be able to what? Help?" Derek interrupted. "To be Anna's confidante? How dare you. She was all I had left after Cooper and Grandpa."

Derek's elevated voice caught the unwanted attention of passers-by, and he reluctantly toned down his volume.

"Whatever, you two deserve each other," Derek glared at Vaughn. "You didn't answer me, why are you here?"

Vaughn couldn't tell Derek the truth.

He'd been paid off by Derek's parents to monitor the Hayes.

He heard Derek had a rough landing into the sixties, so he chose to monitor Derek first.

He agreed to monitor so he could make amends and he was getting paid to do so.

"I've been," Vaughn lowered his voice, "I've been Traveling. This isn't my first destination."

"How many places have you been?" Derek asked. "Travel hasn't been around that long. I've only been here three months."

Vaughn cupped his hands around his mouth and spoke into Derek's ear.

"I'm contracted by TRN to Travel to other eras. I serve as a bridge of communication between TRN and Travelers if needed. I was assigned to the sixties and saw you were here. To be honest, I've wanted to clear the air for a long time," Vaughn explained. "You know I've had a lot of inconclusiveness in my life, moving around and such. Taking Psilopram made me realize I've left a lot of strings untied," Vaughn pulled back. "Look, I was out of line to go behind your back that night. I know it. And I'm sorry. I can imagine how it must have looked to you, believe me, I've replayed it in my head countless times. I wish you would have just talked to me about what happened. It didn't go down how you thought it did."

127

"You kissed my girlfriend. I saw you two laughing while I was going through the shittiest time of my life," Derek said.

"I just wanted to help you, man," Vaughn stated. "I never spoke with Anna again after that night. I only met up with her to try and convince her to stick it out with you, then she went in for the kiss. You've got to believe me."

"Whatever happened, it's over now," Derek softened. "Being here, or *getting* here rather, really changed things. Who knows, maybe cutting ties with Anna was for the best. It led me to Travel."

"The trip really does change everything, doesn't it? Or the things that come with it do…" Vaughn said.

Derek glanced toward Renee at the bar and Vaughn followed his line of vision.

"I saw that girl you walked in with," Vaughn said, "this place is doing you well."

"Should we head that way," Derek gestured to Germain and Renee at the bar, "or are you here with someone?"

"No," Vaughn replied, "I Travel solo."

Just as Derek and Vaughn began to slide out from the booth, Renee signaled them to remain seated then began to cross the dance floor.

"Hold that booth!" Renee yelled, "We're coming over!"

Derek looked around the club. Two tiers of balconies wrapped the perimeter above. Darkened figures looked down and surveyed the dance floor. Derek wondered who may be present.

"Vaughn, you won't believe who I met earlier--" Derek began.

Before he could finish his sentence, Renee and Germain arrived at the booth. They were accompanied by two other

128

individuals; one, a pixie-like, blonde woman, the other, a blonde man who wore a similar haircut to the impish woman. The man had prominent cheekbones and intensity in his eyes. He looked familiar, but Derek couldn't place him.

Renee slid next to Derek. The rest of the crew followed her lead and piled into the booth. Derek took a long pull of his drink. The group chatted and carried on, but the mysterious blondes did not introduce themselves.

Derek attempted to identify the strangers. He continued to scan their faces, but the dim light prohibited a thorough assessment. His evaluation was interrupted when under the table, Renee placed a handful of fleshy objects into Derek's palm. He looked beneath the table.

Renee spoke into his ear. "Pass them around," she instructed. "Then, you have the last one."

Derek did as he was told and distributed the magic mushrooms.

"This will help you realize that you're *a part* of all this," Renee stated and gestured around the club.

Vaughn and Derek met one another's eye.

"It's good," Vaughn mouthed.

Derek trusted Vaughn's experience and hoped for the best.

The dance floor transformed into one organism. A keyboard sounded in colors. Derek scanned the club and zeroed in on Vaughn. The absurdity of his old friends' arrival began to make all the sense in the world. Derek realized that Vaughn had been placed in the sixties to unblock his own flow of love from the universe, to sever the cords of the past.

Derek looked to Renee. She was extraordinary, bathed in prisms. As she danced, a halo shone from the crown of her head.

Derek was delighted when the flowers on her dress ticked from side to side.

Layers of perception to which Derek had previously clung were peeled away. Derek envisioned the planes of time and space. He was overwhelmed by his feelings of connection. Renee was right, he was a part of this. Derek felt liquid on his cheek and realized that tears were streaking down his face.

The overactivity of the dance floor began to tip Derek's mood. He started to panic, wondering how he was to handle the intensity. The gates were open, and Derek was not confident in his ability to endure the complexities which flooded in around him.

The pixie girl made her way next to Derek. The contrast of her deep brown eyes and thick eyebrows against her pure white hair and porcelain skin entranced Derek. As she moved, her impish figure began to morph. Derek grew frightened by the sharp angles of her body and her ability to distort.

He was struck with an urgent need to abandon the dance floor, and Derek retreated to the safety of the booth. There was too much of everything. Derek noticed the blonde man, seated across the table.

The man's presence was sincere and grounding. He gave Derek a knowing smirk, aware of Derek's state. To Derek's relief, the man's expression held no malice. The blonde man leaned in to face Derek. Derek mirrored the stranger and moved in closer. He got a better look at the man's face. His eyes appeared to be different colors: one dark, one light.

"You're not from here either," Derek stated.

The man held his index finger to his lips to quiet Derek. With that, the man stood and walked into the night.

Approbations for *En Blum* continued to intensify throughout the summer. The window incident with Carole and their star-studded night out caused more of a stir than Renee or Derek had anticipated. As a result, Derek grew more accustomed to their high-profile clientele. Derek felt less and less like a visitor to the era as the customers talked to him about the world's affairs.

Now that Grant was in California, Derek began to read the newspaper during the brief, slow periods at *En Blum*. Around the globe, the anti-war movement surged, full speed ahead. One message ran through the veins of society.

Peace.

Derek engulfed himself in articles about the love-ins of San Francisco. He hoped to receive a letter from Grant, detailing his journey to the city by the Bay. Vaughn took Grant's place in Derek's world, hanging around the boutique much like Grant did before departing for California.

During the afternoons when Vaughn wasn't at *En Blum*, Derek began to offer photo sessions to Renee's clients. The back alleyway and Renee's amber-toned office served as backdrops for their clients' shoots. Despite the abundance of celebrities in front of Derek's lens, Renee was still his favorite subject.

On a late-summer afternoon, another iconic star visited Renee's boutique. Derek didn't recognize him, but based on Renee's attentiveness, Derek knew that the client was important. Renee spent an hour and a half on the customer, attempting to put together the right look. The client dodged every attempt to be understood. Renee went through a heap of silk shirts, a pile of trousers, and a half a dozen shoes before he tried on something he found satisfactory, an outfit of black and white.

Derek started to put away the rejected merchandise as Renee rang up the client. The man approached Derek while Renee calculated his total. The celebrity was rather small in stature, but his presence was demanding.

"Who's this one?" He pointed to Derek.

Renee's register chimed.

"This is Derek," Renee answered. "He helps me out here. The two of you may hit it off. He's quite the photographer."

"No kidding," the man gave Derek a once over. "Well, I'd love to see your work. You've got a miraculous subject here," he gestured to Renee.

The man walked up to the counter. He paid then continued to chat with Renee. He made his way toward the front door, then turned to face Derek and Renee.

"You know, both of you ought to spend the long weekend at my property. It's outside the city," he enticed. "There are other friends joining. Get yourselves some fresh air. Listen to the music. Free your minds from daily tasks. There will be lots of beautiful people there, just like yourselves."

"Sounds brilliant," Renee answered for herself and Derek. "Give us the location."

The client wrote down his address and handed it to Renee. He waved goodbye and the doorbell marked another celebrity's exit.

"Lucky for you, I don't have plans," Derek said.

Renee laughed. They both knew that wherever Renee was, Derek wanted to be.

The scene was something out of a fairytale: rose bushes, lazy weeping willows, a broad, sprawling lawn. The fresh air was an unexpected godsend. Derek didn't realize how accustomed he'd grown to the city's lingering fumes.

Their eccentric client's country home was outlined by a vast terrace to which his guests flocked to soak up the sunshine. The outdoor area was meticulously decorated, contrasting the host's erratic methods.

Two of the guests were musicians, accompanied by their current partners. Another guest was a bombshell actress. A film director, working primarily out of Rome, also joined the congregation. The remainder of the guests were collaborators.

Derek scanned the flock of artists on the veranda and found a familiar face. Somehow, Vaughn had already infiltrated the same circle.

"How did you get in so quick with this crowd?" Derek whispered.

"With no help from you," Vaughn teased. "Have you forgotten I was a military kid? I'm used to making fast friends."

The charming chateau consisted of six bedrooms and several gathering areas. Art adorned every corner of the house. Some of the paintings were quite simplistic, composed of abstract circles, strokes, and sporadic lines, other pieces of art were incredibly elaborate depictions of the human form. Oversized prints of their host's favorite photos were hung throughout the space. The walls offered a never-ending stream of visual stimulation.

Luxurious blankets were piled onto each bed. Renee's mouth dropped open as she touched the fabric. Stunning Turkish lamps decorated the nightstands. Derek had never seen such an opulent home.

When the sun on the patio became too hot, small groups rotated indoors through the main lounge. Summer air breezed through the community room's open windows. Gossamer curtains flowed with the living room's air fluctuations creating an ethereal environment.

Throughout their stay, a resident musician kicked off the mornings with his guitar-wander through the soft grass. Between puffs, the artist meandered and played whatever short melodies came to him. The guests often joined him in the ritual, improvising nonsensical lyrics to accompany his lighthearted riffs.

Their host was a catalyst extraordinaire. He held space for people to create. The host captured his guests' most vulnerable truth within his own, controlled environment. Rather than winding through their insecurities, he found the most direct route to their personal essence, making his subjects more interesting. He captured both light and dark.

Derek snapped photos all weekend and was thrilled to see what the roll's development would reveal, though Derek couldn't imagine that any image would reflect a fraction of the utopia.

Derek wondered how long he could surround himself with such impactful individuals. TRN had clearly advised to "not get yourself in the history books." All around Derek was the live version of his most beloved era's music and art and he couldn't force himself to pull away. There was a freedom he didn't know existed and he couldn't decipher whether it was a freedom unlocked by the time or by the falling-away of his self-limitations.

"How long can we do this before TRN intervenes?" Derek asked Vaughn when they were alone.

"*We're* not famous, are we?" Vaughn answered. "We're just around people who are. We have to keep it light; you know. Not get too involved. Just enjoy it for what it is."

On their last evening at the chateau, just before sunset, Renee spread a blanket across the pristine grass and was joined by the golden-haired actress. Some unknown source caused them to laugh with unbridled joy.

Derek watched, knowing that their weekend in the countryside was the best of times. Where Renee's beauty would lead her was a place Derek couldn't follow. The reality stung, but Derek knew what he'd signed up for by Traveling and concluded to enjoy the ride with Renee for as long as possible.

For that moment in time, only love existed, nothing else was real.

Chapter VI

Plink.

The ball landed in the final cup.

"Goal!" EJ high-fived Mia. "Up top! Best pong partner around! Who's next?" EJ rubbed his hands together and scanned the room for their next opponent.

It was Saturday night, the first of November, the night of the Halloween party.

"Should we go for a three-peat?!" EJ asked Mia.

"Let someone else on the table, will you?" EJ's brother, who went by Jaq, said as he nudged Mia.

Since joining the Tuesdaze, Mia had been around EJ's brother more frequently. As EJ challenged the onlookers, Mia studied Jaq's living room. She had only been inside the house on one other occasion. Usually, the Tuesdaze remained in Jaq's detached garage for band practice.

Big brother Jaquez's home was well-decorated for the holiday and Mia was surprised by the welcoming ambiance. Every corner of Jaq's college house was adorned with traditional décor. Mia reached out to touch a hand-painted skull which sat next to an ornate candle.

"My grandmother painted that skull," EJ said. "Ma insisted that we take some of her decorations. That one is my favorite."

"You and Jaq really go all out for the holidays," Mia said.

EJ laughed and replied, "This décor is only a fraction of what ma has at home."

"I wish I had the decorations I remember growing up with," Mia said. "Inherited things are so special. The pieces have seen more celebrations."

EJ nodded, "I can remember the spot where each of these stood at my parent's. Everything had its place. We're still figuring that out here. I'm excited to move in next semester. We didn't expect Jaq to get a house so soon, but it seems his internship is paying well."

"It must be."

Mia noticed thick, glass, candy-filled bowls placed around Jaq's house. Piles of sweets overflowed from serving platters in the kitchen. Before the guests arrived, Mrs. Jaquez had hand-delivered the homemade treats. Mia felt a tinge of homesickness as she noticed the traces of parental care.

"It's on!" Macy shouted, bringing Mia's focus to their pending match.

Macy and Tiffany took their place at the table to oppose EJ and Mia. Macy removed a ping pong ball from the cup and dried it off with the apron of her waitress costume. Just hours before, Mia had hot-glued the apron into existence. Macy didn't prepare a costume, so she made the last-minute decision to dress as a waitress. Macy wore only a black tube top and mini skirt beneath the apron.

"How 'bout this EJ," Tiffany proposed as a group of spectators gathered around the table. "If you and Mia lose, you two tear down after the next gig," Tiffany cackled.

"Let me get this straight," EJ started, "if we lose, I have to tear down my drum set like I do for every gig? Oh no," he joked, "I don't think I can handle that."

The night before, the Tuesdaze headlined for the Lakehouse Halloween Party. They were thrilled to be invited onstage for the venue's sold-out event. Mia was especially relieved for their performance's restoration of positive Lakehouse memories. The only damper was that Lars' influence on the event had somewhat made up for his unacceptable behavior.

On the days leading up to the Lakehouse's Halloween production, the Tuesdaze crammed in practices. When they weren't studying for midterms, they were perfecting their intros and endings. Their setlist covered a few witchy favorites and they peppered in two originals. The crowd was spellbound.

Jaq's Halloween party was the night to finally let loose. The Tuesdaze tossed the pong ball back and forth. After a close game, EJ landed the ball in the last cup and declared the third victory for himself and Mia.

EJ pulled down his hockey mask, threw Mia over his shoulder, and made a celebratory lap around the room. After a satisfactory amount of boasting, they retired from the table. EJ disappeared into the kitchen.

Mia laughed and adjusted her plaid skirt back to a modest length after being paraded around. The grueling practices combined with her studies had left Mia with no time to costume hunt. With convincing from Macy, Mia complied to a last-minute schoolgirl outfit.

Mia felt her clip-on wallet for the outline of the Aid. After her close call with Lars, she heeded TRN's advice to always keep the device within an arm's reach. The party hit a lull, and Mia, Tiffany, and Macy gathered in a corner of the room. They began to relive the Halloween show.

"If only I'd nailed the end of that solo," Mia critiqued herself. "Ugh, I could have practiced so much more if my English paper wasn't due yesterday."

Macy placed her hand on Mia's arm.

"No one even noticed the slip-up," Macy stated. "Hell, I wouldn't have noticed if you hadn't practiced that solo every time we took a break. I was hearing it in my sleep! I think we all need some down time from classes."

"It's so true. I keep reminding myself that Christmas break's right around the corner. I can't believe it's going to be the holidays soon!" Tiffany said. "I'm stoked for the break but—" Tiffany was interrupted as EJ and his brother approached the girls with a plate of shots.

EJ wore his slasher mask and Jaq had a devilish look in his black-rimmed eyes. The liquid inside the small glasses looked cloudy and vile.

"Bottoms up!" Jaq directed. "This mixture is deadly!"

Mia took a deep breath and downed the shot. She did her best to suppress her gag reflex. Tiffany did not hide her expression.

"Ugh! What *was* that?"

"Yeah," Macy said, "that was nasty."

"I call it," Jaq replied, "Zombie Brains." He smirked and walked into the next room to distribute the potion to more guests.

Jaq was a welcome addition to their tight-knit group. Having the space to play and store their instruments was a vital asset to the Tuesdaze, and Jaq asked nothing in return. To let them use his van for gigs was exceedingly generous. After Lars' night of cruel expectations, Mia further appreciated the Jaquez

140

brother's kind demeanor. Jaq even lent his trumpeting skills to play for the Tuesdaze's pseudo-ska numbers.

"You know," EJ put his arms around the girls, "I love you ladies." EJ pulled Mia in closest to himself and kissed the top of her head.

"Especially you, you're the best to have on the team!"

"Hey, you guys cheated!" Tiffany proclaimed. "EJ, don't even think that I missed that elbow of yours over the table's edge!"

EJ ruffled Tiffany's hair.

"Hey! Don't mess it up!" Tiffany pulled away and smoothed her refined curls.

The party's volume increased with the guests' buzzed conversations. The Tuesdaze stuck together and migrated to a card table where an established game was in motion.

"Mind if we squeeze in?" Macy asked a man who was seated at the table.

"Are you kidding? Take a seat! You guys rocked last night! It'd be an honor."

Jaq's enthused party guest pulled Macy's chair out for her. The Tuesdaze exchanged a look of excitement. Macy gestured Mia closer.

"We have fans," Macy whispered into Mia's ear.

Tiffany squeezed onto the chair with Macy. Another guest moved on from the game and offered his chair to EJ. EJ pulled Mia onto his lap, and she scanned the cards on the table. Mia was unfamiliar with the game being played.

"Want to share a hand?" EJ suggested.

"Sure!" Mia agreed.

EJ could smell Mia's shampoo. She felt tense and rigid on his lap. Having been there the night she was nearly assaulted by one of his closest friends, EJ strived to put Mia at ease. He moved his knee to the side and Mia shrieked, nearly tipping onto the floor. EJ caught her and they laughed. He felt her posture ease. Though EJ's kindness was an effective measure to keep Mia from quitting the band, as other members had done before, EJ's increased compassion required him to bottle up his infatuation with the Tuesdaze's guitarist.

Mia had a conscious moment of disconnect from the era. She peered around the table. It seemed that everyone, besides her, knew how to play the game.

The players were dealt cards by the previous game's loser who donned a traffic cone atop his head per the winner's request. To Mia's relief, the game was easy to learn. Just as she got into the game, Mia's attention was pulled away by the creak of Jaq's front door.

Lars.

Tiffany rolled her eyes and pulled up her strapless dress in response to his arrival. EJ squeezed Mia's shoulders.

"He got us the gig," EJ said softly. "Remember what Macy said, we can't let him ruin the night."

The door snapped closed behind Lars, and he stepped inside. Lars' hair was slicked back. He wore a cheap, overly shiny black cape, and his gel-laden hairstyle harshened his features. The perpetual bags under his eyes were enhanced with dark makeup. Lars spotted the Tuesdaze at the table. He revealed a fanged grin.

"Behold," he said and unveiled a bundle of posters beneath his cape. "Tuesdaze posters!"

"Hell yes!" EJ shouted.

He scooted Mia off his lap and went to take the bundle from Lars.

"They're all yours," Lars said and handed over the posters.

EJ went into the next room and showed the bundle to Jaq. Lars smirked at Mia, Tiffany, and Macy, then left the entryway to join the Jaquez brothers.

Lars began his long road to redemption by booking the Tuesdaze for the Lakehouse Halloween gig. Since the venue's opening, Halloween had been one of the Lakehouse's biggest nights of the year. The holiday typically fell one of the last nights that it was warm enough to gather on the dock. The students were fatigued by their studies and year after year, they took advantage of the occasion to go wild.

Macy and EJ were quick to forgive and came to terms with the fact that Lars' behavior had to be excused. Mia and Tiffany barely tolerated his presence, though, in time, they came to accept the reality of his place in their success. Mia agreed to comply only if Lars' antics *remained* in the past.

Lars hadn't gotten belligerent since the night of their first gig. He behaved himself as he claimed he would. Mia began to lower her guard as she continued to drink.

Eventually Mia became less focused on the card game. She saw Jaq bring a boom box down from upstairs.

"Dude, is that a new CD player?" EJ asked his brother.

"Sure is," Jaq replied.

"Damn, share the wealth *hermano*. The internship really *is* paying good."

"The new roomie sprung for it," Jaq stated. "For a subletter, he's really chipping in."

EJ raised his eyebrows, "Wow, no doubt. Where is he?"

"I'm not sure," Jaq answered, "but he's about to miss one wild night."

Macy and Mia made eye contact from across the table. Macy gestured to the next room and leaned in toward Mia. Her breath smelled like watermelon.

"You done with this game?" Macy asked.

Mia nodded. Macy deserted the table and Mia followed her lead. Tiffany remained at the table. Mia grinned at Tiffany's lucky draw as she peeked at her cards on the way to the living room.

Jaq opened his patio door. Mia welcomed the draft into the stuffy living room. A faint smell of cigarettes wafted in with the cool air. Jaq pressed play on the boombox, and his guests began to groove.

They heard Tiffany whooping with her victory, and the game concluded at the card table. EJ and Tiffany disappeared into the kitchen. They emerged with a large tray of shots. The gelatinous contents of the small cups tasted of smooth cherry and went down much easier than the first repulsive mixture.

New guests continued to arrive. The CD spun. Chanting sounded from the card table. Macy placed her hands on Mia's shoulders and sang along with the tune. The whole room belted the lyrics in unison. Then, Jaq turned the lights out.

The room was pitch black and a few guests shrieked. Confused silence spread throughout the party. Jaq flipped a switch, and black lights cut through the darkness, lining the perimeter of the room.

"Oohs" of wonder echoed. Mia and Macy smiled at each other with fluorescent teeth. EJ and Jaq scurried back into the kitchen. They returned to the main area with bundles of neon glow sticks. They nodded at each other, then threw the neon cylinders out to their guests. It looked as though a firework had burst from the kitchen. Some of the glow sticks were caught, many landed on the floor.

Macy bent down to collect a glow stick and, on the way up, drew her fingers along Mia's leg.

"For you," Macy handed a bright pink cylinder to Mia.

Mia wasn't sure if, or how, to pursue the bubbling feelings for her friend. She needed a moment alone to collect her thoughts.

"I'll be right back!" Mia said. "I haven't peed since we got here."

Macy laughed and Mia excused herself to the restroom. She closed the bathroom door behind her. Mia looked at her reflection and couldn't help but laugh. She wrapped her fingers around the Aid, then chuckled at her own paranoia.

Mia adjusted her bra, undid more buttons of her shirt, and rolled the top of her skirt to raise the hemline. She took out her braids and tousled her hair. Mia was just drunk enough to be game for whatever the night brought. If things didn't work out, Mia could retreat to Original Time.

'No strings attached.' She told herself.

Mia's white button-up became too hot as she envisioned Macy on stage. She patted her face with water, smirked at herself in the mirror, and headed back out the party.

Mia beelined to the place where Macy waited. She fell back into Macy's rhythm. Macy was taller than Mia and used her angle to peek down Mia's shirt. It was just the reaction Mia had hoped for. Macy traced the bottom of Mia's miniskirt.

"This isn't just for the shock value, right?" Macy asked and gestured to the small audience watching them dance. She spoke into Mia's ear, "Because I want more than a dance."

Mia responded, "I do too."

Macy pressed her lips onto Mia's. She let her hands wander and felt the warmth of Mia's skin though her clothing. Mia grew

145

short of breath and pulled away to catch some air. She saw Lars watching them.

"I feel a little lightheaded," Mia said and grabbed an unopened beer. She held it to the back of her neck.

Macy rested her hands just below Mia's ribcage.

"You okay?" Macy asked. "Sorry if that was too much."

"No, don't be sorry. I'm just a little…" Mia searched for the right word, "overwhelmed. Want to find a place where we don't have an audience?" Mia gestured in Lars' direction. His eyes were glued to them. "I'm down for more, but we need to be alone," Mia said into Macy's ear.

"Let's go upstairs," Macy said.

Macy helped Mia up the stairwell and led her down a narrow hallway. Mia let out a sigh of relief as they stumbled upon a vacant room. She lay down on the bed, soft and cool.

Mia wondered what other hook-ups were taking place in the Jaquez household. She heard moaning from the next room and the sound served as permission to lean into her lust for Macy. Macy crawled over Mia and opened a window. The fresh air revived Mia.

The incoming breeze rustled a poster which featured an electric blonde in a string bikini. A layering of hemp necklaces hung on one of the bed posts. Rumpled at the foot of the bed was a plaid comforter. The ceiling slanted with the house's peak. Mia began to relax; the room was a perfect hideaway.

Mia and Macy lay on the bed beneath the window as the air flowed in. Mia rolled to her side and kissed Macy. She traced her fingers along Macy's apron seam and felt the softness of Macy's skin. Mia began to round the side of Macy's breast, then pulled away.

"It's okay," Macy assured and pulled Mia's hand beneath the fabric.

Macy smoothed the length of Mia's legs. Any nervous tension was crippled by their magnetic attraction. Macy hooked her finger into the waistline of Mia's skirt.

A sexy guitar riff floated from the boom box as Macy hooked her finger around Mia's inner panty seam. She approached the territory in which many of her previous endeavors had stalled the action. Instead, Mia dropped her knees open. Macy ran her fingers along Mia's silky flesh. Macy pulled off her apron, followed by the rest of her Halloween costume, then pushed herself up and stepped away from the bed.

Mia took in the view.

"What's next?" She asked.

Macy winked and locked the door.

Mia tried to open her eyes, but the room was too bright. Someone was knocking on the door and the crystal doorknob jiggled.

"Hello? Can you let me in? This is my room," the voice on the other side stated.

Mia flopped her forearm across her eyes. Her stomach began to betray her, and her head pounded. She rested her arm above her head and attempted to identify her surroundings. The bikini model poster further confused her internal sense of direction.

Macy lay next to Mia, her nude body draped by the plaid comforter. Macy roused and opened her eyes. She grinned at Mia.

"I think I'm still drunk," Macy giggled.

"Me too. Looks like we got into some trouble last night." Everything came rushing back to Mia. "Oh God," Mia laughed and placed her forearm back across her eyes. "Is this okay?"

Mia's heart raced as she became more rational, and her mind flooded with questions. Between Halloween with Macy and her close call with Lars, she was horrified that she'd put the Tuesdaze dynamic at stake; not once, but multiple times. Laughing off the situation no longer made sense.

"Of course, it's okay," Macy said. "I had fun, didn't you?"

Mia attempted to get a grip on her anxiety.

Macy continued.

"No one's going to be mad about this," she pointed back and forth between herself and Mia. "And people *may* have seen this coming."

"Will you let me in, already?" The voice on the other side of the door persisted.

Macy sighed, "Here we go."

She wrapped herself in a sheet and unlocked the door. Mia pulled the covers over shoulders. Standing before them was the man whose room they occupied. The morning sun whited out his face.

Macy groaned, "Sorry man, will you give us a few more minutes?"

"Yeah, a little privacy would be awesome," Mia said. She sat up and searched the floor for her clothes.

The man picked up his backpack. "I just needed my bag," he said and sauntered back out to the hallway. Mia caught him doing a double-take on his way out of the room.

Macy zipped her skirt and put on her apron. Mia dressed and Macy continued to search for her missing tube top. Mia looked down at her plaid skirt and cropped button up.

"Think they'll let us into the Diner like this?" Mia asked.

The tenant knocked on his door again.

"Come in," Macy answered. "It's unlocked."

"I need to grab a sweater. It's chilly out there this morning," he said.

"Thanks for letting us crash," Mia offered.

"I didn't really have a choice, did I?" He chuckled and avoided eye contact. "Not that I would have opposed."

Now that the tenant was out of the sun's glare, Mia could see him more clearly. She recognized him, but in her state, she couldn't put forth the effort to figure out where from. She started a conversation to distract herself from her sour stomach.

"Hey, I didn't get a chance to meet you last night, are you Jaq's roomie?" Mia asked.

"Yeah," he answered as he dug through his clothes, avoiding eye contact.

"How do I know you?" Mia asked. She craned her neck to catch another glimpse of his face.

"You and I, we met last night. I was," he paused, "at the card table!"

Mia attempted to recall him at the table, but her recollections were blurry. Her stomach turned and she winced.

"I need food," Mia stated.

"The Diner?" Macy asked. "I'm not feeling so hot myself."

The tenant was just about to exit his room when Macy stopped him.

"Hey Jaq's roomie, you got a sweatshirt I can borrow? I'm not sure they'll let us go in like this," Macy looked down at her tattered apron and black mini-skirt. Macy's black tube top was lost in a heap of bedding and the hot-glued apron exposed the sides of Macy's breasts.

"Sure thing," Jaq's roommate answered.

He fished a sweatshirt from his dresser and tossed it to Macy. "Thanks, dude!" Macy said.

Mia was envious of the cozy article of clothing. Her button-up felt stiff in comparison to the soft sheets from which they emerged.

"Can I have one too?" Mia asked. The tenant tossed her a worn-in hoodie. "Thanks, you're a lifesaver."

"No sweat," he said. "I've gotta split, I'm running late. I'm sure we'll bump into each other again." With that, he rushed out the door.

Macy and Mia trudged down the stairs. Mia hoped that, at the bottom, minimal interrogation awaited. She gripped the handrail to maintain her bearings.

EJ and Tiffany were asleep on a futon bed. Jaq lounged in his recliner and flipped through the channels. He gave Mia and Macy a thumbs up and mouthed, "Nice."

Beer cans lined the kitchen countertops. Sticky liquor bottles were grouped together by the sink. Two plastic ghost face masks were left for dead at the card table. The broad daylight added an extra level of tackiness to Halloween's evidence.

A loud scene on the TV jolted EJ awake. He gasped and turned to face the kitchen, making eye contact with Mia and Macy. At that moment, he understood where they had disappeared to the night before. EJ nodded his head in approval.

"Nice," he said with two thumbs up.

"Do you have to be so loud?" Tiffany sat upright.

She glanced down at the ensemble she'd slept in-- a baggy t-shirt and basketball shorts.

"Ugh, that was one crazy Halloween," Tiffany stated.

"We're going to the Diner. This one needs food stat," Macy pointed to Mia.

Mia's chills intensified. Her residual buzz was quickly wearing off.

"Give us two minutes, we'll be right out. Go get some fresh air," Tiffany waved them outside.

Mia and Macy stepped onto the front porch. The screen door banged behind them, aggravating Mia's headache. Once they were outside, the cool November air began to take the edge off Mia's hangover.

"Fresh air always makes me feel better," Macy said.

"Me too," Mia agreed. "I meant it earlier. I don't know if it's the hangover or what, but my anxiety is skyrocketing. Is this okay? Us, I mean?"

"Mia," Macy said, "it's *so* okay. One night doesn't mean you have to turn your world upside down. I'm comfortable with this. I wouldn't take it back. I stopped letting my own shame get to me a long time ago. There's enough people out there to put the guilt on people like us," Macy placed her hand on Mia's shoulder and squeezed.

Macy pulled a pack of cigarettes from her handbag. She offered one to Mia, but Mia declined. They waited in silence for Tiffany and EJ and digested the autumn scene. Overnight, the world had gone from active to dormant.

The leaves' vibrancy had peaked the week before Halloween. After the consecutive nights of hard frost, the leaves fell like ticker tape.

"Gorgeous, isn't it?" Macy asked.

Mia was silent. She was reminded of the day, approximately a year ago, when she'd lost her virginity. Mia's unofficial boyfriend of the time, a basketball star her previous bandmates had set her up with, invited Mia over to his house. His parents were gone for the weekend. After hours of effort on his part, Mia gave into his advances. She saw the loss of her virginity as something she wanted to put behind her. She felt nothing after the encounter and, eventually, her and the jock passed each other in the hall as acquaintances.

Being with Macy was different. Mia remembered the potency of her feelings from the night before. She was falling fast, and the drop was exhilarating.

EJ and Tiffany emerged from the house.

"Let's do this," EJ stated. "I need some hash browns ASAP."

The four of them piled into EJ's car and headed to the Diner.

"Oh wow, look at that bright tree," Tiffany said and pointed to a golden-orange maple, still reveling in Autumn's brilliance.

As they drove through the neighborhoods, Mia fixated on her parent's upcoming visit. She hoped their process was smooth and their acclimation brief. Mia couldn't wait to show them everything she loved about Birchmont, including Macy.

After a drive which seemed longer than it was, the Tuesdaze arrived at the Diner. Tiffany dropped her head back in frustration. Lars was seated on the curb outside.

"Did you call him?" Tiffany asked EJ.

EJ sighed, "Yeah. I figured I'd get him breakfast for hooking us up with the Halloween gig. Did you see those posters? He had those made with money from his own pocket."

Tiffany shook her head.

"He was supposed to be making-up to us. Not the opposite way around."

They pulled themselves from the car and approached the Diner. EJ and Lars greeted one another with their signature handshake. Lars faced Mia and Macy. He raised his eyebrows.

"Crazy night?"

Mia cringed at his question.

"We should ask you the same," Tiffany quipped. "I saw you leave with that poor young thing last night. How old was she? Fifteen?"

"Give me a break. She was eighteen," Lars scoffed. "That's what she said at least."

Their usual booth was vacant and the five of them took their seats. Mia was in dire need of sustenance. She looked around the restaurant in search of a distraction. Halloween window clings were beginning to peel away from the glass. The mystical spirit of the holiday had passed, leaving behind its kitschy décor. Mia thought of the Jack-o-lanterns, soon to distort upon the neighborhood porches.

"So, Parent's Weekend is coming up," Lars started, "would anyone's folks like to see their little girls on stage? I'm talking to you too, EJ," Lars teased.

Mia imagined how thrilled her parents would be to see her perform. Though they weren't fans of her past band's setlist, Jon and Ellie never missed one of Mia's shows.

"My parents would love that!" Mia said.

Lars grinned and Mia regretted letting him see her open enthusiasm. She hated the obligation to let him get away with more satisfaction than he deserved.

"Alright then, here's the situation. The Loop's Friday night openers dropped out. They mentioned something about a conflicting show in the city," Lars shook his head. "Kind of shitty to cancel last minute if you ask me. Anyways, I know the Loop's a smaller venue than the Lakehouse, but are the Tuesdaze interested?"

They nodded in unison and agreed to play the gig. Lars beamed. Even without his vampire teeth, he looked like a cunning monster.

"Want a lift?" EJ asked.

Mia's apartment was within walking distance of the Diner, but drizzle began to fall, and she was already under the weather from the boozy Halloween.

"Now that we have another gig around the corner, catching a cold isn't worth the risk," EJ enticed. "No one can fill in for you."

"Sure, thank you," Mia agreed to the ride.

First to drop off on EJ's route was Mia. Next was Tiffany, and last was Macy. EJ pulled up in front of Mia's apartment complex and put his car in park.

"EJ, I'll be right back. I left my makeup and craft stuff upstairs," Macy said.

Mia and Macy ran inside and climbed the stairs to Mia's unit.

"Are your parents coming next weekend?" Mia asked on the way up.

Macy seldom talked about her family. From past conversations, Mia had collected that Macy's father was a realtor and her mother a nurse, but Mia knew little else about them.

"Nah," Macy answered. "They won't be able to make it. Mom can't get the time off and Dad is always showing houses on the weekends. I guess he's trying to close on a few properties before the holidays. They're going south for the winter this year."

"You can hang out with me and my parents. They're pretty cool." She paused. "Even if they knew about us, they wouldn't be mad."

Macy was silent. Mia turned the key and opened her front door. Their party preparation the night before left the living room in shambles. Macy fumbled with a plastic grocery bag. She crouched down and collected her hot glue gun and remainder of apron fabric. Macy tied the bag and looped the handles around her forearm. She stood and took Mia's hands.

"Last night was incredible," Macy said. "Tomorrow's my heavy class day, but I'll be excited to see you at practice Tuesday evening."

"I'll be excited too. Tuesday practice gets me through Mondays," Mia stated. "Hey, I've got to ask, because I'll be thinking of it all day, when my parents visit, how do I introduce you?" Mia asked. "I haven't done anything," she paused, "like last night before. I've dated people, but I've never felt like this. We're so much more than friends at this point."

Macy sighed, "I agree, we have something special, but not everyone needs to know about it. You mean a lot to me too, but I'm not gonna go telling my parents," Macy said, "they just don't need to know. The Tuesdaze are cool with it. That's enough for me." Macy kissed Mia's cheek. "I'll call if I'm not drowning in homework tomorrow," Macy smiled and opened the entryway door. "Happy November, take some time to chill," Macy turned and walked down the hallway.

Mia watched Macy wrap down the stairs and out of sight.

The crowd erupted.
"Touchdown Birchmont!"

That fall was playing out to be the college's best football season in decades. Hours before the game, Mia and her parents got up and, with thermoses of coffee, stumbled to the tailgating lot from Mia's apartment. The night before was the Tuesdaze's Parent's night performance at the Loop.

As openers, the Tuesdaze only played three songs, but Mia's parents displayed the same enthusiasm as they would for a stadium concert. The Hayes sang along to every one of the covers and Macy was impressed that Ellie knew all the lyrics to the "new" songs of the era. Mia respected Macy's wishes and introduced Macy to her parents as a friend.

After the show, Jon and Ellie stayed in one of TRN's new, exclusive hotels.

"The Time Regulatory Network has lodging for Travelers who don't want to reside in their destination for long periods of time," Ellie had explained to Mia. "Their hotels have made Travel way more casual by lightening the commitment. That Adrian Glass, he's changing the whole Time Travel landscape."

"I'm so happy your acclimation went smoothly," Mia said. "I didn't know how it would be for you two based on… the last few years."

Jon shrugged, "We're surprised too. That drug is a miracle-worker."

After the game, Mia showed her parents around Birchmont's campus. She took them along the same path where she and Macy had held hands earlier that week. Although the branches were no longer decorated by leaves and the colors had faded to shades of sepia, the Hayes admired their daughter's stomping grounds.

Mia told her parents about the gigs the Tuesdaze had played that fall. She assured them that her grades were holding steady and informed them of the Aid's arrival. Mia began to see their worries fall away. She debated whether to elaborate on Macy and her relationship, but decided against it,

"I've been going on about myself for so long," Mia said. "What have you two been up to?"

"Work," Ellie stated.

Their family business began with Ellie's parents, Les and Valerie. Throughout the Hayes' childhood, even into their teenage years, King's Music Lounge served as a second home.

Les often went on about the "Three kings of the blues," and how "they started it all." The name of his store, King's Records, was derived from the legends. In Original Time, when Mia's band attempted to flavor her musical taste with bubble gum, Les took it upon himself to keep Mia's musical integrity in check. Les and Mia became so close that even left his collection of band tee shirts and acoustic guitar to Mia.

"Why don't you sell those shirts?" Mia's cousins would ask.

The shirts were sacred to Mia. When she pressed her nose into their fabric, she could still smell Les' pipe tobacco. Losing her grandpa was one of the final pushes to leave Original Time. The world felt strange without him.

Growing up, Ellie worked at King's Records. As she matured, she came to run most of the daily operations, and in Original Time, she shared the responsibility of the business with Jon.

In the early days, a pool hall took up the floor below King's. Over time, the pool hall's business dwindled, and the owners were forced to close the doors. King's Records took a rent increase and absorbed the lower level.

Les and Valerie transformed the space into a small music venue. They named it The Court. On nights when they held concerts, they opened King's before and after the shows. The concertgoers ventured upstairs and flipped through the stacks. The community began to refer to the tiered establishment as 'King's and the Court.'

King's Records required constant evolution due to the everchanging way in which society consumed music. There were many years when King's struggled to keep up with the swift change of pace. King's supplier provided stacks of no-name records faster than they went off the shelves. Les and Valerie panicked when other established record stores resorted to disposal of the enormous shipments. King's inventory grew as their customers diminished.

With the release of eight tracks and cassette tapes, it seemed Les' love for records couldn't stand up to technological advancements. In the 1980s, the demand for music systems vastly overshadowed the public's desire for records. It was then that Les and Valerie received the offer; a national music supply store wanted to purchase King's Records.

Les insisted that they turn down the offer to sell. The venue gave him just enough hope that their business would not fail. Meanwhile, when Ellie turned old enough to drive, she bought CDs in secret and listened to them in her car. Despite Les' initial disappointment upon finding out, Ellie finally sold her father on the essential change he needed to make if he didn't want to lose everything.

"Dad, you have got to let go of this vinyl purism," Ellie told him.

Les caved and King's began to sell CDs. Time passed, and their customers purchased vouchers for music downloads via the World Wide Web. Just when their desperation peaked enough to reconsider the chain's offer, vinyl collectors came out of the woodwork. Les struggled to keep his boxes of wax filled. Even new artists etched their music onto vinyl. Reliable old rockers and hipsters came to King's not just to expand their collection, but to sit and chat the afternoon away with Les.

"That crackle and warmth, you can't beat it," Les said. "*That* is how an album is meant to be experienced."

With age and stabilization of the venue, Les loosened the reins on the business. Ellie took full autonomy of daily operations shortly after her marriage to Jon. Les put-up posters of legends and Ellie brightened up the décor. They blocked off a large storage room which Ellie had finally organized and titled the nook, "the listening room" with a neon sign over the doorway.

Radio stations broadcasted from King's listening room and the Court became a notorious place to find the next up-and-comer. Les and Valerie relaxed into semi-retirement.

Then, the virus hit, and stability became a luxury of the past. Mia was born six months after the illness spread to the United States. Jon and the twins couldn't even accompany Ellie to her doctor's appointments.

"What if I get sick while she's in my belly?" Ellie fretted.

To endure the required shutdown of all non-essential businesses, King's offered curbside pickup and online orders. The Court was a financial drain as they were forced to cancel more and more concerts. Jon and Les expected the virus to go into late summer, but it persisted into the colder months, and the business hung by a thread.

Finally, the system got a grip on the virus and Jon, Ellie, Les, and Valerie planned a re-opening party for King's and the Court. They reminisced about that party with a happiness that Mia couldn't comprehend.

"It's still such a treat to go to any show," Ellie said as she sat across from her daughter at the Diner. "Especially when you're onstage."

The last day of the Hayes visit arrived too quickly. Every evening that week, Mia visited her parents in their hotel. Her homework load was light, so Mia showed them the Lakehouse, the practice shed at Jaq's, and her apartment. The Hayes finished their visit with breakfast at the Diner.

"Grandma and Grandpa would be so proud of you, Mia," Ellie smiled at her daughter. "And *we* are so proud. It's not easy to let your baby go so far away, but you're doing great, and we love seeing you this happy."

Jon and Ellie held hands. Mia smiled. It had been years since she'd witnessed their affection.

"It's no surprise you like it here. We loved being young during this era. Although it is different now, as an old man."

"You're not an old man," Mia laughed. "This has been wonderful. When can you come back again?"

"Well, we're aiming for next year. We would love to come back for the holidays but there's not enough TRN staff to support the volume of Travelers for the season," Jon stated.

He lowered his voice.

"There's word of a TRN employee shortage. If you want to come back to OT within the next year, I'd get a visit on the books soon. You know where your hub is, right?"

Mia nodded.

"We were lucky they got us on the books months ago at your final TRN appointment or we wouldn't have been able to visit until spring," Ellie said.

"I'm so glad you booked when you did. Have you guys thought of visiting Derek?" Mia asked.

"We'd love to, but the volume of Travelers going there is even higher than here. I don't know, we've finally gotten our numbers back up at King's & the venue," Ellie looked at Jon. "Maybe the right time will come. We just don't feel right leaving now that the business is back on its feet."

"She's just as married to that store as she is to me," Jon joked.

Ellie nudged him, "I'm getting better."

After a drawn-out breakfast, Mia and her parents exited the Diner.

"It's time for us to go, Mia," Jon said. "Fifteen minutes until we're due at the hub. It's been nice not having to pack for this kind of trip."

"That's right," Mia said, remembering her fully stocked apartment upon arrival. "This has gone too fast; I've missed you both so much."

A tear slid down her cheek.

"We miss you too, but we're glad you did this, right?" Jon said and waited for Ellie's confirmation.

"Right," Ellie said. "We would barely get to see you and Derek anyway with how crazy business has been."

They walked down the street and stood in front of TRN's hub which was disguised as an insurance agency.

"I guess this is it for now," Jon said.

Ellie reached into her cargo jacket.

"Here, before we go, this is for you," Ellie presented Mia with a blue box. "TRN customized my Shell so I could hang onto it. Mom would have wanted you to have what's inside."

Mia knew what the box held. For years, she had adored its contents. She opened the jewelry box, and Valerie's charm bracelet looked exactly as Mia remembered. Les added a new piece to the bracelet for every year they were together, and the keepsake was heavy with charms. Mia examined the dainty figures which were held together by a silver chain.

"It's been so long since I've seen this," Mia said.

"Well, Grandma has been gone for a while now," Ellie stated.

Mia held the charms between her fingers; the pointe shoes for Valerie's short time as a dancer, the eight ball for Les' love of pool, the tongue and lips for their favorite concert.

"Thank you," Mia said. "It feels good to have a piece of home with me."

Autumn's bright sunlight glinted off the silver.

"We love you. We know you're doing amazing here, but if you ever get the urge to come back, we'll make sure it can happen," Jon promised. "Even if we have to pay a little more money to get you back, King's and the Court can make up for the difference right now."

Ellie stroked Mia's hair and gave her a long embrace. Mr. and Mrs. Hayes walked into TRN's secured Travel hub. They turned and waved good-bye to their daughter through the storefront.

Mia lingered at the door and watched her parent's check-in. Ellie and Jon looked out at their daughter. Mia kissed her hand and pressed it to the window.

Chapter VII

'*Don't make history,*' Derek repeated to himself.

Renee's portfolio began to burst at the seams. It seemed all eyes were on her. Every photographer in London knew her name and Derek could barely keep *En Blum's* shelves stocked once word got out that she was the owner. Renee's growing fame paralleled Derek's increasing worries.

Despite TRN's repercussions for deterring from their guidelines, Derek continued to play with fire.

'*In Original Time, I haven't heard of her,*' Derek told himself. '*But, when will my star's descent begin?*'

Renee's ambiguity in Original Time was the only reassurance that Derek wouldn't be ripped from the sixties by TRN. Derek's heart rate spiked every time a camera was pointed at him and Renee. The thought of Renee fading from the limelight saddened Derek, but it was the only way he could validate continuing their courtship.

Derek could see that Renee was trying to maintain an upbeat mood, but she was overcommitting herself and she began to grow edgy. The lazy, summer breeze sharpened, and Derek too found his attitude declining, but he was determined to make his life in the sixties better than his life in OT. Derek kept himself busy and began to assist with *En Blum's* books. Within weeks, he'd come to control every aspect of the boutique aside from the apparel itself.

The spike in *En Blum's* traffic allotted a raise for Derek and provided the means to hire more staff. Derek became the manager while Renee was out at shoots. He oversaw two young, part-time employees. Both new hires were huge fans of Renee.

En Blum's two enthusiastic fashionistas had just started Uni. They were grateful for the extra money provided by the part-time job. Both Derek and Renee were refreshed by the employees' youthful energy. The new employees wore *En Blum's* apparel around the city with pride, attracting even more clients to the boutique than Renee thought was possible.

Somehow, Renee still found the time to construct a few custom pieces and continued to hand-select every article sold in the boutique. Derek watched Renee carry out her seasonal ordering ritual, and, for the first time in months, saw her relax. The glimpses reassured Derek that Renee still had her feet on the ground. He wished to spend time on Renee's chaise in her amber-colored office but couldn't imagine that Renee had the time when she was busy occupying the pages of every magazine in England.

Derek and the two young employees struggled to keep up with *En Blum's* increasing demands, especially since Renee's final approval was necessary for many interactions. Derek found himself waiting after hours for her to sign off on this or give advice on that.

One day, shortly after noon, Renee rushed into the boutique.

"So sorry for being late, love," she apologized.

Derek looked at his watch, "Only by three hours this time."

Renee gave Derek a peck on the cheek.

"Come with me," she said and led him to the backroom.

The Uni girls lingered around the corner to eavesdrop.

Renee went on to tell Derek that she had spent the morning with the host of their chateau getaway.

"He invited me for coffee, and I thought I'd be back in time to open. He walked me here and, on the way, began to snap photos. We just had so much fun and lost track of time, but now here I am, late again," Renee said. "There's nothing going on though, you know that, right?"

"I know, I'm not worried," Derek stated.

Renee brushed her fingertips along Derek's face. She heard rustling around the corner and peeked through the door at the Uni girls. "Darlings, would you give us a moment?"

"Of course," they said and scattered to the boutique floor.

"The reason I'm telling you all this is because he's got me convinced that I need to ride this wave," Renee said. "I know you're already doing so much, but I want you to start making more decisions. I'll still do the order, but if there are ever questions regarding the financial end of things, I'm giving you permission to speak for me."

In the weeks that followed, Derek's heightened responsibility offered relief to Renee's balancing act. Renee had more time for photo sessions. Her head space cleared, and the lowered stress translated into her modeling. Within weeks of stepping back from the boutique, Renee appeared in international publications and cosmetic campaigns.

Delighted makeup artists painted intricate designs around Renee's green eyes, inspired by her beauty. Her elegant figure was draped in the seasonal collections of luxury designers. Renee was an adaptable canvas, but never dull.

Derek had seen women who were the epitome of perfection yet left something to be desired. They lacked a certain element; some quality of which Renee held an endless supply.

Then came *the* photo; the image of Renee wrapped in a brilliant turquoise dress. One side of the dress' neckline had eased its way down Renee's shoulder. A dark lock framed Renee's face, reminding Derek of her wild hair after their first night out together. The color of the Paris chiffon cut through the era's residual black and white, and the world fell in love with Renee Blum.

Derek began his closing duties. Only two shoppers remained, so he flipped the front door sign to *'Closed.'*

"Got plans tonight?" One of the Uni girls whispered into Derek's ear as he eyed the shoppers.

He chuckled, "No, just tired. Ready to go home for the night."

Finally, the remaining customers exited the boutique with heaping bags in hand. Derek began to count the cash register but was distracted by the sound of Renee entering through the back door. The two young employees discussed their evening plans, oblivious to Renee's entrance, so Derek released them for the night.

Derek heard Renee opening her desk drawers and walked across the empty showroom floor. He leaned against the backroom's door frame.

"A little late for your shift, aren't you?" Derek teased.

A smile spread across Renee's face. Derek's drab, weeknight mood was lifted with Renee's apparent enthusiasm.

"Derek love, you will not believe this!" Renee said. Her heels clicked as she paced back and forth. "I've received the best news!"

"Well don't leave me hanging," Derek said.

"An American men's lifestyle magazine asked *me*," she trembled with excitement, "to star in their publication! They want to interview me and everything."

Derek was at a loss for words. He was one of the lucky few who knew that Renee's unmatched sense of style was rivaled by what was beneath her clothing.

"My goodness," Derek replied. "You've never done that type of work before, have you?" Renee hung her head and Derek backtracked. "You'll be great at it! I just hope—"

"I know what you're thinking," Renee interrupted, "but this magazine's executives really are decent. They gave me their word that they publish with taste and class. They said they wouldn't make me do anything I'm not comfortable with. The man I spoke with was a real gentleman."

Derek nodded, "I hope so."

"The magazine has far more substance than the public recognizes. They feature articles about America's Civil Rights movement, sexual liberation, the War," Renee explained, "they're a *part* of it. That's all I've ever wanted to be," Renee nodded, "a part of it."

"I understand," Derek said, "I've wanted to be a part of it as well, now, thanks to you, I finally am. I'm not here to shoot down your dreams."

Renee placed her hand on Derek's shoulder.

"Those who want to criticize me can fade away," Renee said.

"I am thrilled for you," he held Renee's waist and looked into her eyes.

Renee smiled, "Thank you, my sweet Derek. And I know there's a lot going on here at the boutique right now, but this frenzy may be temporary. I've got to take these opportunities while I can, you know. I may not be so fortunate as the years pass. I just feel pulled in so many directions. It's as though I'm letting *Grandmere* down but--"

"Don't worry about the boutique. I know what it means to you," Renee's eyes welled as Derek spoke. "I can go on with operations and supervision of the girls. If anything starts to slip don't hesitate to mention it."

Derek smoothed a dark strand from Renee's face.

"Another thing," Derek said, "You best consider an agent or assistant to be with you more often. They'll make sure you're safe and that you earn what you deserve. I don't want you making a cent less than they promise."

"I'll look into it. And I wouldn't feel comfortable putting *En Blum* in anyone's hands but yours," Renee said. "Remember," she emphasized, "personal style always prevails over trend. Help the individual find what suits *their* identity."

"I will do my absolute best," Derek promised.

What began with turning heads of passers-by swiftly turned into news periodicals stalking Renee. An unflattering photo of Renee, emerged. She was sweaty on the dance floor, her body held upright by a man Derek didn't recognize.

Though Renee brushed off the unwanted attention, her agent did not. He encouraged Renee to attend private events only. Derek kicked himself for suggesting an agent as they grew further apart.

One late-September day Renee arrived at the boutique near closing time. Renee joined Derek in creating a window-display when she was spotted. Two young fans pointed at her through the glass, mouths agape.

The pair of teens rushed into the boutique. One of the girls, a gamine redhead, blurted, "Renee, you are so beautiful. My mum won't let me go to the salon, but Kitty," she gestured to her friend, "she's going to dye my hair dark like yours."

"You are beautiful just as you are," Renee said and stroked the redhead's hair. "You keep that brilliant copper crown, that's *your* calling card. Now go along, you sweet girls."

Before departing, the fans procured two sheets of loose-leaf paper from their backpacks. Renee signed their crinkled papers and they scurried away, ecstatic. Renee sighed as the girls flashed her signature down the street.

Within fifteen minutes, the boutique was at capacity. Derek played the role of bouncer and kept an eye on the merchandise. Darkness fell as Derek hustled the last few customers from the boutique.

"I feel absolutely awful about this Derek," Renee said, exasperated, "but I can't be here during normal hours of operation anymore. This is just too much," Renee held her head in her hands.

"Renee, people can feel you when they walk in, whether you're here or not. We can handle this place," Derek assured. "You've done all the work needed here."

"Meet with me for drinks after work."

For weeks, during his afternoon stop at *En Blum,* Vaughn had invited Derek out. Derek consistently refused.

"I can't tonight, there's too much to do around here," Derek said.

"So, take a night off. I don't know why you're getting so wrapped up in this. We have some things to discuss," Vaughn stated.

Derek's curiosity piqued, but he was drowning in work. To top off the chaos, Renee was in and out of the country indefinitely. Pending decisions were piled high on her desk. Derek did his best to answer the questions presented to *En Blum*, but vendors and their high-profile clientele weren't there for Derek's opinion. The only contribution they desired from Derek was that of a camera click or a signed check.

After an especially stressful week, Derek accepted Vaughn's invitation for a night out, and they met at a quaint pub. The old friends purchased their ales and settled into an open booth.

"So, you and Renee," Vaughn inquired, "are you guys exclusive? I mean, you practically run the boutique, she obviously digs you."

"I'm not sure," Derek shrugged. "I haven't been with anyone else, but I suppose she could be. I wouldn't blame her. She's getting booked for more shoots, she's started attending galas and," Derek paused, unsure of whether to share her potential centerfold status, "she's *it.*"

"Sorry man," Vaughn started. "That's got to be hard with the no fame rule."

"Think about this, where we are from, have you heard of Renee Blum?" Derek asked.

Vaughn raised his eyebrows. "Good point," he replied. "I haven't, but you never know. The course can change based on *one* new person coming into her life." Vaughn tipped his beer toward Derek. "That's you."

"I don't know what I could do to change her course. She was meant for this. You've seen her, she's a vision. She's got the look for right now too," Derek quipped, "but maybe her time is *limited* to right now. She's admitted she may not be able to take the pressure forever."

Renee's look unified every component of the moment— the Carnaby swingers, New York beatniks, and Haight-Ashbury

172

flower children; she summed all of them up. But Derek knew the future. He knew Renee's iconic look may not translate to the decades that followed.

Vaughn placed a hand on Derek's shoulder and looked him in the eye.

"You've got to be careful. You're spending less time together, right?" Vaughn asked.

"Right," Derek said.

"Good. Be smart. You know the consequences," Vaughn warned. "I can see how hard this is for you, it would be hard for anyone to pull away from Renee, but *everything*, this whole life you've created," he paused, "it's *all* on the line."

The pub grew warmer with the increasing crowd. Vaughn removed his jacket and tossed it into the corner of the booth. Derek caught Vaughn fumbling a silver gadget into his pocket.

"What was that?" Derek asked.

Vaughn leaned in and spoke lowly, "Mine is the UpgrAid. They've updated the shape from the original, round Aid."

Derek shook his head, "What are you talking about."

Vaughn was equally confused, then it hit him.

"Haven't you gotten yours?"

"Gotten what?" Derek asked.

Vaughn's eyes held concern. "Everyone has one. I got mine months ago, and most Travelers have gotten one by now. It's an emergency device. If you get into trouble, just flip the little switch on the side, then TRN is alerted." Vaughn looked around to make sure no one was within earshot. "It's called the Aid. I'll see what I can do about getting one for you."

"Wait, every Traveler has one?" Derek asked.

"Shhh," Vaughn hushed.

"Sorry, I'm just confused. Why don't I have one? Was my acclimator supposed to give it to me?"

Vaughn took a deep breath.

"No, they weren't quite out yet when you arrived. When you Traveled here, there was a high volume of people destined for this era," Vaughn shook his head. "Glass warned of a stall in production. He must have been right."

"Can you get one for me?" Derek asked.

Before Vaughn could answer, a head of blonde corkscrews pulled Derek's attention away from the conversation. Vaughn welcomed the distraction from the unexpected situation.

Derek lay his eyes across the pub on a familiar face. She leaned forward into brighter lighting and her identity was undeniable. The poet. At last, Derek had confirmation that she wasn't a figment of his post-acclimation haze.

Surrounding the poet was a group of fellow beatniks. The lot of mavericks occupied a booth near the front window. Her golden ringlets had grown since Derek last saw her.

"Do you know them?" Vaughn asked.

"Not yet," Derek explained, "but I recognize the one with the blonde curls."

"Go on," Vaughn prompted.

"When I got here last spring, I was wandering around the city, high, and went to a poetry reading at a café." Derek said, "I was pulled in by her words. I tried to talk to her afterwards, but never got her name."

"Dude, this is your chance," Vaughn encouraged. "Go talk to her!"

"I don't want to interrupt them," Derek evaluated the group. They were deep in conversation with raised voices and active gestures. "I would ruin my chances if I joined them uninvited. And what about Renee?" Derek asked.

"What about Renee? Man, you have to understand," Vaughn reiterated, "she *can't happen*. You must move on from Renee. Not just to follow the guidelines," Vaughn hesitated, "but for your own good. Famous people jump around from one relationship to another, and I know what you've been through this past year. I want you to enjoy this time, not to be reliant on someone else for your happiness. There's no good ending to your story with Renee."

Derek sighed, "You're right. Even though I hate to admit it."

"Sorry," Vaughn said. "It's just that I've seen people get ripped from their destination and it's ugly. I don't think they'd do that to you, but they might if things progress. I would feel responsible if something bad happened to you when I was around. Plus, you don't need to get sucked into anything permanent here. Remember why you left, to change your circumstances, not to recreate them in a new place."

Derek nodded and gave Vaughn a halfhearted smile.

"Right again."

"I've got to come clean, the reason I've invited you here tonight is that I want you to know," Vaughn continued, "if I ever leave without notice, it's nothing personal. I have some commitments elsewhere. I have to say though, before I got here, I never expected we'd work out our shit. It's a relief."

"I'm glad we've worked it out too. Sorry it's taken me so long to meet up with you. Running the boutique has taken more time than I anticipated. I guess it's easy for me to get caught up in the day-to-day."

"The longer you stay, the more Psilopram wears off, the more it happens," Vaughn stated.

"What did you mean by 'commitments elsewhere?'" Derek questioned.

Vaughn evaluated his surroundings. The crowd had doubled in size since their arrival and a barrier of space no longer remained between their seats and the limited standing room.

"More on that later," Vaughn assured Derek. He changed the subject. "Everything else aside, I think you should go talk to her."

Derek looked toward the window and accepted Vaughn's advice. The poet's circle was still speaking passionately amongst themselves. A break in the conversation seemed unlikely.

"I'll go over when the time is right," Derek stated.

"We're not leaving until you give it a shot," Vaughn smirked. "Be right back," he said and excused himself to the restroom.

Derek monitored the window table for a break in their discussion. As he sat alone, his thoughts wandered back to the Aid. TRN had been so trustworthy throughout his Travel process, and Derek couldn't imagine the organization leaving an entire era of Travelers behind.

Vaughn made his way through the busying bar and returned to the table. He grinned and looked behind Derek.

"She's coming this way!" Vaughn said.

The remark pulled Derek from his fretting. He looked, and there she was. Derek and Vaughn's booth was placed in the middle of the poet's route to the bar. The poet squeezed her way through the bodies.

"It's now or never," Vaughn said.

"Miss," Derek started. He addressed her louder over the crowd's volume. "Miss!"

The poet turned to face Derek. Derek had forgotten how light her eyes were, verging on hollow.

"Yeah?" She responded.

"I'm Derek," he extended his hand. "Early last summer, I was at your poetry reading in a cafe."

She remained silent.

"You know, the cafe on the end of Carnaby," Derek explained further. "I hoped we'd run into one another again."

"Ah yeah, maybe I remember. Let me think about it. Sorry, I've got to split. My table's dry. Talk after a bit?" She asked.

Derek responded, "I'd like that."

"Thank you for stopping by the cafe. I'm still there every week. Now that I'm thinking about it, I recall having told you that. I wish you would have come by."

With that, she squeezed by Derek and Vaughn's table to join the mass of people gathered around the bar.

Derek cradled his head in his hands.

Vaughn patted Derek's shoulder, "You threw it out there. You would have regretted saying nothing."

A few minutes passed, and he and Vaughn watched the poet gather all six pints. Derek was prepared to offer a hand, but she managed the beverages and ventured back to her table.

"Do you think they're a group of couples?" Derek asked Vaughn. "I feel so stupid. I should have just let her pass without bothering her."

"Quit worrying, she said she'd come back in a bit," Vaughn laughed, "Be cool," he stated and lounged back in the booth.

Derek changed the topic.

"You mentioned having to leave," Derek started, "when might that be?"

"We'll see what happens," Vaughn replied.

"If you stay, maybe we could travel around this era together. Like you said, I don't have to remain stuck here," Derek said. "I'd like to go to San Francisco, just to see it at this time, you know?"

"Isn't your friend there? Grant, right?"

"Yeah, but I'm not sure when he's coming back," Derek stated.

"Has he written you?" Vaughn asked.

"No," Derek said, "not a word. I hoped for a postcard. He got there just in time for the Summer of Love. With how things are going lately, I regret not joining him."

"What?!" Vaughn shouted, unable to hear Derek.

Derek repeated himself, "I should have gone to San Francisco with Grant!"

Vaughn shook his head, frustrated with the noisy pub. He resorted to makeshift sign language. Vaughn patted his pocket where two small joints were nestled then pointed toward the pub's exit.

Derek nodded. The whole purpose of the evening had been to catch up with Vaughn, and it was impossible in the loud setting. They abandoned their booth and stepped outside.

Derek looked around to ensure they were alone. He followed Vaughn's lead and lit the end of his joint. The rip hit them rapidly.

"What's it like Traveling through the eras?" Derek asked.

Right after the question left Derek's lips, he and Vaughn were startled by a belligerent drunk who was thrown out of the pub onto the sidewalk. The drunk mumbled nonsense at them, and Derek and Vaughn faced each other, considering an escape to Vaughn's nearby apartment.

Instead, Derek turned to see the golden-haired poet, glowing through the front window. Her expression had become more jovial since their previous interaction. Derek guessed the round of drinks had something to do with it, but he didn't care. He looked to Vaughn for encouragement.

"Let's get back inside," Vaughn said. "I'll explain more another time."

"Just go for it, give it one more shot," Vaughn told Derek. "You talk to her. I'll work on getting us a booth."

Derek mustered his confidence and walked up to the golden-haired woman. She was now separated from her group, waiting for the bartender to fill another round for her table.

"Sorry to bother you again," Derek's words flowed smoother after the smoke-break. "Am I upsetting anyone with my interest in you?"

The poet gestured to her table with a nod.

"See for yourself," she said.

A man watched the poet from beneath his heavy, blonde fringe. The suitor glared at Derek.

"He tries too hard," she shook her head, "Seems my friends don't know whom I fancy as much as I had hoped. He can't take a hint, so I keep excusing myself for another round," she laughed.

Derek saw Vaughn secure a booth.

"Well, there's plenty of room with us," Derek gestured to Vaughn. "Your friends can join too," he offered.

The poet extended her hand.

"Angelene," she introduced herself.

Derek took her hand in his.

"Derek."

"Glad to officially meet you," Angelene smiled. "Well, it remains to be seen if they will relocate. They're all pissed. Been knocking 'em back since early afternoon."

Derek looked at the clock.

'10:30.'

"Stay tuned," Angelene said.

She turned away to join the iconoclast rag tag.

Derek watched as Angelene's admirer fussed with his hair. Every time the man spoke, he looked around the table for a response. Derek saw Angelene gesture toward his booth.

The suitor responded to Angelene's suggestion with a look of disdain.

"Been buying your drinks all night and this is what I get," he shouted.

He rose to his feet and stormed out of the pub. A young lady from their group went out after him. The remaining four stood and made their way toward Derek and Vaughn.

"Mind if we join?" a wild-haired brunette asked.

"Plenty of room," Vaughn made space on his side of the booth.

The brunette slid in, accompanied by a man with dark rimmed glasses. Angelene and the remaining man, who was very quiet, sat on Derek's side of the booth. They made their introductions. The ale continued to loosen their lips, and the strangers became further acquainted.

"Americans," David, the man with dark rimmed glasses stated. "I'd watch myself if I was yous," he said in a thick accent. "Just 'cause you're here don't mean they won't bang on your door when you get back and serve you those Vietnam orders. Given your age and build, you'd be first pick."

"We don't intend on returning to the states," Vaughn answered, "for the time being, at least."

"Oh, give it a rest Dave," Angelene said. "We've spoken of the war all evening."

"Forgive me for discussing the predominant issue of our world," David replied.

"So, what brings you two across the pond in the first place?" The brunette asked. She hadn't taken her eyes off Vaughn since she sat down.

"Well," Vaughn explained, not one to miss a cue, "we went to the same university in the States. We heard this is where it's happening, and now," he winked, "here we are."

"Is he ever going to show?" The quiet man asked Angelene. "Or is he on Yank time now," he looked at his watch.

"We must have missed something," Derek stated. "Are you expecting someone else?"

"Give him a break. He just flew back this morning. My brother," Angelene explained, "just returned from a holiday in the States. West Coast."

The brunette piped up, "I can't wait to hear about that groovy area he was staying in." She paused and turned to Vaughn, "What's it called in the Bay? Hashbury?"

"It's Haight-Ashbury," David corrected. "Some New Yorkers refer to it as Hashbury. The flower child Mecca apparently," he stated and pushed his glasses up the bridge of his nose.

"You just wait Ang," the brunette laughed, "Grant's going to come back with flowers in his hair. Have you heard from him?"

"Not a word," Angelene answered.

"Me either," Derek said.

They looked at each other and Derek laughed in disbelief. "You're Grant's sister?"

181

Grant awoke, still jet lagged. He returned to his flat around 8:00am BST. Grant was home, and summer was over.

Night fell, and Grant looked out his window. The scenery his flat overlooked was starkly different from that of the Bay view. Friday night traffic bustled through a cold rain.

Grant had quickly grown accustomed to San Francisco hills and constant music in the air, and he began to come down in many ways. The first leg of his flight consisted of a layover in Denver, then New York City. Once he arrived in London, he coordinated for Germain to drive him home from Heathrow.

Grant cracked open his living room window, and the air refreshed his senses. He smiled as a group of young ladies rushed along the sidewalk. Grant's long, sun-bleached hair blew back from his face, and he drew in the night's thin air.

He was swept into the reality of the changing seasons, not just in the time of year, but in his life. Since the moment his feet touched the ground in San Francisco, he'd lived in a dreamland. The Monterey Pop Festival, love-ins, and occasional trip across the bay to the University had all been one sunny blur.

Then, he remembered his obligation for the night. He was supposed to meet his little sister.

"10:00 at the pub," she'd said. "My friends will be there to welcome you as well."

He read the clock, *'10:15.'*

Grant had been clear for too long and craved something to soften his perception. Adding to his come-down, Angelene's friends always proved to drain Grant after a night in their presence. He plucked a joint from the table and lit it up.

'Thanks for the welcome home gift, Germain.'

Once the joint was cashed, Grant slid on his cargo jacket. He felt a bulge in his pocket and remembered the acid-dipped cigarettes he'd smuggled across the ocean.

They were a gift from the charismatic man who had given Grant a place to stay. The man was generous throughout Grant's time on the coast and had a constant abundance of drugs and women. Though Grant remembered little of their nights together, he knew, in his being, that the charismatic man was a part of something bigger than himself.

Grant slid the dipstick pack from his coat and stashed it in his nightstand. Upon exiting his apartment building, Grant looked up to the sky. Above him, a heavy, full moon glowed.

He smiled at her mysterious beauty. Grant felt connected to his brothers and sisters in America through the moon. He realized that the same astral body also beamed down upon young men in an unfamiliar jungle.

As Grant started toward the pub, he wondered how Angelene had spent her summer. His little sister's writing was impactful, and Grant was proud of her for sharing her words with the world. He wished he could have introduced Angelene to his California family.

Grant stepped into the pub and spotted his sister. As Grant grew closer to Angelene's table, he was thrilled to see another familiar face.

"Derek! I didn't know you'd be here," Grant said with open arms.

"So good to have you back," Derek said. "My friend Vaughn and I just happened to be here, and we met your sister. I went to one of her poetry readings a while back, so I recognized her from that."

"Right on," Grant said.

After hugging Derek, Grant reunited with his little sister. He embraced her and picked her up off the floor.

"Shame on you, Grant!" Angelene joked. "You didn't write any of us, did you?"

"I didn't, I was just living in the moment. You must know though, I thought of you there. You would have loved it," Grant stated. "They're creating their own society, free of the classist rubbish we have here."

He went on to greet Angelene's friends, then turned to face Vaughn. They made their introductions. Grant got settled and was uncertain where to begin in describing his holiday.

"Is it as groovy as everyone makes it to be?" The wild-haired brunette asked.

Grant nodded, "It's the beginning of a revolution."

A week after his homecoming, Grant was fully rested and ready to get back to his old scene. Derek suggested they go out that Saturday night, and Grant agreed to join without hesitation.

The evening was off to a great start. They went to the Ace and the club's crowd was the perfect size, not packed, but busy enough to keep the energy high.

En Blum hit a quieter, in-between season before winter festivities, sparing Derek from exhaustion. Derek leaned into the scene, but Grant appeared stiff and discontent.

"I'll be back in a few," Grant stated.

"Wait," Derek said, "I'll join you," but it was too late, and Derek was detained by a tenacious dance partner.

Grant stepped out back with the smokers. Before leaving his flat, Grant had stashed an acid-dipped cigarette in his shirt pocket, saving the rest for another night. He slid the dipstick between his fingers and flicked his lighter.

He remained outside as the acid kicked in. Grant found himself enamored with the revolving door of humans who stepped out of the club. A couple joined the mix. Grant recognized them. They were famous, musicians on the rise.

The lady towered above her partner. The length of her legs stretched beyond her knee-high boots. She and Grant met eyes.

"You alright?" she asked.

"Sorry," Grant stumbled, "you're just so…stunning."

Her partner went on to pull out a pair of cigarettes. He kept one for himself and handed the other to his date. He pulled out a lighter and wrapped his thumb across the starter multiple times but produced no flame. Frustrated, the man rattled the bum igniter, and shook his head.

The woman turned to face Grant, her silky black hair fanning across the air.

"Got a light?" She asked with a contralto voice.

The other-worldly beauty of her face turned Grant mute. The goddess' partner continued to shake his lighter in despair. He repeated his date's question.

"You got a light?" He asked and looked to Grant for an answer.

"We are all light," fell from Grant's lips.

The man nodded.

"Far out," he grinned, "it's all love brother."

Another smoker overheard the couple's inquiry and jumped at the opportunity to provide fire for the celebrities. Grant watched the flame pop from the match and transfer its brightness to the couple's cigarettes. The goddess's cheeks hollowed as she inhaled.

After a few more minutes of fresh air, Grant was ready to go back into the Ace. He followed the couple inside.

"You cool, man?" The man asked.

Grant nodded.

They entered and a bouncer stalled Grant. Grant watched the couple diffuse into the crowd. Light glared off the bouncer's bald head.

"You're not going to cause a fuss now, are you?"

Grant shook his head no.

"All right then, go on," the bouncer scoffed.

Inside, the bass pulsed through Grant's being. A familiar song was amplified by the speakers. In San Francisco, he had seen the graceful woman behind the voice. Grant moved with no restrictions and the song brought him back home to a state of pure freedom.

He was transported back to the dirty house in San Francisco. Grant could still smell the patchouli and see the billowing clouds of incense. He recalled sitting in his charismatic friend's living room, smoking one of his dipped cigarettes, and being told to clear his mind of any beliefs or thoughts.

"What good is the 'self' anyway?" he could still hear the man say.

Grant let himself drift into the ether. He ebbed and flowed with the waves of music as they crashed over the dance floor. For the remainder of the night, Grant ceased to have another conscious thought as he locked into a state of non-existence.

Derek could see that Grant was experiencing the club from a different plane.

"Sorry love," Derek made it a point to break away from his persistent dance partner, "I've got to check on my friend."

"Find me later," she said and disappeared into the crowd.

"Hey man," Derek got Grant's attention. He evaluated Grant's state and laughed. "I wish I could have stepped out with you. What'd you have?"

Grant leaned in close, "Acid," he said into Derek's ear.

"I'll be right back. I'm going to try and get on your level."

Derek stepped away from Grant to order a drink and was disappointed that Grant's substance of choice that night wasn't something in which he could partake. While Derek waited at the bar for his order, he scanned the club, keeping an eye on Grant. After a few minutes, the bartender supplied Derek's cocktail, and just as Derek took the first sip, he noticed a celebrity couple dancing near Grant. He looked for a place to set down his drink and join Grant on the floor. Derek claimed an empty high-top table.

He set down his mixed drink and watched Grant extend his long limbs to their full span. Grant's movements became inconsiderate, and the surrounding dancers distanced themselves from him. Derek scoped the club's perimeter for authority figures, but his surveillance was interrupted.

Angelene and a handful of her beat friends entered the club. Their somber presence was contrasted by the club's ruffled edges and short hemlines. Derek approached them.

"I see you decided to brush off the dust and join the fun tonight," Derek teased.

"Here to watch," Angelene stated, "Not to participate. Where's Grant?"

"Come with me," Derek said, "I've got a table at the edge of the dance floor. I'm not sure whether to laugh or be concerned about him."

"He's out of control again?" Angelene asked.

"I wouldn't say out of control," Derek responded. "I think he's just having a really good time."

Derek led her to his table. Angelene and her friends joined Derek at the high top and watched Grant sway with the music.

"I don't want to come off square," Angelene began, "but has Grant seemed a bit off since getting back?"

"I haven't had much of a chance to talk to him. Some of us have complied with society's nine-to-five," he joked. "This is mine and Grant's first night out together since he got back."

"Well, I spoke with Germain earlier this week, he said that Grant has… treated him differently. He's never been *like* that," Angelene said. "I'm meeting up with Germain tonight. He said he'd be at a pub around the corner, but I wanted to check in on Grant before meeting Germain there."

"That explains why Germain said he was busy tonight," Derek said. "Why don't you just approach Grant directly rather than sneaking behind his back and talking to Germain?"

Angelene sighed, "Grant won't want to hear it. Imagine, your friends and family are concerned about your behavior after the best summer of your life. The situation is delicate to approach."

"Fair enough," Derek replied.

Angelene and Derek continued to watch Grant. Angelene's friends snickered.

"Give it a rest," Angelene snapped at them.

A dancer got too close and was struck by Grant's elbow. Derek stood and gestured for Grant to join them at the table. Grant took the most direct path to Derek with no regard for the crowd and ran into several people along the way. He rested his forearms on the table and looked at Derek with a blank expression.

"You've got to *understand*, man," Grant said. "It's bigger than just us."

Fear struck Derek as he remembered the similar words which TRN had spoken. He was momentarily paralyzed. Meanwhile, Grant walked around the table and rested his hands on Angelene's shoulders.

"We've got to go now, sister. You're not prepared."

Grant guided Angelene toward the Ace's exit. Angelene's cheeks reddened as Grant caused her to bump multiple people on the way out.

"Grant, you're not making sense," Angelene struggled away from her brother.

Nearby clubbers whipped around to see what the fuss was about.

"Watch it!" A woman yelled as Grant stumbled into her, causing her drink to splash across the floor.

"Fine," Angelene seethed, "we're leaving. I'm going to wrap things up with Derek and the crew. Keep it together."

Angelene walked back to the table where Derek was preparing to leave.

"What's wrong with him?" Derek asked. "He wasn't like this before."

The Ace's security bee-lined toward Grant, stalling Derek and Angelene's conversation. The guard gripped Grant's arms and ejected him from the club. Angelene cut through the crowd. Derek attempted to follow but fell behind, not wanting to disrupt the assembly and get himself ejected as well.

Derek overheard the security guards.

"Been knocking people around all night, the wanker. Hippie freaks god-dammit."

Derek reached Angelene and Grant.

189

"It's okay Grant, there's no reason to be frightened," Angelene assured and put her arm around her brother. "Let's go home."

"Can I walk you?" Derek offered.

Angelene shook her head no.

"Something messed with him out west," Angelene said into Derek's ear. "Go, meet Germain and tell him what happened. Tell him I can't meet with him tonight," Angelene turned to face Grant. "It's okay, come with me," she said and walked her brother down the street.

Derek's heart pounded as he walked to meet Germain. He entered the establishment and found both Germain and Vaughn seated at a booth.

"Hey! Glad to see you mate!" Germain greeted Derek. His expression changed when he saw Derek's face.

"Be glad you didn't come out tonight. Grant freaked out at the Ace. Angelene told me Grant's been acting weird all week?" Derek paused for an explanation. "I wish I would have known."

"Sorry, I couldn't tell you in the boutique. You get so busy there and I didn't want to make a scene in front of the customers," Germain said, "but it's been bad."

Vaughn sighed.

"There's some shady shit happening on the Bay right now." Vaughn wasn't sure how much to say. TRN could tap into his conversation at any moment through his upgraded device. "They're messing with people's minds, planting stuff in their heads," Vaughn said with a lowered voice.

"That bad acid," Germain shook his head, "I have heard of it warping people's minds. We gotta look out for Grant. I just needed a break tonight. I love my brother, but he's becoming a liability. We've known each other since we were babies and I've

190

never seen a shred of violence from him. He's avoided me. Acted suspicious. Did Angelene get him home?"

"I think so," Derek said. "She wouldn't let me walk them."

"She's probably embarrassed of him," Germain concluded. "She's a little guarded if you haven't noticed. It's been her and Grant taking care of each other for so long, she probably didn't want you to tell Renee or get anyone besides me involved."

Vaughn looked at his watch. He felt the place in his coat pocket where, Derek knew, the Aid was stored. Derek was distracted by Vaughn's fidgeting.

"Do you have somewhere else to be?" Derek asked.

"I, uh," Vaughn said with a wavering voice, "I do. I'm sorry, I'll explain another time. Come over tomorrow and we'll talk."

With that, Vaughn stood and left the bar.

Germain raised an eyebrow, "Wonder what that's all about. Strange guy he is."

"Strange indeed," Derek agreed. He wondered why, if Vaughn wanted to meet up so badly, he only once asked Derek to his flat. Derek grew sour. Vaughn had given Derek a hard time about being busy, but Derek often failed to contact Vaughn by telephone. The only time they spent together was at a pub or the boutique.

Vaughn wished he could tell Derek the whole story. He hoped one day, Derek would understand.

Derek splashed cold water on his face then ventured into the kitchen. He poured himself a glass of water and began to call Grant. He hung up with one digit left to dial.

Instead, Derek called Vaughn. The phone rang ten times before Derek hung up.

Just as Derek put on his jacket to go to Vaughn's flat, his phone rang.

"Hello?"

"Derek," Grant said on the other end, "I don't know what to say, man. Angelene told me what happened. I don't remember anything past stepping outside to smoke," he rambled.

"It's fine," Derek said. "I've gotta go. I'll come over later."

Derek started toward Vaughn's apartment. When he arrived, Vaughn's building was locked, so Derek waited outside. His fingers began to go numb. Finally, he caught the door as another tenant was leaving.

Derek rushed to Vaughn's unit. He knocked but there was no answer. Derek turned the doorknob, and to his surprise, the door was unlocked. Derek's stomach turned with the eeriness of the vacant apartment.

"Vaughn?" He said into the emptiness.

Derek walked beyond the entryway, into the kitchen. He noticed a sheet of paper on the table. A round, iridescent piece of glass weighed down the paper. Derek picked up the translucent circle and couldn't believe his eyes.

The glass piece revealed words on the sheet.

'Derek,

I figured you would come here after my abrupt departure last night. I didn't have time to call you before I had to go. They needed me somewhere else. I'm sorry I didn't answer some of your questions. There were always people around, and they listen in to be sure I'm compliant with their guidelines.

I've notified them, and you can expect a quarterly newsletter delivered to your flat. There is a significant shortage of employees right now, so it's best for you to stay put in here until they can meet the demand.

I'll do my best to get you a device. I checked in with the nearest hub, and they're completely out. I'd give you mine, but they would have my ass if I didn't respond to their every call.

Hang tight. Don't get yourself in too deep.

Vaughn'

Chapter VIII

Mia cranked down the Cav's window. She exhaled the smoke from another cigarette, wondering why she kept taking Macy's carcinogenic offer. Weeks had passed since Halloween, and Macy and Mia agreed to pick up EJ and Lars after bar close. EJ's month-long high surrounding his twenty-first year's arrival was in full swing. The boys offered Mia and Macy a case of beer for the ride.

Mia and Macy passed a koozie-wrapped beverage back and forth. Macy drove over a bump, and Mia's beloved charm bracelet tinged against the beer can. No matter how far she felt from her childhood, from anything familiar, the bracelet brought comfort to Mia. Offering further peace-of-mind was another silver charm; she'd hooked the Aid to her bracelet. The device blended perfectly into the other trinkets.

Mia took a drag of her cigarette.

"Everything okay?" Macy asked. "You're quiet."

"Yeah, I'm good, it's just school," Mia bluffed.

That morning, Mia received another one of TRN's newsletters. The quarterly update shocked Mia as she read that there were still eras of Time Travelers who had not received an Aid. The sixties were one of the decades included in the mishap. TRN claimed there was a production error and vowed to make it right for Travelers left without the gadget. They promised an increased supply by Original Time's year-end.

Before Mia could fully digest the newsletter's information, Macy had arrived to pick her up. Mia stashed the letter in a box under her bed and joined Macy for the day.

"You should have said something if you had homework. I could have picked you up later," Macy said as she drove.

Mia kicked herself for not requesting more time alone. If she'd had the day to herself, she would have stopped by the TRN hub. She would have asked if Derek had a device and ensured that her parents had arrived home safely.

That week, furthering her homesickness, Mia and the Tuesdaze had gone to downtown Birchmont's tree-lighting festival. For the first year in her life, a Hayes family Christmas was not on the horizon. Mia understood the distance she'd put between herself and her family was the product of the decision to Travel, yet she struggled to let go of the memories of holidays passed. She guessed it was Psilopram's effect wearing off.

Every time Mia considered going home, her friendship with the Tuesdaze kept her from departing. Mia was reminded that going back solely for the dose of familiarity would lead her back into restlessness. Her mind had been stretched and no longer fit into the perimeter of its former confinement. Plus, there was no way to bring Macy home.

Though conditions had been ideal for Macy and Mia to hook up again and their nightly ritual was still going strong, Macy had grown increasingly distant since Parent's weekend. Mia regretted mentioning coming out to her parents. When she apologized to Macy for getting too serious, Macy blew it off and changed the subject.

Contrasting Mia's growing commitment to the nineties, Jaq's roommate, who had just moved in before Halloween, announced that he planned to relocate after winter break. Mia didn't know the details of his departure, but shortly after Mia and Macy's Halloween escapade, Mia realized how she knew Jaq's roommate.

He was Vaughn, her brother's college friend, or enemy as Mia knew him after Vaughn's interference with Derek's girlfriend.

Mia met Vaughn for the first time when she was in high school. Derek was home from college for the day to gather his winter clothing and picked Mia up after she was released from class. Vaughn was in the front seat and Mia couldn't keep herself from stealing glances at him in the rear-view mirror.

When Mia saw Vaughn at Jaq's over Halloween, she barely recognized him. His hair had grown longer than she remembered, but his signature dimples were still irresistible. Though they saw each other in passing, the privacy or reason to discuss their familiarity had not yet presented itself. Neither Vaughn nor Mia could risk revealing their true identities and they didn't want to provoke the attention of TRN. In spite of Vaughn and Derek's issues, Mia saw Vaughn as a welcome addition to the nineties. He served as a reminder that the era wasn't Mia's native home and she hoped that at some point, she could confide in him about the challenges of Travel.

Furthering her fluctuating emotions, a commitment loomed in Mia's immediate future. Earlier that week, despite the demise of their physical relationship, Macy asked Mia to be her roommate. Macy's mixed signals left Mia feeling lost as to how to move forward.

"If I can sublet my apartment, we could move in together after winter break," Macy had said. "I cannot *stand* my roommates anymore. They're a bunch of sticks in the mud."

"We'll see what happens," Mia replied. "Let's see if you can find a subletter and we'll go from there."

Between the shortage of Aid devices, college courses, and the impending layer of bonding to the time, Mia's mind reeled as they wove through Birchmont.

"I know it's a long way off," Macy said, "but once we're done with finals, want to do something crazy? Like get a hotel in the city for the weekend?"

"I'd be so down," Mia replied. Macy's question drew her from introspection. "Just you and me or the whole crew?"

"Whoever wants to go, it'll be cheaper with more people. I don't care, I'll sleep on the floor," Macy said. "We just need to get you out of your head for a night."

"I can think of some ways to clear my mind," Mia began. "And we wouldn't even need to leave town."

Macy sighed.

"Mia, I've been meaning to talk to you about this, but everything's been so crazy lately; I didn't want to add to the stress," Macy rested her hand on Mia's wrist. She fumbled with Mia's bracelet. "I like that we've pumped the brakes a bit. Don't get me wrong, Halloween was freakin' sexy. I'm just not sure we're looking for the same thing. I can see how close you are to your family. You spend every waking moment with them when they were here," Macy broke contact with Mia and put her hand back on the wheel. She took a puff of her cigarette. "I'm not looking for something… serious."

"I'm not either," Mia said.

Macy chuckled, "C'mon, Mia. You thought about introducing me as your *girlfriend* or something. We are two different types of people. I *can* have a night like Halloween and keep it light. You *can't*. You're deep. Honestly, I'm afraid if I'm not clear about what I'm looking for, I'll hurt you, and I don't want to do that. What we've got, or what we could have, has the potential to up the band."

Mia's heart dropped, but she respected Mia's straightforwardness. She gulped down the lump in her throat and took a drag.

"You're right," Mia admitted. "Especially if we're moving in together, we should set some boundaries. Things could get complicated with the band too. We're both adults, we can just move forward as friends. I suppose focusing more on school wouldn't be bad for me either."

Mia was extremely bright and in Original Time, hadn't dedicated much effort to her studies. If she missed something in class, there was always a backup— a recorded lecture or online supplement. However, in the nineties, Mia hated the old, bound, textbooks and droning lectures. Whenever Mia cracked open the musty volumes, she had to repress daydreams of performing and resist the desire to call Macy for company. It was painful to put her guitar to rest and shift her attention to gen-eds which served as the foundation for a life she wasn't certain she wanted.

Mia took another swallow of her beer and began to unwind. She was perked-up by the energy of the youthful city as they cruised along Birchmont's side streets and watched off-duty students trudge through the sharp air, pressing on toward the homes of their friends. Mia wondered if there were other Travelers posing as era collegiates in Birchmont.

"Let's see if Tiff's around," Macy said and drove toward Tiffany's apartment.

In Original Time, Mia would have texted Tiffany to see if she was home but here, that wasn't an option. Showing up without notice was an adjustment for Mia at first, but she grew to enjoy the spontaneity.

Macy's headlights shone on the front of Tiffany's apartment building. Tiffany's roommate walked outside. Macy put the car in park and rolled down her window.

"Hey Claire!" Macy shouted. "Is Tiff inside?"

"Yeah! Last I knew she was attempting to study," Claire replied. "What are you ladies up to tonight?"

"Just a little cruising," Macy said with a wink. "How 'bout you?"

Claire answered, "The library, lame, I know," she turned to show Macy and Mia her loaded backpack.

"Lame, yet very responsible," Macy gave a thumbs up, "I admire the discipline."

"Ugh, something like that. Well, have fun tonight! Have a drink for me," Claire said and unlocked her car.

Mia and Macy walked up to the building and buzzed Tiffany's apartment.

"Hello," Tiffany's voice crackled from the speaker.

"Hey bitch," Macy shouted, "wanna cruise?"

Silence.

Then, they saw Tiffany make her way down the stairs. She held a large, black CD case under her arm and a bag of red licorice in her hand.

"Ready to go!"

Mia and Macy slid back into the car and Tiffany settled into the backseat. She flipped through her CDs. Macy drove out of the parking lot and Tiffany leaned forward to feed a disc into the player.

"Just what I need," Mia stated. "Thanks for bringing the music selection to wake me up. I'd be in bed right now if we hadn't agreed to pick the guys up later."

"That'll change when we move in together," Macy said. "I'm a night owl!"

Tiffany spoke up from the backseat.

"I love ya Mace, but I'm not sure I could deal with your shit everywhere."

"Hey! I've gotten better," Macy replied.

"We'll keep working on it," Mia laughed.

"Guys," Tiffany said a half hour into their drive, "I have to tell you something. I think Vaughn is crazy hot. He's so…mysterious. I'm mega-bummed that he's moving away. Think I should make a move before he goes?"

Mia thought back to the crush she'd had on Vaughn when she was younger. During her visits to Derek's college, she always hoped to run into Vaughn. She used to fantasize that Vaughn would come home with Derek. Mia imagined herself and Vaughn, alone, making out on the couch. Despite the steamy reveries of her adolescence, Mia didn't want to disturb the friendship that she and Tiffany had cultivated.

"I say go for it! Especially since he's leaving soon. What have you got to lose?" Mia asked.

Macy pointed out her window, stealing their attention.

"Look at these cuties!" Macy shouted.

Lars, Vaughn, and EJ strutted down the campus-town street of bars.

"Ow, *ow*!" Macy called out.

The guys looked toward the slow-rolling car. They strolled with their heads held high, mistaking Macy's catcall for some new, hot chick's compliment. EJ clapped his hands together and laughed when he saw it was Macy.

"Back that beast up, babe!" EJ taunted.

Macy found a spot along the boys' trajectory and parked.

"You done with the bars?" Macy asked.

"I don't know guys," EJ answered, "are we?"

"I am," Vaughn said. He made eye contact with Mia and grinned.

Lars shrugged, "I'm not, but I can always come back down here later."

"We could go to Hayden's pond," EJ suggested.

Macy gestured to her back seat, "Hop in!"

Hayden's pond was one of the few places outside of town that the cops had yet to discover. The owners of the property lived forty-five minutes away and rarely checked in on their piece of decaying land.

"There's not room for all of you!" Tiffany said as the boys piled into Macy's car.

"Mace," Lars leaned into the front seat, "Can I bum a smoke? Man, it's crammed back here, Tiffany, just lay across us."

Tiffany shot Lars a glare.

"Or," EJ said, "Tiff, you could sit on mine or Vaughn's lap."

Tiffany scooted onto Vaughn's lap. She stretched her legs across EJ, and her boots landed on Lars. Tiffany chuckled to herself as she remembered the mud on her soles from walking across campus.

Tiffany handed her CD case to Mia. Mia accepted the large magazine of CDs and opened it like a book. She thought of her parents; the case was full of music they listened to at her age. She selected an album, and the CD player drew in the disc.

Music burst from the speakers. Mia heard a can crack open behind her. A few months ago, she would have panicked at her friends' comfortability with an open container, but Mia had become accustomed to the ninety's recklessness.

Mia glimpsed in the rear-view mirror at Tiffany who cozied up to Vaughn. Mia wondered if Vaughn was interested, then suppressed the curiosity.

'It's none of my business.'

"I don't know how many more shows I'm going to get booked for the Tuesdaze this winter," Lars uttered. "Especially if you're not careful with your shoes, Tiffany."

Lars shoved Tiffany's feet off his lap and brushed off his jeans.

"Take a chill pill, Lars," Tiffany replied.

"Why don't I take one of yours, Tiff," Lars quipped. "Clearly you haven't taken your meds today."

"I would have doubled my dose had I known I'd be dealing with you tonight," Tiffany said.

"Go ahead, drop me off downtown. Go to Hayden's. I have his number. He might want to know if under-agers are drinking on his property," Lars threatened.

"Everyone calm down," Macy intervened. "Do I need to pull over?" She joked.

They drove out of town. The only sound was that of Mia's selected CD.

"Hey Lars," Vaughn said, "wasn't that the owner of the Lakehouse you were schmoozing tonight? Lots of people go out over Thanksgiving."

Mia turned down the music to better hear Vaughn.

Vaughn continued, "You keep saying you've got all these hook-ups, when was it the Tuesdaze headlined last?"

"Halloween," Tiffany answered. "And it's not like we're making money. Most people pay more for their bar tabs than we get to put in our pockets."

The song ended and the CD looked back to the beginning. Mia searched for the next sound to fill the silence.

"I-I guess I'll see what I can do," Lars said, not accustomed to being called out.

Mia looked back to see Tiffany stroking Vaughn's hair. Mia wished she could do the same. After standing up for the Tuesdaze, he became even more attractive.

Mia settled on an album. Though the songs were overplayed, a smile crept onto her face as the pop quintet started in. One by one, the car couldn't help but sing along with the opening track.

Vaughn's motive to be in the era remained a mystery to Mia. She couldn't surmise that, by chance, they'd ended up in the same year, in the same town. Mia looked in the side mirror and caught Vaughn's eye. She knew when the time was right, they had a lot of catching up to do.

They approached Hayden's pond, and a bright, full moon illuminated the rolling hills and barren trees. Macy ignored the *Private Property* sign and put her car in park. Hayden's pond spread across a clearing downhill from the curve of the gravel road.

Lars tapped Mia's shoulder. He leaned in from the backseat and spoke into her ear. He smelled of cologne and cigarettes, reminding Mia of the night she saw his true colors.

"I found this place when I was introducing EJ to fishing," Lars said. "Then, I realized that most cruisers go to the other side of town and thought, 'what a perfect spot to party.' Old man Hayden throws crazy shindigs out here once it warms up. I got to know him last summer. He's got a huge cabin just over the ridge," Lars stated. "I'll have to bring you next year."

"Thanks for enlightening us, Lars. We had no idea you knew Hayden," Tiffany said, her tone dripping with sarcasm.

Though Hayden's was more discreet than other drinking hot-spots, Mia kept her guard up. She knew that Birchmont's police would crash their party if there was a drought of action within the city limits.

Macy powered down her lights and engine. The path to the water was a steep, brushy hike. Tiffany struggled with her footing on the way down and Vaughn lent his hand. Tiffany giggled and Mia smiled at her friend's lovesickness.

After a precarious hike, the six of them reached the clearing. Their jaws dropped at the glass-smooth water bathed in the full moon's light. They admired the elucidated scene.

While the rest of them talked, Mia remained silent, processing everything that had happened that day. She considered asking Macy for another cigarette. Vaughn approached Mia.

"What's on your mind?" Vaughn asked.

"Playing again," Mia answered. She looked around to see if her friends were within earshot. Lars' eyes were on Mia and Vaughn, so she delayed sharing her true concerns. "We don't have anything else on the calendar."

"I've been meaning to talk to you about your set list," Lars said, inserting himself into the conversation. "We might want to look into some more modern options, yeah? Less hippie covers. I've got a few song seeds. I'm not a musician myself, but maybe we could work together sometime," Lars paused, "alone."

Vaughn rolled his eyes, "Their setlist is fine. They need to have gigs on the books before they can make tweaks anyway."

Lars ignored the remark. Mia was grateful for the sound of crickets to alleviate the silence.

"What is it, you don't have as many connections as you claim?" Vaughn prodded. "You ruin your relationships by being an ass?"

"Get bent man," Lars responded and secluded himself to pout near the water's edge.

Tiffany patted Vaughn's back, "Thank you."

"You deserve so much better than that douche. Your Halloween show was recommended to me right after I moved in," Vaughn said, "by more people than just Jaq. After I saw you, the way you worked that crowd, I want to help in any way I can before leaving."

"I'm bummed you have to go," Tiffany said and put her hand on Vaughn's shoulder. "I don't want to pry, but Jaq mentioned it was a family thing. I hope you know; I'm here if you want to talk."

"Ah," Vaughn dodged her advance, "you don't want to hear about it. It'll bring down the mood."

'Keep it light,' Vaughn told himself. 'You're here on business.'

Vaughn's email chimed. He took a swig of his coffee and opened the message.

Monitoring Opportunity
- *Ensure safety of siblings, Derek and Mia Hayes.*
- *Shadow their social circle for 2-6 months.*
- *Destination: 1967 (Derek), 1997 (Mia.)*
- *Bonus offered with project success.*

Vaughn jumped at the opportunity. He knew that no one could fulfill Jon and Ellie's wishes as well as he could; with or without the financial incentive. He waited outside Dr. Lowell's door with his resume and was offered the opportunity on the spot.

Vaughn still couldn't shake the guilt of leaving sixty-seven so hastily. He'd hoped to stay longer, but was getting caught in Derek's social web and consistently skirted TRN's guidelines on their nights out. TRN was concerned with Vaughn's overcommitment to the assignment, so they decided the time had come for Vaughn to move onto Mia's era.

"He knows Renee is off-limits, right?" Dr. Lowell had asked.

"Of course," Vaughn answered, hoping he was right.

"Well then, you've fulfilled your responsibility of keeping safe. Hopefully the poet will cement him into the time."

"I told him not to get too involved. He's gotten hurt by overcommitting in the past," Vaughn explained.

"Shit," Dr. Lowell said. "Glass is hoping more people *stay* in the past. We've had a lot come back lately. I can see him growing concerned that our efforts here in OT will be for naught should too many Travelers return."

"I-I'll try to get Mia to stay without getting too…well-known," Vaughn promised. "I left Derek so promptly because he

208

doesn't have an Aid. I had to come back and see that the shortage was resolved."

Vaughn knew he owed Derek more explanation than the letter he left behind. He was pained to leave the sixties but had learned in his childhood that goodbyes were best when swift and painless.

Vaughn grew up in a military household. From kindergarten through high school graduation, Vaughn was enrolled in eight different schools. During college, Vaughn spent more time in one city than ever before. His roommate, Derek, was the closest friend Vaughn ever had, so the Hayes occupied a special place in his heart. He'd seen other employees take the money and run, barely paying attention to those they were incentivized to protect. Though Vaughn was paid to keep the Hayes safe, he made it his personal mission to monitor their well-being, even after he got his bonus.

Vaughn attempted to remain detached from Mia, but that became difficult after seeing her onstage. He planted himself in her friend circle by coordinating a friendship with Jaq and offering to pay rent until EJ moved in.

"You couldn't have asked at a better time," Jaq said. "My brother's lease isn't up until next semester."

Monitoring the Hayes increased Vaughn's standing with TRN, and he was next in line for a promotion. He was about to make the leap from monitor to recruiter. TRN was in dire need of employees. With little to bring Mia back to Original Time, TRN saw that she was cut out to work for them, so Vaughn posed as a double agent. He fulfilled Jon and Ellie's investment in their children's safety while gauging Mia's aptitude to work for TRN, though getting Mia alone proved to be a challenge. Just like her brother, Mia had melded into the social scene of the time. Vaughn found humor in the parallels between Mia and Derek's draw to the spotlight. In Original Time, they didn't shine, but Vaughn chalked their new bravery up to Psilopram and the opportune era.

Mia looked at home on stage and Derek was drawn just close enough to the celebrity's circle to make Vaughn sweat. Vaughn had flirted with the edge of fame himself, but always knew when to leave the era behind for his own good.

Vaughn eased his own concerns by telling himself that even if the Tuesdaze were to become well-known, notoriety put so much strain on bands that they often imploded. Vaughn had seen the ego-ignited disintegration of musicians through many eras. Rather than concern himself with the Tuesdaze popularity, Vaughn concluded to use his limited time in the nineties to offer an out from Lars' toxic hold or better yet, to charm Mia into becoming his co-worker.

As the rest of the Tuesdaze spoke, Vaughn looked over his shoulder to keep an eye on Lars. Vaughn relaxed after seeing that Lars had not yet finished sulking and remained out of earshot. Vaughn took a seat on a large boulder. A side conversation formed between EJ, Tiffany, and Macy, so Vaughn beckoned Mia closer to him.

Vaughn lowered his voice and spoke into Mia's ear. She felt her cheeks warm.

"Looks like you've got it made here," Vaughn started, "the band, the friends, the look, you must have been styled by Rae," he said. "Your brother would be glad for you. He's doing very well for himself," Vaughn paused, remembering Derek's missing Aid device, "for the most part. My last trip was to... where he is," he chuckled, "talk about a good time."

"Get out!" Mia said in disbelief, "You have to tell me everything."

From the clearing's edge, Lars glared at Mia and Vaughn, scanning them with a suspicious eye. Mia realized she had spoken louder than intended and lowered her voice to a whisper.

"I'm surprised you and Derek patched things up," Mia said to Vaughn. "There must be some good drugs where he's at. I never thought he'd forgive you."

"I'm glad we're cool now. The whole thing with Anna," Vaughn shook his head, "it was all a big mess. A major misunderstanding. I was out of line to meet with her, but I had no idea she was trying to get with me. I just thought she needed a nudge back toward Derek."

Vaughn glanced around to assess their discretion. He saw that Lars lurked closer to himself and Mia. Their privacy dwindled with every passing minute.

"We've got company," Vaughn said with a subtle gesture toward Lars. "Before we move on, I've got to tell you something that's been on my mind. Derek didn't receive the Aid."

Mia gasped, unable to hide her reaction.

"I'd hoped he wasn't one of them."

211

Her worries had become a reality. Before Mia could verbalize her questions, Lars further encroached on their conversation. Mia and Vaughn looked at one another.

"Later," Vaughn whispered.

Mia nodded. Her hatred for Lars doubled for interrupting their discussion. Mia proceeded to create a decoy conversation with Vaughn about boy bands. Lars rejoined their group just in time to hear Mia and Vaughn scheme.

"Let's plan a music video night," Vaughn said.

The conversation went from a ruse to a real discussion dedicated to the appreciation for the lost form of visual entertainment. Eventually, Mia and Vaughn's side conversation fizzled, and the group reconvened.

"What's everyone doing over Christmas vacation?" Macy asked.

Tiffany sighed, "Off to the 'rent's. You know how much I look forward to being plagued by the little step-monsters. My mom spoils them. I never got away with half the shit they do."

"On the way here, Mia and I were saying we should all get a hotel in the city," Macy said as she pulled out her lighter. "Hit a rave or club, yeah?"

"And how do you propose we get into this club?" Tiffany asked, "Do you have a fake ID? Because I don't."

"I can get you fakes," Vaughn offered.

Mia raised her eyebrows.

"How is it that you've only been here for a few months, and you can get fakes?" Lars interjected. "Seems a little sketchy to me."

Tiffany glared at Lars, then turned to face Vaughn.

"Sold," Tiffany said. "Just let us know how much we owe. And mine better have red hair."

Vaughn broke out his knee-weakening smile.

A car made its way around the curve and the five of them snapped around to face the main road. Lars surveyed the area while the rest of the Tuesdaze searched for places to hide. They threw their beers into the tall weeds and Macy reluctantly tossed her remaining third of a whisky bottle into the brush.

Mia, Macy, and Tiffany were all under twenty-one. Vaughn, EJ, and Lars weren't immune either. Despite their legal age, they were on private property and had supplied alcohol to minors. They looked at each other with wide eyes.

"Hide," EJ instructed the girls. "Lars, please tell me that's Hayden's car."

Lars craned his neck.

"It's not looking good."

Mia, Macy, and Tiffany scattered into the thick grass lining the water. The girls crouched down, concealed by the dry, scratchy weeds. A beam of headlights rounded the corner then, the vehicle came into clear view.

Cops.

The cherries flashed. Two officers exited their vehicle and zeroed in on the clearing. EJ, Vaughn, and Lars froze in place. The officers approached the brush.

"Get on up here. What are you fellas doing out here?" the cop asked with a gruff voice. "Whose car is this parked on private property?"

"Sorry sir," Lars began as the guys struggled up the incline, "Hayden said we could come out here anytime. You can call him if you want, I have his number. We just needed to get out of the city, away from the books for a night. Take in some fresh air, you know?"

"IDs and registration," one of the cops barked.

The three of them handed over their driver's licenses.

"Where's the vehicle's registration?"

"I just renewed it," Lars answered. "My girl trashed the inside of this thing. She stole my CDs and cleared everything out of my glovebox."

"That girl's gonna be the death of you," EJ said. "Got any advice for this guy?"

"You really wanna know?" The cop began. "Get that young, college tail while you can kid," he advised. "But be careful with those crazy chicks. They may be fun now, but they'll wear on you as the years pass."

The other officer laughed at his partner.

"Head on back to town," the officer added, "we'll follow you."

Mia, Macy, and Tiffany shared a look of alarm. Tiffany and EJ made eye contact.

"Be back," EJ mouthed.

The guys drove away with the police behind them. Dust from their departure hung in the air. Once the taillights disappeared, the girls abandoned their grassy post.

"That was way too close," Macy heaved and held her hand to her chest.

"What a nightmare," Tiffany said. "Who knows what kind of wildlife is out here?"

They gathered around the large boulder where Vaughn sat just minutes before.

"I know this isn't ideal, but I am psyched that there is not a textbook in sight. I can't even think about classes for a while" Macy stated. "I have no idea if I'm headed in the right direction. School is hard man," she hung her head. "I just can't wait until we graduate. What then though?"

Mia thought back to the discussions she and Derek had during his college days. As a student, her brother had the time of his life, but after graduation, he seemed more stressed than ever. Mia remembered his constant, existential contemplation.

"You're right, Macy, what *do* we do after graduation?" Mia asked.

"Don't ask me," Macy answered.

Rather than go down the uncertain road of the future, Macy flicked her lighter and pulled a cigarette from behind her ear.

"Good thing I kept one on me," Macy stated. "See, Mia, you make me get too deep."

"Ooh," Tiffany stood and meandered through the long grass, "let's find that bottle of whisky!"

"Mind if I have a drag?" Mia asked Macy.

"And to think you never smoked when we met," Macy smirked.

Macy shared her cigarette with Mia. She sucked in and felt her body relax. The buzz ushered Mia into a state of serenity.

They finished the cigarette and went on to join Tiffany in her hunt for the discarded whisky. As they sifted through the brush, it dawned on Mia that any urgency surrounding her life's path was only an illusion. A sense of relief replaced her previous despair. Mia locked to the same mindset of acceptance she'd felt after her Psilopram-fueled journey. Though months had passed since taking the drug, with focused efforts, she could often access the same psyche she possessed upon her arrival. The scope of time and space in which to explore was unlimited.

"I cannot believe the guys made it out of that pickle!" Macy remarked. "I'll take temporary abandonment to legal trouble any day. My parents would kill me!"

"True," Tiffany agreed. "I hope the guys are back soon though."

"Here it is!"

Mia fished the dirty whisky bottle from the weeds. She used her shirt to wipe the bottle clean, then screwed off the lid and took a long pull. The warmth of the spirit fused well with the sharpness of November's air.

"Share the wealth," Tiffany said, snatching the bottle from Mia.

As Macy and Tiffany took their swigs, Mia paused to gaze at the smooth body of water. As she stood by the water's edge, her eyes settled on the gentle ripples. Before Travel, Mia often floated through her days, letting events unfold around her. She always felt like a spectator as people came in and out of her life, absorbed what there was to offer, and left. In that moment, Mia honed in on her strong sense of control.

Rather than settling for the mysterious unfolding of Original Time with no guarantee that she'd be satisfied with her life's outcome, she was crafting her own experience, blazing a new trail. Original Time wouldn't have offered the same opportunities that Mia had in Birchmont, and she felt a renewed validation for her decision to Travel.

Mia gazed at the sky. Her eyes followed the Milky Way. She remembered Dr. Chandra's comment on Traveling to the nineties.

"In the nineteen-nineties, they discovered that the universe is expanding faster and faster, not slowing down as we anticipated."

"Interesting," Mia had responded.

"The previously unnamed force causing everything to expand was the key to Time Travel," Dr. Chandra paused and smiled. "Every evening when we looked at the night sky, it was right there, waiting for us."

Mia came out of the memory and realized had been standing alone, staring at the water and the sky. She wasn't sure how long it had been. Mia looked back at Macy and Tiffany; certain they would wonder if she'd smoked the countryside's ditch weed. They were still deep in conversation as though no time had passed.

With admiration for her ever-expanding universe, Mia savored a few more moments of solitude. Her trancelike state was broken with a rustle along the tree line and Mia hurried back to her friends. They passed the whisky around and the three of them reminisced about their semester at Birchmont. They began to set plans for their New Year's trip to the city.

Finally, headlights cut through the night as EJ's car emerged around the bend.

"We're rescued!" Tiffany cheered.

They parked and EJ stepped out of the vehicle's passenger side. He burst out laughing when he saw the girls passing around the whisky.

"Here," EJ said, "pass that over! I need a drink!"

Vaughn stepped out from the driver's seat and reached for the whisky. Mia waited for Lars to ruin the mood with his sourness, but she didn't see him in the car.

"Where's Lars?" Mia peered into EJ's backseat.

"Well," EJ explained, "he wasn't too happy someone," EJ nodded toward Vaughn, "put him in his place. Wanna be our manager, Vaughn?"

The group of five laughed.

"You're going to have to take better care of us though, manager. You're lucky I didn't freeze to death out here." Macy shivered, "Will you pop the trunk? I need a blanket!

Inside EJ's trunk were boots, two ice scrapers, snow pants, and chunky winter gloves.

Mia laughed, "Wow, do you foresee a bad winter?"

EJ looked at Mia with a confused expression. "Don't you have an emergency kit in your trunk? I know it's not bad out yet, but it's good to be prepared just in case I ever get stranded."

Mia had forgotten that cell phones were not yet a staple. Earlier, on their way to Hayden's, she was astonished at the amount of space in the countryside. Commercial and residential developments hadn't yet gone underway. Online delivery warehouses and shopping centers had yet to purchase acreages and family farms.

In this era, vast stretches of no-man's land still sprawled across the country. Macy pulled the outerwear from EJ's trunk and doled it out to the group. They sat at Hayden's for another five minutes and took pulls under the moonlight.

"We better be going before our luck runs out and the cops come back," EJ stated. "It wouldn't surprise me if Lars called them on us after ditching him at the bars just now."

They piled in the car and began their return to Birchmont. Heat blasted from the vents, and they grew tired. It dawned on the students that, with every mile, the evening's reprieve from their studies waned.

Tiffany whispered into Vaughn's ear and Mia closed her eyes. Wrapped in the blue flannel blanket from EJ's trunk, Mia drifted to sleep and the five of them rode into the final days of the semester.

Chapter IX

From a screen across the ocean, Derek watched protestors gather. His conscience was struck by the intense discord, and in his heart, Derek understood what it was like to be a native of the time.

Derek knew how history would be written, but he didn't know how much longer he could separate himself from the events, unfolding before his eyes. Derek watched the crowd multiply by the hundreds on the black and white television. Mothers demanded to know why their sons were shipped off to die. Meanwhile, Derek was using the era as a vacation from his own life, which held no immediate danger, but was dull.

"One American could be laid to rest as payment for three hundred enemy soldiers," Grant had told Derek. "And they're fighting a desperate enemy, putting their back against the ropes. The soldiers are seen as a percentage, a ratio rather than eighteen-year-olds. Most of them had yet to board an airplane prior to their deployment."

Derek couldn't comprehend how his home country had been so irreversibly woven into the disastrous conflict. He thought back to his first grasp on the concept of war.

As children, Derek, Cooper, and Mia spent a lot of time at their grandparent's house. Derek remembered the day when they discovered the dusty, yellow-bordered stack of magazines in Les and Valerie's basement. They spent an entire afternoon flipping through pages of historical images. Derek could still smell the distinct musk of the old publications as he watched the live version of the articles play out before him.

Les nearly served in the Vietnam war. Due to a chronic heart condition, Les was spared from the draft. His twin was not so fortunate.

As they got older, the Hayes siblings were curious about their grandpa's close call, but they were under strict instruction from their mother to avoid the topic. Ellie had made the mistake of bringing up the war when she was a child. Despite Ellie's innocent interest, Les broke down and Valerie made Ellie promise to never bring up the war again.

As Les aged, he began to speak more openly about his family's tragedy. With the right therapist and Valerie's patience, he dealt with his loss. Les even went on to speak of the war with his grandchildren.

It started when Les walked down to his basement and found an abandoned electronic tablet laying in the center of the floor. Les scanned the room and saw the grandkids gathered around one of his old magazines. They had pulled the publication from its corner shelf and were reading together in silence.

"I'm glad we didn't sell those," Les said. "Whatcha reading about? There was a casualty on the floor by the stairs," Les said and held up their abandoned tablet. "Something more interesting than those games, huh?" He teased.

Les leaned forward to see what issue the siblings had stumbled upon.

Vietnam.

The kid's eyes widened, then they turned in to face one another.

"You ask," Les overheard from their hushed debate.

"Grandpa Les," Mia asked as she used a nearby end table to pull herself from the floor. "Mom said you almost had to fight in the Vietnam War. She said your brother had to go, but you didn't."

Mia procured the magazine from the ground. Les was struck at the juxtaposition of Mia, his sweet grandchild, speaking of such heartbreak. She wrapped her fingers around both sides of the magazine and turned the cover so he could see it. A child, Mia's age, peered into the photographer's lens.

Les didn't know where to begin. He gritted his teeth and swallowed the lump in his throat. He wished he could have distracted them with the tablet. Les looked at his twin grandsons, Derek and Cooper, and remembered his own mirror image.

"It's true," Les started. "My brother was called to fight. I almost went over there with him."

Les and his three grandchildren got comfortable on the sofa. The boys sat on each side of Les, and Mia plopped down on his lap. Valerie overheard the conversation and joined.

"Everything okay?" She asked.

"I'm telling them about Vietnam," Les answered.

Valerie nodded.

Les explained how the draft worked and went on to tell them about getting the call that his brother was missing in action. Les pulled a box from storage. The top half of the box was filled with letters from Les' twin.

'This is hell,' was written in black ink and Valerie snatched the letter away before the kids could read it.

"Let's look at these instead," Valerie dug deeper into the box. "These letters were exchanged between your great-grandparents before they were married. They're more romantic."

The scrawl was barely legible, but the children discovered that their great grandparents were engaged to be married through a letter delivered by V-Mail. Derek ran his fingers over the threaded texture of a uniform patch.

"Dad was a part of the ninety-fifth infantry," Les explained. "The 'Iron Men of Metz.'"

Les continued to reveal treasures from the box, pulling frontline letters from their discolored envelopes.

"Letters were how they communicated during the World Wars. Can you imagine that?" Les asked. "My brother and I could at least call each other, though I wish I had spoken with him more. But what would I have talked about?" Les asked. "I felt helpless. I still get sick to my stomach when I think about it. There was nothing I could do but watch the horrors on the news. They lied about it at first, but I knew. Every night, I went to my clean, dry bed, I thought of my brother on the spongy ground of the jungle. When he left," Les took a deep breath, "I knew that was the last time I'd see my mirror image outside my own reflection."

Derek studied the faces of the young soldiers. He couldn't imagine what Les must have experienced. Derek's world of color was darkening. It seemed society's problems were stacked so high that at any given moment, they were due to crumble.

Derek's mind wandered to his own tragedies. The image hadn't surfaced in a while, but Derek remembered walking into Cooper's room and seeing his twin's body on the floor, lifeless.

Derek longed for something to fix the eeriness of his inner and outer world.

Vaughn's abrupt disappearance exacerbated Derek's sense of uneasiness. Though Derek was thankful for the decryption glass and promise of an Aid, he continued to process Vaughn's swift departure. He wished he would have made the time to meet up with Vaughn sooner.

The activity in Derek's head began to spiral out of control and he clicked off the TV. Derek gathered the items needed to get out of his flat, and more importantly, out of his head.

Germain flipped on his television to view the United States' Pentagon protest. He watched as the scene intensified. He thought back to his own heritage and remembered the story of how his family came to live in England.

Germain's grandfather, Leon, was a soldier in the First World War.

Leon was not a fighter, but quite the opposite, a musician. Leon's father, Germain's great-grandfather, was a musician himself. He raised Leon and his siblings in the United States' South. Leon's mother had died during the birth of her sixth baby, Leon's littlest sister.

To keep a roof overhead, Leon and his siblings found jobs early on in life. Leon's father put his whole being into becoming the best horn player in the Big Easy. As Leon grew up, he became more frustrated with the limited opportunities where he lived. He saw his father, struggling to make ends meet and dreaded meeting the same fate.

The family was pummeled with discrimination on the city's fringe, endured flood after flood, and the memory of their lost matriarch lingered in every corner of their home. Once all the siblings were grown and stable with their own families, Leon and his father took a leap of faith and hopped a train to New York City. As they pulled into the Big Apple, the city lights reignited the dim fire in Leon's father's eyes.

Two weeks after their move, Leon was drafted to serve in the First World War.

Oliver, Renee's grandfather, couldn't keep his jaw from dropping. A lifetime of music halls had never led any sound so wonderful into his ears. Leon played a warm, heartfelt solo, which nearly brought Oliver to tears. The noble sound cut through the wall Oliver had constructed around himself, protection from the terrors of the trenches. Oliver felt worthwhile emotion for the first time in months and was determined to make acquaintance with Leon, the musician turned soldier, once the show commenced.

Oliver cut through the crowd to pay his respects. Just as Oliver reached Leon and began to lay on the plaudits, orders were barked for the artists to transform back into pawns. The musicians were robbed of their accolades and ripped back to the barracks.

Leon's division, the 369th Infantry, came to be known as the Harlem Hellfighters. In addition to introducing Europe to jazz, the division was also awarded the Medal of Valor. Shortly after the war's end, before the ships were homeward bound, Leon developed a cough followed by a climbing fever.

He'd gotten to celebrate just one day of the war's end when Leon was struck by another mass devastation, the Spanish Influenza. Leon was quarantined and went on to miss his last free ticket back to the United States.

The Influenza years presented another period of darkness to an exhausted world. Once again, Leon fought for his life. His brothers-in-arms departed, and his ship home sailed.

Leon lay in the infirmary bed, barely conscious. He was roused by a new patient being placed in his neighboring cot. Leon mustered the strength to turn his head. Through blurred vision, he saw a familiar face. Leon recognized the kind, British soldier who had complimented his musicianship.

"Out of the frying pan," Leon paused to catch his breath, "and into the fire," he said to the fellow veteran.

The English soldier attempted to respond, but his words gave way to a heavy cough. The Brit remembered Leon from the Hellfighters' performance. Life trickled back into the Englishman as he relived the energy of Leon's troupes' show.

After days without the strength to speak, the British soldier finally introduced himself to Leon.

"Oliver Blum. I didn't catch your name. We met at your performance. Hell of a horn player, you are. Your infantry's sound," Oliver paused, "I've never heard anything like it."

"I remember your compliments," Leon replied. "And thank you. I'm Leon Chery."

"I never imagined this is where we'd meet again," Oliver said, "I rarely fall ill."

"Me either," Leon said. "Alright place to be though, after where we been."

Oliver nodded. "You can say that again. When everything is all settled, I think I'll stay in France. I want to *really* see it now that the war is done."

"No family?" Leon asked.

"Sore subject," Oliver sighed. "Father would have me work at the factory upon my return. Mother's passing left him more bitter than ever. We all do miss her. My elder sister is recently married. He's high society, looks down on where she came from, so we've lost touch. How about you?"

"My father and I barely sunk our teeth into the Big Apple, then I was drafted. We're musicians. Didn't even have time to book a gig before I got my orders."

The soldiers recovered with the passing of time. One day, during their afternoon card game, their designated nurse approached them.

"Looks like you're ready to go back out into the world," she commented.

"Thanks to you," Oliver nodded at the nurse with reverence.

As the soldiers gathered their few belongings, the nurse asked, "Where will you go from here?"

Oliver and Leon looked at one another.

"We're not quite certain ourselves. I will remain in France," Oliver said. "There was a town we passed through during combat. A beautiful Opera house stands near the village square. Once this bloody illness passes, I hope to enter it as a spectator. Rent there is likely more affordable there than it is in Paris."

"I know the theatre you speak of," said the nurse. She described the opulent structure. "My aunt lives near there. I worry about her. I don't want to ruin your plans, but I don't know if the town endured the war. My obligations here are heavy, as you can see, but I've written her with no reply. If you mean to go there, will you give her my current address and ask her to write me?"

"Of course. By any chance, does she have a room for rent?" Oliver asked.

"I can't speak for her, but I do recall an old shed behind her house. Perhaps she would be willing to rent it out to a couple of victorious soldiers. Please, tell her to write me back," the nurse said. "She's all I've got left."

Oliver and Leon began their journey toward the village. Though they were no longer symptomatic, they were hard-pressed to find lodging that would allow guests during the illness. At night, when they grew exhausted of walking, the soldiers settled in abandoned barns to survive the winter nights. After the long trek, Oliver and Leon scaled the final hill leading into the village. Leon grew quiet as they approached the city limits.

"This theatre would be lucky to feature the likes of your music," Oliver said to Leon.

Leon grinned.

"What do you say we stick together?" Oliver suggested. "It's gotten us this far, right?"

Leon's French came in handy as he guided them to the home of the nurse's aunt.

"You say you know who?" She asked, skeptical of the soldiers.

Oliver pulled the nurse's letter from his pocket. He handed it to the elderly woman.

"Wait here," she said and closed her entryway door.

Leon and Oliver shivered. The daylight waned and their breath made clouds in the frigid air. The aunt's footsteps grew audible, and she reopened the door.

"The writing on your letter from her *is* identical," the aunt said. "Looks the exact same as her letters from last year. You said she's been trying to write me?"

"Yes," Leon replied. "She worries about you. This is her new address," Leon offered the scrap on which the nurse had scrawled her address.

The aunt invited them inside and agreed to let the unlikely duo rent her detached shed. The space was very simplistic but provided two beds and a small wood-burning stove. Leon and Oliver helped the town to make repairs and shared rent in the French village.

With no belongings but Leon's horn and the clothes on their backs, they made a long-awaited home out of their nurse's aunt's shack. They played countless card games throughout the winter as the Influenza ravaged the outside world. Toward the end of winter, Oliver entered his and Leon's small home in a glorious mood.

"You've been gone a while," Leon said.

"I believe I've been sleepwalking," Oliver explained. "Tonight was a dream. I met a woman named Sylvia. Her eyes resemble precious emeralds. We spoke and she is not married. We mean to meet at the same place two nights from now."

Over time, the illness faded, and Oliver made Sylvia his wife. Their nurse's aunt eventually passed, leaving her home to the young soldiers who never missed their rent during the days of the Influenza.

Leon, Sylvia, and Oliver continued to cohabitate for the cheap rent. With the Opera house restored, Leon was often gone performing in the evenings now and frequently stumbled home into the outbuilding. When Oliver and Sylvia weren't attending Leon's shows, they had plenty of privacy to be newlyweds.

A year after their wedding, Sylvia announced her pregnancy. Oliver and Sylvia relocated to a house across the way from the soldiers' first French home. Leon remained in the aunt's home, still close by. Sylvia gave birth to her and Oliver's first and only child, a daughter named Vivienne. A new darkness began to unfold just after Vivienne's arrival to the world.

Whispers of abduction circulated. All who were Jewish, black, homosexual, Roma, or in other disagreement with Hitler's army were plucked from their homes, vanishing from their friends and neighbors.

"The stakes are so much higher with Vivienne to protect," Oliver said one night when he and Leon met for cards. "I hate to leave all we've built here, but I think the window to escape is closing."

Within a week, Oliver, Sylvia, Leon, and the baby relocated to England. They left just in time to beat the rumored genocide's manifestation into horrific reality. The four of them took the first housing offer they could find and settled into a downtown flat in Soho. From there, they watched World War Two explode around them.

Leon wrote to inform his father of his new address with no reply. Though he was troubled by his father's unresponsiveness, he wasn't alone in the world. The Blums continued to view Leon as family. Leon filled society's need for distraction from the darkness and gained residency at an intimate, neighbourhood jazz club.

There, he fell in love with one of the club's singers. V-Day came, and Leon asked her to marry him. Leon and his wife moved into their own flat in the same building as the Blums.

The families got by with each other's help. They prevailed through anything the world threw at them. Years passed and their grandchildren, Germain and Renee, upheld the families' longstanding friendship. They remained a constant support for each other in an ever-evolving world, keeping one another's secrets from those who would use their identities against them.

Derek was equally grateful and guilty for the mental cushion accessible to him in the unsteady destination of his choosing. No matter how bad things got, Derek had an out. Grant was not so fortunate and dwelled on his changing psyche.

Derek took a walk with Grant on an autumn day, hoping to clarify the source of Grant's change in behavior. As they strolled, Derek looked up at the blue sky; only wisps of feathery clouds interrupted the pristine vastness. The chill in the air seemed to have taken a hiatus for the day. Sunlight warmed Derek's dark hair, and he listened to Grant's recollection of his euphoric summer on the bay.

"The music was crafted perfectly for the crowd. The artists curated a psychedelic adventure, just for us. You would have loved it. A group of musicians shared a big, grey house near my own place of residence. It was just up the intersection from Haight and Ashbury. Their tunes floated through the air. We all joined them in their home. We had a rotation of kind, gentle people. When they played for us, it was like they were *with* us in our minds. You could *feel* their music. Their melodies made these," Grant paused, "harmonious prisms. We were all together."

"I would have loved to have been there," Derek said.

"This middle-aged shrink was always around as well. He wasn't like other doctors. He supported our trips and was there to guide us. You have to look, but a few of the older generation are open to exploring all aspects of consciousness."

Derek thought of Dr. Lowell's progressive demeanor.

"We gathered in parks nearly every day. It feels like a dream now, after the last few days' gloom," Grant looked down at his feet as he walked. "I'm still sorry for my freakout, man. It's like I'm chasing a feeling I had in California. I long to be back at

232

Monterey, to witness the deterioration of any barrier between myself and the universe," Grant trailed off. "Man, I don't know what came over me the other night. The last thing I recall was feeling a bit paranoid," Grant said. "But then this blinding sensation took hold. Maybe it was the travel back, the lack of sleep, you know? Maybe being tired or something about Ang's friends provoked me. They can be quite pretentious."

Derek chuckled, "I know. Her wit is captivating, but her friend's elitism challenges my tolerance for intellectual conversations. They discuss everything as though they are writing a thesis on the topic."

"I can't explain it," Grant said. "At the club, the last thing I remember is feeling driven to make the world understand something, something I don't even understand myself."

"Don't sweat it," Derek interrupted.

"You say that, but you don't know what it's like to feel disconnected from yourself, to *want* to feel disconnected from yourself. That night, I stumbled into bed and found no rest, just bad dreams."

Grant hung his head. They walked in silence. Grant's inability to account for the lost time at the Ace stirred another painful recollection. Grant quickly stuffed the memory back down, not wanting to relive the foggy, summer morning when he awoke among mad humans along the beach, expelling the Bay's water from his lungs.

Grant excused himself.

"I'm heading home," he said. "I've got to get some food in me. Not sure I've eaten all day."

Derek continued to walk in solitude. He absorbed the final warmth of the late-season sun which began to sink below the horizon line earlier and earlier. The streetlights flickered on, and, to his surprise, Derek ran into Germain outside of a pub. Germain was with a small group of friends. Derek recognized Lorraine but was unfamiliar with everyone else.

"Derek, my man," Germain said with a smile and handshake. "Care to join us tonight?" He gestured to his crew. "We're going to Tom's pad. It's not a far walk from here."

"Yes, the more the merrier," one of the gentlemen replied. "Tom," he stated, introducing himself to Derek.

Tom was tall and rail thin. He had disheveled, copper hair with an angular, acne-scarred face. Tom resumed conversation with the group. Derek was refreshed by Tom's apparent sense of humor as the girls giggled at Tom's jokes.

"I've got no plans," Derek said, and agreed to join them for the night. "It's been a crazy week."

They walked just a few blocks and arrived at Tom's pad. He welcomed them inside then broke away to start a record. Derek and the rest of the crew hung their jackets on a coat tree. Derek caught his own reflection in the mirror of Tom's last-look room. During their walk, the wind had picked up and blown Derek's hair into a mess. He attempted to put his shaggy mop back into place.

Derek was impressed with the large flat. He wondered what Tom did for a living. Shiny black-and-white checked tiles led the guests from the entryway to a sunken living room. The small group filtered into the red conversation pit. Wood paneling covered the walls and geometric art-pieces adorned the room.

Tom entered the conversation pit, balancing a cocktail tray. He presented his guests with a faux-wood ice bucket, drink glasses, and various supplies to craft their beverages. The tray clinked as Tom placed it on the center table.

Their host had just begun to take beverage orders when the doorbell rang.

Tom shouted over his shoulder, "Come in!"

Grant and Carole entered the flat. Tom was preoccupied playing bartender, so Germain and Derek stood to welcome their friends.

"I must have just missed you, Derek," Carole said. "I ran into Grant on his return to his flat. I was on my way to freshen up and come over here, and he agreed to join. Lovely place, isn't it Grant?" Carole stated.

"So groovy," Grant mumbled as he chewed the last of a deli sandwich.

Tom was an excellent host. He engaged in conversation with Derek, and they got more acquainted. Tom multitasked and wove his guests' conversations together with ease, keeping their drinks full all the while.

"How do you know everyone, Tom?" Derek asked.

"Germain and I frequent all sorts of venues together," Tom explained, "auditoriums, dives, jazz clubs, dance halls," he topped off Derek's scotch on the rocks. "You should join us mate. It's a real trip going out with Germain. He knows everyone," Tom paused. "How come we haven't met?"

"I guess I've been busy," Derek shrugged.

Tom smirked, "You work for Renee, don't you?"

"You guessed it," Derek answered.

"She does have a way of drawing people in," Germain remarked, "though I like to think I'm immune to her charm."

The guests continued to sip their cocktails and Tom slipped away. He emerged less than a minute later with a glass dish. Tom placed the bowl in the center of the table.

"If anyone cares to take a little trip," Tom said.

The guests quieted and turned their attention to the center of the table. Inside the quaint dish was a collection of tiny, square papers. Derek was conflicted. He hadn't tried acid post-Shell. Though it had been months since the Psilopram was in his system, Derek was determined not to take the risk. He remembered the clarity of his thoughts right after acclimation compared to his thoughts before Traveling. Psilopram's effects led Derek to a broader, more connected way of thinking and he couldn't risk the step backwards.

"Care to trip, Derek?" Tom asked, his casual tone causing Derek to feel naïve about his cautiousness. "Have you done it before?"

"Yeah," Derek answered. "Well, sort of. It was part mushroom, part something else," he fumbled with the explanation of Psilopram. "I'll pass tonight though."

Tom nodded, "All right," and moved on to Carole and Grant.

Derek looked to his left and there she sat. He didn't know her name, but earlier in the evening, she joined them outside the bar with the rest of Germain's crowd. She and Derek made eye contact.

"I *know* you," he said.

She laughed and responded, "I know you too."

Derek watched in awe as she floated around the table, her canter smooth as glass. He shook his head in disbelief.

Derek had passed on the acid, yet the world around him was morphing. The woman arrived at the center of the living room and poured herself a cup of water from a glass pitcher. Rather than pour into gravity, the water wouldn't stay put. It kept evaporating from her glass like liquid nitrogen. The mystery woman shook her head, frustrated.

She caught Derek witnessing her struggle. The acknowledgement was enough to break her frustration and they began to laugh. The strange occurrence became an unspoken joke between the two of them.

'Why is the water misbehaving?'

Germain was intrigued by their laughter. He floated over to Derek and involved himself in the spectacle. The woman handed the pitcher to Germain and offered him a glass. She looked to Derek as if to say, *'Get a load of this.'*

Germain poured the water and his jaw dropped. His laugh burst through the room. The three of them roared while Tom's other guests viewed their antics, suspicious.

"Are you laughing at me?" Grant asked and smoothed his hair.

Derek shook his head no, unable to answer through his laughter. Once he gained composure, Derek gazed around Tom's living room. He fixated on a diamond-shaped lamp stand. The stand was silver and was formed into the shape of a diamond with smaller diamonds progressing down into its center. The diamonds were twisted at an angle to create a three-dimensional effect.

Derek watched in awe as the diamonds ocellated. The center diamond birthed a new diamond which eventually grew to become the outermost layer. Then, the shapes spun on their axis so quickly that Derek feared the lamp would blast off, like a rocket. He stood and went to stabilize the fixture.

Tom looked at him.

"I saved your lamp," Derek said.

Suddenly, Derek had to use the restroom. He went to Tom for guidance and Tom led him upstairs. Derek stepped into the bathroom, but as soon as he grabbed the handle to close the bathroom door, Tom stood in the frame, blocking the doorway.

"Whatever you do," he looked Derek dead in the eyes, "do *not* look in the mirror."

Derek agreed and closed the door.

Tom returned to his sunken living room and addressed the group.

"Who dosed him?"

Derek put down the toilet lid then paused. He studied the toilet paper. He couldn't tell if the lighting was playing tricks on him or if the paper was, indeed, rose-hued. Derek looked down at his feet as he washed his hands. To avoid his reflection, he focused on the herringbone pattern of the rug beneath his feet. The pattern became active, and Derek lost his balance. He stumbled then grabbed onto the sink to steady himself; in doing so, he came face-to-face with his mirror-image.

Derek watched his own reflection morph into Cooper. He reached out to touch his twin's hand. In the mirror, Cooper pulled away from Derek and his face went from handsome to pale and lifeless. Derek was drawn to vacate Tom's home with the same urgency as an avian was drawn to migration. He had to get away from Cooper. Cooper embodied death and Derek was there to live.

Derek opened his eyes. His telephone rang for the third time. He stumbled toward the noise and lifted the handset to his face. A voice on the other end wailed. Derek recognized Grant's voice and panicked.

"Help me remember, Derek. I've lost another night."

Seared into Derek's mind was the strangeness of his visuals the night before; Cooper's reflection, staring back at him in Tom's bathroom. The image in the mirror wasn't the handsome, unscathed Cooper that Derek liked to remember, but the ashen-faced, vacant-eyed corpse. Cooper wasn't supposed to be at Tom's, he wasn't supposed to be anywhere.

"I'll be right there," Derek said.

"Yes," Grant's voice cracked. "Hurry."

On the way to Grant's flat, Derek attempted to recall the events of the previous night. Though his memory was extremely hazy, Derek recalled spurts of the swift trip back to his own apartment the night before. The rest of the night was a blur. He had no idea how Grant, Germain, or the rest of the group's evening had concluded.

'I was dosed.'

Derek shivered. Grant's flat was cold. He hadn't noticed the weather on the way there, but as Derek looked outside, an icy drizzle fell on the other side of the glass. The day was appropriately dreary.

Grant was seated on the floor. He was wrapped in a blanket and stared blankly at Derek with bloodshot eyes. Derek sat next to Grant.

"What's going on? You called me over, now you won't say a word," Derek put his arm around Grant. "I'm here, you can talk to me" he assured. "You should kick on the heat, it's cold. I've got some coins to loan you."

"I can't accept anything from you after what I've done," Grant said. "Everything is so backwards."

Derek stood and walked to Grant's entrance; the floor creaked beneath his feet. Grant's mood was alarming. Derek slid the metal door chain to ensure privacy.

"After you left last night, something happened."

Grant pulled his arms out from the blanket and revealed the back of his hands to Derek. Grant's fingernails were lined with blood. Derek further digested Grant's ragged appearance and noted a maroon stain on the corner of the blanket.

"Dear God," Derek said, "what happened?"

Grant's face was pale, his eyes brimmed with tears.

"I don't know."

"I shouldn't have run out on you," Derek said. "Damnit, I knew I shouldn't have looked in the mirror, but I couldn't help it. All the sudden, *he* was in front of me. I was freaking out. Someone must have dosed me."

Grant pressed his lips together, fighting to maintain composure.

"I can't remember *anything* after arriving at Tom's flat," Grant said. "I had such a good day, walked in the morning with you, caught up with Carole, had a great start to the party," then a sob broke Grant's sentence.

Derek patted his friends' arm.

"Whatever happened, we'll figure it out," Derek said.

"No, we won't. I remember arriving at Tom's, seeing you there," Grant's voice broke again, "Then I lost it. I woke up and found my hands like this. Me, violence, it's like I'm Jekyll and Hyde, an absolute monster. I can't even tell you everything."

Grant cradled his head in his hands. Derek stood and began to pace. Derek hoped that his friends' worst fears were less severe than imagined.

"Look in the kitchen," Grant said.

240

Derek's heart raced as he walked into the next room. He suppressed the urge to run. Then, Derek saw it. A knife lay on Grant's kitchen table, partially submerged in a pool of dried blood. Derek's stomach churned; he felt his face blanch. Grant's agony echoed from the next room.

"I've become a monster, *a monster*," Grant repeated.

Derek stared at the weapon, stunned. He heard Grant walk into the kitchen. The look in Grant's eyes caused Derek to snap out of his paralysis and he instinctively backed away from Grant.

Grant pleaded to Derek, "Help me, I don't know what to do. I might as well stick that knife straight through my heart," Grant reached toward the blade.

Derek shoved Grant back into the living room, causing Grant to collapse onto the floor. He looked helpless wrapped in his blanket, his body shaking with each sob. Derek's thoughts raced. Then, anger replaced Derek's fear. He wasn't horrified with Grant, but by the manipulation practiced by those "in charge." Derek's trust in TRN plummeted. He'd been fed a drug, just as Grant had been. Derek worried he would lose his mind too if he hadn't already lost it the night before.

Derek and Grant jolted at a frantic knock at the door.

Rap rap rap.

The fist in the hallway was swift and impatient.

"Grant," a familiar voice shouted. "Grant, open this bloody door!"

Derek and Grant locked eyes.

Angelene.

Grant wrinkled his brow; he was on the brink of another meltdown. Derek grabbed both sides of Grant's face and pulled their foreheads to touch.

"You have to keep it together," Derek said. "At least until we know what really happened."

Derek threw a worn kitchen towel over the knife and Grant went back to his corner. He continued to rock back and forth. Derek walked to the entrance and took a deep breath. He unlocked the door and backed away.

Angelene burst inside and the door cracked against the wall.

She seethed, "Grant you *have gone mad!* And *you,* what are you doing here?" She pointed at Derek.

"He called," Derek explained, bewildered. "He asked me to come over."

Derek placed a hand on her shoulder to redirect Angelene from Grant.

"I don't know what happened, I was dosed last night. But there's got to be more to the story," Derek said.

Angelene jerked away from Derek's hand and faced Grant.

"You've got an enormous amount of explaining to do," she pointed at Grant.

"I-I wish I could explain any of this madness," Grant sniffed. "Give me the knife Derek, give me the knife," he reached out and his hands shook.

Angelene's eyes widened.

"The knife? *What knife?*" She looked to Derek for an explanation.

"Angelene, I know this is crazy, but they *did* something to Grant in California," Derek stated as Grant shivered. "Whatever happened last night, it wasn't *our* Grant."

Derek turned to face his friend.

"Grant, those people you met," Derek shook his head. "They weren't all your friends. I know what happened, I," he tried to rationalize how he knew without giving away his perspective

242

from Original Time. "I heard," Derek said, "that someone, someone very bad, is using acid to discover alterations they can make to the human mind. They're brainwashing people to benefit their war."

Derek knew how crazy he sounded, but Grant finally began to catch his breath. Angelene's fit of rage subsided. Derek continued.

"Grant, those houses in San Francisco where they gave you the drugs and women, those houses were run by this... evil."

Tears welled in Derek's eyes as the reality set in.

"I can't believe they did this to you. I can't believe someone tried to do it to me."

"It... it may have been me," Grant admitted. "It's hazy, but I can see myself having dosed you. They did it to people all the time. We were encouraged to do it, to see how spiritually sound our brothers and sisters were."

"How could you, Grant? That's how people go crazy!" Derek shouted.

Angelene and Derek were quiet as they processed the information. Derek realized how different it was to live in a conspiracy's unfolding as opposed to learning about it from a distance. His blood boiled at the fact that the demonization of the sixties spirit had been an inside job.

"Someone on the coast messed you up, Grant. It's the only thing that makes sense," Angelene said. She knelt to her brother's eye level. "Grant, for my entire life, I've adored you. Even when I wouldn't listen to you through my teenage years, you've never shown an ounce of anger. For you to dose your friend, for you to be dishonest and violent, Derek," she looked up to face him, "you must be right about what they did."

Despite Grant and Angelene's narrow age gap, Grant had found the help he and his sister needed when they were neglected and starving. When she was a child, Angelene read books about pixies and elves and Grant told her how the little green circles in the grass of the countryside were made by fairies dancing in the moonlight.

"Whatever happened Grant, it wasn't you."

Both Carole and Germain called Angelene that morning.

Carole told Angelene how Derek vanished from the party with no warning.

"The last I saw of Derek was when he sprinted out the front door. He acted so strange. He covered his eyes as he passed the entryway mirror," Carole had explained. "Derek kept saying, 'he shouldn't be here,' and kept saying, 'Cooper.' I didn't even see him take acid. I stepped away to use the restroom, and when I got back, Grant had vanished as well. No one saw him leave. One minute Grant was there, the next he had disappeared."

"And you went after them, right?" Angelene asked.

"Of course. They fled into downtown Friday night. I was ten minutes into hunting them down when I bumped into Germain who had also left Tom's party in search of Derek and Grant.

We stopped at Derek's flat first. We had to wait outside for a while before another tenant let us in. We walked up to Derek's apartment, and it was unlocked. We found him asleep on the sofa. We searched the whole apartment, but Grant was absent. Germain shook Derek awake and asked him where Grant was. He didn't know."

"Oh my," Angelene said, "God help us."

"Ang, we searched for two hours before spotting Grant. He was wrapped in a blanket, sitting alone on a park bench. His face was ghastly white. I couldn't help but scream when we saw him."

Angelene was speechless.

"Grant was shaking so badly. I think he was in shock. I had to leave, Angelene, I just had to," Carole blurted on the other end of the line.

Before Carole could explain more, Angelene hung up the phone and was out the door.

"Bloody hell Grant," Carole shook her head in disbelief. After her summer spent at Renee's side, Carole didn't know who could be lurking behind the bushes with a camera and a microphone. "Germain, there's no doubt that this scene will lead to a scandal should it reach the press," Carole moaned.

"I know sugar, get outta here. I'll get him in a cab," Germain instructed.

Germain pulled out his handkerchief and began to wipe the blood from Grant's hands.

"Don't you touch me!" Grant said through gritted teeth and began to spout nonsense.

"Stop it! You know me, Grant," Germain put his hands on Grant's shoulders and looked him in the eyes. "You know me. Now, look at yourself, man."

Grant looked at his hands and a tear streaked down his cheek.

"We've got to move!" Germain knew the clock was ticking. He looked at his own hands, now stained with blood. "Brother, get up here to the edge of the sidewalk, let's get you a cab," Germain said. "It's too far to walk with you like this."

Grant looked down and noticed that his corduroys were wet with blood. The stain sat right where his pocketknife was stored. Grant slipped the blade from his pants. His pocketknife wasn't quite closed and was slick with blood. Grant felt his leg again.

"There must be a cut, somewhere. I must have cut myself," Grant said.

"Put that thing away!" Germain demanded.

Grant evaluated the park and spotted a trash can. He began to run toward it.

"No," Germain growled, "It's got your prints on it! Bring it home and figure out how to get rid of it there."

Grant trembled.

"Sorry I yelled. Calm down man, breathe, in and out," Germain exhaled with Grant. He scanned the area for any sign of authority. "Man, I can't be tied up in this, you've got some cab money," Germain said.

Grant heaved. Germain sat with him and breathed until their rhythm slowed. Grant forced a controlled façade.

"You get out of here, I'll call when I get home," Grant stated.

"You sure?" Germain asked.

Grant pressed his lips together and closed his eyes.

"Go."

"What do you remember of last night?" Angelene asked Derek. "I need you to dig."

"I remember sipping my drink at Tom's flat. After that, I can't decipher what was real and wasn't," Derek began to tremble as Grant had, just minutes ago. "Was I an accomplice to Grant?"

"Germain said that little time had passed between your departure from Tom's and his and Carole's visit to your flat. You had no blood on your hands when you awoke, right?"

"Right," Derek agreed. "They visited my flat?"

He vaguely recalled a dream from the night before involving Carole and Germain. He was relieved to hear that it was reality, and they hadn't left him to the darkened city streets. Derek's urgent desire for an Aid subsided as he took comfort in his friends' loyalty. They were proving to be even more reliable than TRN.

Derek looked to the kitchen table and saw that the blood began to soak through the towel. He chose to unveil the knife to Angelene.

"No," Angelene uttered, horrified.

Derek's eyes wandered to the window. The darkness of the world seemed to close in on him from all sides. The bright colors of summer faded, reduced to a fraction of their former potency. He saw a parallel forming between Grant and his situations; both involved uncharted trips and the unfulfilled promise of a better life. The grey consumed Derek and he was stunned by his inability to feel anything at all.

Chapter X

"I can't do my job when you don't do yours!" Vaughn shouted.

For a short window of time between monitoring Derek and Mia, Vaughn made a pit-stop in Original Time. He was desperate for answers which no one at TRN could provide.

"I can't keep everyone safe, there are too few of us. When nearly an entire *decade* of Time Travelers is without an Aid, we can't just chalk it up to a bug in the software! This is the kind of shit that makes people want to leave their destination. *This* is the shit that breeds distrust!"

The tech lead hung his head, "It's been such a mess. I understand your frustration."

"No, you don't!" Vaughn fumed. "You fix technology, a non-living thing. I'm held responsible for Travelers' lives! Families have paid us to make sure their loved ones are safe, and you've screwed up a whole batch of devices! I've seen your team in here during the day, fucking off. Get them in order and get that bug fixed as soon as possible. We promised the Travelers it would be out by the new year; the clock is ticking!"

Vaughn stormed out of the room. In the hallway, he ran into a passerby, scattering the contents of her bag. Combs, clips, and tubes of makeup littered the floor.

"God, I'm sorry," Vaughn said and helped collect her belongings.

He looked at her face. Tears streamed down her cheeks. Vaughn's heart dropped.

"You're not the only one who has bad days," she said.

Vaughn identified her as one of TRN's stylists. She caught his eye whenever he passed the salon. She always had someone in her chair.

"I'm sorry. You know how it's been around here lately."

"You mean crumbling? Chaotic? An absolute shit-show?" the stylist asked. "Yeah, I know." She strapped her bag onto her shoulder. "Guess it's good to find someone who admits it. Rae," she introduced herself.

"Vaughn."

They shook hands.

"Are you just coming in for the day?" Vaughn looked at the clock.

2:00.

"Leaving actually," Rae said. "I hoped to make a stealthy departure then…" Rae gestured to the floor where her supplies had fallen.

"Sorry again," Vaughn said. "There's just so much that needs—"

"Mending?" Rae said.

Vaughn nodded.

"So," Mia sipped her coffee, "where do we begin?"

Rather than meeting at the Diner where the rest of the crew could make an appearance, Vaughn took Mia to a bakery located uptown from the college-based area of Birchmont.

They chose their pastries from behind the glass then sat at a corner table. Vaughn chuckled at the oddity of Time Travel. He would have never imagined having breakfast with Derek's little sister in the nineties.

"Let's start with the Tuesdaze," Vaughn began. "I remember Derek saying you knew how to play guitar, but man," Vaughn's eyes widened, "that Halloween show was dope!"

"Wait, you were at the show?"

Mia peeled back the layers of her croissant and contemplated the logistics of Vaughn's arrival. She knew Vaughn was at Jaq's the morning after the Halloween party, but Mia didn't know he was at the Lakehouse show. She still questioned his motive for being in the same town, in the same year.

"Yes," Vaughn smiled. "God, you guys were good. It was hard not to mention the Halloween concert when you saw me at Jaq's, but I had… a crazy morning that day."

"It means a lot that you like our music," Mia blushed. "Thank you, Vaughn. Lars has really jerked us around lately. It was cool of you to back us up last night. You've got Lars in a tailspin," she laughed. "He acts like he doesn't care about your opinion, but your push for us to perform has done more for us than we could have done on our own. I get the feeling he was about to drop us and tell the venues not to book us."

"He's certainly a piece of work," Vaughn said and rolled his eyes.

"I think he's just sour no one would hook up with him. Lars tried to come onto me you know," Mia averted her eyes from Vaughn, zoning out at her steaming coffee.

"Are you serious?" Vaughn asked. "What happened?"

"He cornered me at the Lakehouse and tried to," Mia paused, "tried to do everything. It was awful. And get this; the headlining guitarist saw Lars trying to get with me. I was humiliated. It looked like I was sleeping with our connection, like I don't have real talent. Like I was a puppet."

"Wow, Mia," Vaughn said and shook his head. "I knew he was bad news but not that bad, I'm so sorry that happened. Didn't you want to leave after that?" Vaughn paused. "You have a… device, right?"

"I do, but I didn't have it with me that night. The rest of the crew stayed with me afterwards to make sure I was okay. Ever since, they've been more supportive of me than they have been of Lars, someone they've known for years. The Tuesdaze make it hard to leave because of one bad situation. Aside from gigs and occasional nights out, I rarely run into Lars. Once I move in with Macy, I think I'll feel even safer, not being alone at night and all."

"I had a feeling about him from the very beginning," Vaughn narrowed his eyes. "Now I'm even more motivated to make some connections in this town's music scene before I go."

"Luckily the guitarist was enough to distract him that night. If more had happened, I'd probably be back in OT," Mia stated.

Vaughn took Mia's hands. Her grandmother's bracelet jingled on the table. Vaughn fidgeted with the tiny metal charms.

"If you ever feel in danger here, there's a way you can tell me," Vaughn said. "You can communicate with *me* directly through this," he pointed to the Aid which hung off her bracelet. "Since I'm the nearest employee right now, I'd be the one helping you out. There's more I have to tell you," Vaughn stated, "it's about why I need to leave. I can't tell you here though," He paused and surveyed the crowded bakery.

The waitress arrived to refill their coffee creating a lull in Vaughn and Mia's conversation. They used the silence to devour their pastries. Mia laughed as cream from Vaughn's éclair lingered above his lip. Vaughn still had the same, knee-weakening smile she remembered from the first time she saw him. Though Vaughn's familiarity set Mia at ease, there were aspects of him that had changed. She guessed the Psilopram had something to do with his new characteristics.

Vaughn gazed at Mia and remembered running into her the morning after Halloween. He was caught off guard with how stunning she had become. When he had met her for the first time, Mia was awkward with big teeth and fuzzy hair.

Mia had grown into her wide grin. She had developed a quiet confidence. In all his Travels, Vaughn hadn't found anyone with whom he could speak so naturally. Their conversation flowed as if they were more than acquaintances.

Mia dreaded dampening their upbeat cafe date, but a question had been rattling in her brain since reading TRN's most recent newsletter.

"Is Derek okay?" Mia asked in a hushed voice. "I'm worried about him all alone without the device."

"I think he's good for now," Vaughn replied. "I'm working on getting him connected. Other than that, he's doing well. Frankly, I'm not sure if he'll ever want to leave his destination. I could see him just looping in that era for a while. He has a hard time moving on, doesn't he?"

"He sure does," Mia said. "Do some Travelers do that? Just relive one time over and over?"

Vaughn chuckled, "People do about anything you can imagine with this new mode of travel. They loop, vacation, shuffle. That makes it harder to ensure they have the security device."

"Does it worry you that he and all those people didn't receive one?"

Vaughn weighed the benefit of giving his honest answer. He opted against it.

"Not really," he bluffed. "Derek arrived at his destination during a very high-volume spurt of Travel. It's not his fault, but the more concentrated a time is with Travelers, the more people there are to keep track of," Vaughn stated. "They don't always have the capability to monitor *everyone* efficiently."

"How do you stay so updated? Do you report to the hub often?"

Vaughn gestured to the crowded room.

"Another time," he answered. "We've probably spoken about too much already. I might have gotten myself into a little trouble talking with Derek too openly in a pub."

"Understood. I'm curious, what's Derek been up to in his day-to-day life? If you can say, that is."

"He's met a couple of girls. He's going to a lot of clubs. I don't need to tell you how incredible the music is there," Vaughn said.

Mia sighed. While she loved nineties music, the sixties sound wrenched her heart. There was nothing else like it.

"If acclimation wasn't such a process, I'd go visit Derek," Mia stated.

Vaughn smirked.

"You get used to the process over time."

Before Mia could ask questions, Vaughn continued to tell her about Derek's life in the sixties.

"Derek's working at a clothing boutique."

"A clothing boutique?" Mia remarked. "He's never been into fashion."

"He is now." Vaughn grinned, "One of the girls he's seeing is the owner. She's why he started working there. He's doing some photography too. He always did like that class in college."

"*One* of the girls? How many is he seeing?"

"Well, I should clarify, the girl that he *was* seeing is the owner. Now that she's getting famous, he's taken a step back. She's a model," Vaughn shared.

Mia's mouth dropped open and Vaughn laughed at her surprise.

He continued, "She's gotten too well-known for Derek to continue dating without possible repercussions, plus she's too busy. Right before I left, he was pursuing a poet," Vaughn explained. "Leave it to Derek to be oblivious to his charm. It must run in the family."

"I'm glad he's having fun," Mia disregarded the compliment. "It's probably good for him to get back out there," she said, "dating, you know."

"He's out there alright," Vaughn said. "He's been brushing elbows with legends. He's clubbing. He's opening his mind," Vaughn smirked. "I'm just glad to see him letting go. There's so much more I need to tell you, but somewhere else."

"And I have more questions for you," Mia said. "Want to come back to my place?"

Vaughn answered, "I thought you'd never ask."

Mia and Vaughn spoke with little breaks until the sun began to lower. She heard new college tales about her brother and got the uncensored version of Vaughn's time in the sixties.

"I wish I could just do that," Mia stated.

"Do what?"

"Live like you, with no strings attached. I expected Travel to be," Mia paused in search for the right word, "different. Don't get me wrong, I'm not disappointed by what I have here. I just expected to be less invested in everything. Time passes though, and it's hard not to engage."

"We hear that a lot at TRN. Some people even come back to Original Time because of the commitments they made while Traveling. They see themselves creating the same stressors they had in Original Time. For me, the way past all that is to Travel more often. To let Psilopram do its job."

"You're giving me the Travel bug," Mia said. "I'm not sure how long I should stay here. The band is fun, but college is really kicking my ass. I wish I could just be here and enjoy it without having to study."

"Remember, you always have an out," Vaughn assured. "It doesn't have to be so serious."

"You're right. Sometimes, I just need someone here to put it into perspective for me," Mia said. She remembered Macy's comment about being too deep.

The solace of being inside on a cold evening began to permeate Mia. She laughed to herself and evaluated the state of her living room; blankets were strewn about, a half empty bag of chips was abandoned on the coffee table, and several upside-down CDs were placed atop the kitchen counter.

"Vaughn, why are you here?" Mia asked. "First the sixties with my brother, then the nineties with me. It doesn't seem random."

"I'm here because, despite my own desire to leave Original Time, I still like to see familiar faces now and then. As an employee, I can check in on everyone I've met over the years and make sure they're okay in their new era and—" Mia's phone rang, interrupting Vaughn,

"Hold that thought," Mia said. "Do you mind if I get that? I want to make sure I'm not missing anything with the band."

"Go ahead," Vaughn said, relieved by Mia's distraction. He realized recruiting Mia would be more difficult of a task than he'd expected.

"Hello?... Econ? Yeah, I don't know either... Can I call you back in a little bit?... Thanks Mace, let me know if you figure it out... bye!" Mia hung up the phone. "Sorry, where were we?"

"I was just saying it's been nice to see the people I care about in other eras, in the periods of time where they were meant to live." Mia's clock struck ten. "Wow, today has flown. I'd better be going," Vaughn said. "It sounds like you've got homework to do."

Vaughn gave her a half smile and started toward the door. He wanted to expand on the benefits of working for TRN, but after Mia's skepticism surrounding his intentions, he decided to rework his recruiting pitch. Vaughn needed to further gain Mia's trust.

"I'll walk you out," Mia said. She couldn't help herself.

They made their way down the stairs, and Vaughn locked his fingers with Mia's. Vaughn turned to face her when they reached the bottom of the stairs. Mia stood one stair up, eye-level with Vaughn. His long hair really served him.

"See you at our next show?" Mia asked, then sighed, "Whenever *that* is. Or we can go to breakfast again. Why did you take me out anyway? We couldn't *really* talk about anything."

Vaughn shrugged, "To distract you from your homework," he teased. "No really, I did it because you deserve to be taken out. Just because you're in another time, don't let their misogyny go unchecked. We can make a difference, you know, maybe not in the future, but at least in the present." Vaughn promised. "I'll keep trying to get Lars out of the picture."

Vaughn put his hands on just the right part of Mia's waist.

"Is TRN *making* you leave next month? Or is there someone else in another time?" She asked.

"There's no one else," Vaughn answered. "Duty calls."

Mia wrapped her fingers in the hair at the nape of his neck and pressed her lips against Vaughn's. He held her face in his large hands. Mia pressed her hips into his and felt his body tighten, then, the lobby door of Mia's apartment complex opened.

"Wow, sorry to interrupt," a startled resident blurted as she stepped inside.

Vaughn and Mia looked at the resident and she and beelined to her apartment. Once the door closed, Vaughn and Mia burst out in laughter. Mia grabbed him by the hand and led him back up to her apartment.

"Mia, I don't know about getting involved before I leave," he said. "It's not fair to you."

"I'll decide what's fair."

Vaughn gave in. Getting physical had worked for recruiting in the past, but he was trying to do better at avoiding his recruits' heartbreak. Within seconds of stepping into Mia's apartment, they were intertwined in her sheets. They paused to catch their breath. Vaughn used the moment to slow down the progression, desiring more than a hookup.

Vaughn needed to know if Mia would join him, but it wasn't the time to ask. Final's week had arrived, and despite his urge to ravish every inch of Mia's body, Vaughn forced himself to wait for the right time.

"I gotta go," Vaughn peeled himself from Mia, "and you," he tapped her nose with his index finger, "need to study."

Physics.

Mia procrastinated for hours before pulling the massive textbook from her backpack. The bold letters on the front of the outrageously priced textbook seemed to read, 'waste of your life.' Every assignment felt like an attempt to solve problems that resisted solving. Mia thought of Dr. Chandra and the doors that physics opened. Despite the advancements which allowed Mia to Travel, she didn't see the subject as an essential component, necessary to join the workforce.

Mia felt trapped and knew, deep down, that she only enrolled in college because she was expected to go. As she sat through countless lectures and attempted to adhere the material to her memory, Mia couldn't help but fantasize about dropping out. Her completed gen-eds from Original Time urged her to press on.

TRN allowed education in any college after 1983, the dawning of the internet, to be considered fluid with education in Original Time.

"We want the college experience to be one which most fulfills its alumni," Adrian Glass had stated. "There are skills from each time in history that can enrich our youth in different ways than the education offered by our current era."

Mia knew that she needed to keep her grades up. Though her thoughts fluctuated between gratitude for her education and pondering the necessity of college, she always resolved to see it through. So far.

Mia understood the value of money. She'd seen her family's business on the brink of bankruptcy. Mia bought her own way to the nineties using every penny she had earned from her days at King's. In high school, while Mia's friends slept in until noon on Saturdays, she was pricing dusty attic record collections. She envied the kids that didn't have to work every weekend, but, once she walked into King's and the Court, she didn't feel like she was working.

Les and Valerie started King's with just a few crates of records. In time, they transformed the space into an institution. Their obsession with music seeped into every corner of their lives.

Mia realized she had been zoning out at a paragraph in her textbook and she sighed. She longed for a crystal ball to tell her if she *needed* to go to college to make a comfortable living. Her grandparents lived their dreams and neither of them went to college. Mia wasn't even sure if Les had completed high school. Mia questioned whether the investment of her time and money would be more useful if spent on her band or her education. She thought back to an interview she heard.

Mia remembered the host's question, "How did you get your start in the music business?"

"When I was coming up in the industry," the artist answered, "you just *did it*. If you wanted to be a singer, you sang. If you wanted to perform, you found a stage, it didn't matter how big it was. If you wanted to be a writer, you wrote. Simple as that."

Of course, the artist didn't mention the years he spent sharing a small flat with five roommates. It never came up that there were weeks when he and his mates rummaged through the trash in search of scraps, fit to consume. Mia expected that the brightness of his success killed any remaining shadow of his journey to get there.

Mia feared that if she didn't have a back-up plan, she would have to live in survival mode until her big break. She was disappointed in herself for clinging so tightly to the idea of having a plan B, but she wasn't brave enough to free fall into the narrow landing of a music career.

Mia switched out her physics book for economics and cracked down.

After four straight hours of studying, from a book rather than an interactive screen, Mia was in need of reprieve. She was unconvinced that she was doing enough to prepare for Finals, but her brain was incapable of taking in any more material.

As she paused from her studies, Mia's thoughts drifted to Macy. Mia was excited to move in together and looked forward to spending less time alone. She had adequately assimilated to the nineties and was no longer concerned that she would give away her origins.

Macy and Mia saw less of one another with the uptick in their academic demands and Mia had resolved to give Macy the space she'd requested. Now, rather than reliving the rush of Halloween with Macy, Vaughn crept into Mia's mind. Mia did her best to shut down any hope of something substantial with him and distracted herself with the TV.

'Just one set of 'Unplugged.'

Her phone rang. Mia remembered she couldn't pause the onscreen performance.

'Ugh, right in the middle of the solo?'

Her prickly response lifted when she heard Macy's voice on the other end of the phone.

"Mia, our streak is over," Macy said, elated.

"What do you mean?"

"We're playing the Loop's holiday bash!"

Mia shrieked, "Shut *up!*"

"I know!" Macy said. "It's not the Lakehouse, but the holiday bash is always packed. It's the Loop's busiest night. Last year, you could barely move in the place. I know how Lars is," Macy paused, "but he really hooked us up this time."

'Only with Vaughn's push.'

"We'll celebrate soon," Macy promised.

Mia hung her head, "Not soon enough."

"Chin up buttercup," Macy encouraged. "Hit those books, then we'll go all out in the city over break."

Their conversation ended. There was a mountain of class material to climb, but Mia didn't have the energy. The gig before Winter Break stole the last bit of her attention span. Mia watched the artists, onscreen under the hot stage lights, and imagined what it would be like to make it big. She knew it was forbidden by TRN, but couldn't help her daydreams.

'To hell with college,' she thought.

Mia's desire to gamble on a career in music became less theoretical as she thought of the reverse of inflation for Travelers. Her funds could go further. Mia knew the Tuesdaze wouldn't end up in the history books. She never envisioned them playing to a stadium of fans, but she did feel they could hover at a mid-level status, enough to make a living.

Mia watched the featured artist flood the television's stage with his heart's contents. Emotion welled in Mia's chest. She thought back to her and Vaughn's date and realized she was bothered by Vaughn's ability to disconnect from his Travel destinations. Mia's recognition of that part of Vaughn's personality caused her to reflect on her own moral code.

Shortly after ten o'clock, Mia clicked off the TV. The quiet of her apartment was contrasted by her racing thoughts. Mia resolved to cave into the ultimate distraction from her classes and called Vaughn to come over.

Vaughn knew that the night had come to lay his cards on the table. Just days before, he'd left Mia's apartment when things got steamy to respect her academic priorities, but tonight's invitation suggested she wasn't as cemented to the time as he thought.

He knocked on her apartment door and took a deep breath. Mia opened the door and her contagious grin spread to Vaughn.

"I'm so glad you're here! I had to share the exciting news with someone, and Macy is studying for the night," Mia said.

"I'll be your second choice," Vaughn teased.

"Sorry, that came out wrong," Mia led him to the sofa. "We got booked to headline at the Loop's holiday bash! Things have been so rocky with Lars, I had no idea if we'd even play until next semester, let alone headline."

"That's wonderful news!" Vaughn said with a half-hearted grin.

Mia studied his face, "Something's up with you," she said. "Is everything alright?"

Vaughn hesitated to dampen her spirits with his heavy proposition, but with more gigs came a decreased chance that Mia would work for TRN.

"You caught me. There is something I want to discuss. I was going to wait until you were done with Finals, and I know you don't need more stress right now, but you have to know something."

'Spill it.'

"I've used my position with TRN to look out for you and Derek," Vaughn omitted the part about being paid extra to do so, "but you're both doing fine. You know I'm always here if you need anything. I'll expedite Derek's requests for a new Aid device once they're available. I'll do my best to get you both access to impromptu departures and anything Travel related. You have made an amazing start to your adult life here, but I want to talk to you about joining me, joining TRN, as an employee."

"Me? Become a TRN employee?" Mia laughed. "Do you really think I'd be a good fit?"

"Yeah, it's a great gig, but there are too few of us. We need more. You can visit any era you want. Hubs make sure that every couple of days, there's a block on the schedule for employees to depart if needed. Sometimes it's like a work trip where you have someone to monitor or a situation to evaluate for TRN, but most of the time, it's like a vacation.

When Travel started, we were fully staffed but now, many employees have drifted off into the ether. TRN has brought some of them back, but others have just found their favorite place in history and stayed. They were the ones I was talking about when I referred to looping.

I worry we will be left short-staffed, and I think you would fit the job description perfectly. You're young, Mia. There is so much to see. Plus, I wouldn't be mad about spending more time with you," Vaughn admitted. "We could go to other eras together. I could train you."

"This is a lot to consider," Mia stated. "How did you get into this position in the first place?"

"Well, when Time Travel was brand new, I offered to be a test subject," Vaughn said. "I've done this for a while now."

"That's *crazy*!"

Vaughn laughed, "It really was absurd, even for me. For the next year, I am bound to TRN by contract and must go to a new destination for two-to-three-months. I make sure things are going smoothly, then I leave."

"And you've requested an Aid for Derek?" Mia asked.

"He's due to receive it soon, though not as soon as I'd like. They said by the year's end," Vaughn said. "There was a huge glitch in distribution during the sixties. Many Travelers didn't receive the Aid or the TRN decryption glass piece to read their newsletters," Vaughn scoffed. "Hell, most sixties Travelers still haven't received a TRN newsletter at all. The high volume was anticipated, but tech prepared for it terribly. Then, they screwed up a batch of two thousand devices."

"Holy shit. I expected them to be more organized," Mia stated. "Are you sure Derek will receive one?"

"Absolutely," Vaughn said. "I'll see to it myself if needed."

"Where are you off to next?" Mia asked.

"I'll stop back in Original Time for a bit. Maybe see my parents for the Holidays. From there, it all depends on my assignment. I'll check on Derek if needed, then I'll go wherever they tell me. If I do well enough on these next few assignments, I might even get a promotion," Vaughn said.

"What would a promotion involve for you?" Mia asked.

"A pay raise, but I don't care about that. When you drift and monitor like I do, you want for few possessions. Plus, the rate of exchange for us humans from the future is almost criminal. I'm hoping the promotion gives me more free time. I'll be there to advise new TRN employees of course, but I'd like to Travel more often with no obligations. I think TRN is realizing that time is the most valuable currency."

"I bet you miss a lot of people in other eras," Mia said. "I hope you get the promotion and can stay put wherever you'd like. You've probably gotten used to the lifestyle though. Your family moved a lot, right?"

"They did. But it wasn't all bad. I learned a lot about myself by moving. And about the world," Vaughn stated. "It's true, I do miss certain people, but I have to force myself not to dwell on their absence. Every time and place has an expiration date. Had I stayed anywhere longer, things may have ended on a bad note."

"What brought you to TRN's doorstep? I know you're used to new scenery, with how you grew up, but didn't you want out of that kind of life as an adult?"

"I had no clue what I wanted." Vaughn remembered the day he walked through TRN's front doors. "A techy guy, who lived on the same floor as me and Derek, told me that Travel was really going to take off and gave me the Hub's address. I was fresh out of college with mediocre grades," Vaughn explained. "Not a lot of jobs around, no bright future. Derek and I- well you know what happened."

Mia nodded.

"I didn't feel that there was anything on the horizon for me, so I joined the trials for Time Travel," Vaughn smirked, "I was one of the first twenty people to do it."

Mia's mouth dropped open.

"That is insane! Was losing my brother's friendship enough to make you be okay with getting stuck in another time? Or worse…" Mia trailed off. "It was *so new*. So strange. When they told me about the Shell for the first time, I nearly had a panic attack."

Vaughn looked for the words to explain his draw to Travel but could hardly explain his state of mind before Psilopram.

"I went through a *really* down time in college," he stated. "There were days I couldn't get out of bed. Nothing seemed

266

worth it, *I* didn't seem worth it. I had no idea what I was doing with my life. When I learned that TRN was looking for test-Travelers, when I handed them my resume, I wasn't afraid to die. I knew I was doing something meaningful with the life I was given. Even if it didn't work out for me, it might help others."

Mia recalled her brother mentioning Vaughn's moods. When the dark clouds rolled in, Vaughn would hole up in his room for days. Derek grew concerned as piles of dirty clothes accumulated on his roommate's bedroom floor. The trash would have overflown had Derek not taken it out. Vaughn's dishes stacked in the kitchen sink and Derek washed them out of necessity.

"I also got to test the Psilopram," Vaughn shared. "That was a big part of what got me the job. My state of existence was so miserable, Dr. Lowell offered me the job on the spot. 'If Psilopram could fix me, it could fix anyone.' That's what Dr. Lowell told me."

"Do they ever deny people the opportunity to Travel?"

"Yes, they do," Vaughn answered. "Though not often. The applicant would have to be a felon or a psychopath. Psilopram gets most people out of their own way. If I'd run into Derek before Traveling, I would have looked the other way. When I went back to the sixties, I made it a point to be in the same place as him. Some part of me, a part birthed by Psilopram, drew me to Derek. I had to make things right. Not for my own ego, but to correct some," Vaughn searched for the right word, "karmic thread. Every time I come out of acclimation; I have a new draw to fix something I'd damaged before understanding the big picture."

"I haven't thought of my acclimation process in a while," Mia shrugged, "you know, with finals and the band. But I remember that feeling. The clutter cleared away to the purest state of mind I've ever experienced. I sometimes wish I could remember the Shell. How on Earth I confronted Cooper and Grandpa's loss. The weight of death, hopelessness, existentialism, Original Time's problems, it was all lifted by Psilopram."

Vaughn shook his head, "They've created possibilities never anticipated by any of us. People are skeptical, and I don't blame them. It feels too good to be true. But I don't *try* and fuck up such good things anymore."

"How have you survived so many acclimation periods? The vitamins and supplements to recover, the acclimator's care, it's worth it, but seems very taxing if done repeatedly."

"It gets easier and easier," Vaughn replied. "The Psilopram eventually runs out of things to fix."

"So, you're perfect?" Mia joked

"Not exactly," Vaughn said, feeling guilty for the payment he received to monitor Mia and Derek.

"I'm happy for you," Mia said.

"I'm happy for you too. You seem good here. I have to ask though, that first morning we saw each other at the house, right after you and Macy were in my bed," Vaughn paused with the reddening of Mia's cheeks. "Are you two together?"

Mia sighed, "No. I dove in too deep, and she got freaked out. The more time has passed, the more it's come to light as a one-night thing. I've noticed that sexuality is so rigid in this time. When we kissed in front of everyone at Halloween, it was considered a novelty. People here either condemn girls together or don't take it seriously and use it to get off."

"That has to be tough," Vaughn said. "Not to drive home the appeal of working for TRN, but sexual fluidity might be easier for you in other times."

"Original Time *does* have that going for it. Maybe I should just go back there," Mia joked, "where everything is perfect."

Vaughn laughed.

Mia stood and opened her living room curtains. Snow began to fall outside the glass. Delicate water crystals were illuminated by the streetlamps. The gleaming flakes descended and multiplied over the next few minutes.

"Come with me?" Came out as more of a question than Vaughn intended. He restated, "Come with me."

Mia froze.

"At least think about it," Vaughn said. "I don't expect an answer tonight, but I wouldn't ask if I didn't think you'd love seeing all the eras. They'd be lucky to have you. I see all that you have here, but remember, you can't get famous with the Tuesdaze," he stated.

Mia lay down, encircled in Vaughn's arms. She couldn't help but wonder why, after so little time together, Vaughn was inviting her to drop everything and join his team at TRN.

"Vaughn," Mia began, "that's a lot to ask. Here, I have so many opportunities that I wouldn't have had in Original Time. How would I play with bands in other eras with such brief spurts of time in each place? Let's be real, the Tuesdaze probably won't get famous. Even in the nineties it takes a lot to make it."

"I realize this must seem like a dramatic move. You've got the band, your education, your friends, and I understand wanting to continue on this track." He sighed. "I'm also asking you from a selfish place. I've been on my own for a long time, and though I feel young, time is passing, and not just because I'm drifting from one year to another."

A draft came in from the window and Vaughn tightened Mia's blanket around her.

"My college days are behind me. Most people my age are in a relationship or married. Wildly successful in their career or starting a family. Traveling the world or perfecting their home. Derek and I are exceptions to the classic sequence of life, which drove us to Travel in the first place. Like I said before, I don't have many possessions, but I have eras worth of experiences and for me, those are worth more than millions to my name."

Mia stretched one of her legs and kicked the magic eight ball which sat on her coffee table. She smirked at Vaughn and reached to pick it up. Liquid splashed inside the sphere as Mia shook the ball.

"Should I stay or go?" Mia asked the cheap oracle.

Vaughn raised his eyebrows in anticipation for the answer.

'TRY AGAIN LATER.'

"Wow," Mia laughed, "okay then, I guess I'll think about it."

They looked out the window, mesmerized by the snowfall. Vaughn kissed the top of Mia's head. Time, she just needed time.

Macy pulled into Mia's parking lot and glanced at her dashboard clock.

'10:20'.

Macy double-checked her purse to make sure she'd brought the first flyer to the holiday bash. The Tuesdaze name was written across the top of the bright red paper. She couldn't wait to show Mia.

Mia and Macy's nightly trash TV and veg-out sessions had taken a sharp decline since the academic demands took priority. Macy looked forward to reconnecting and celebrating their holiday gig. She regretted her aloof attitude following their hook-up and hoped it wasn't too late to reignite their intimacy.

Macy rolled down her window for a quick cigarette. She sparked her lighter and drew in a deep inhale. The crackle of the burning paper and rush of nicotine soothed her overworked brain.

Just as she was ready to discard the butt, a familiar face approached the apartment entrance. He buzzed a room, and the door clicked open. The light hit his face and Macy identified the figure.

Vaughn.

The hypnotic mellow of her cigarette wore off. Her heart dropped. Macy understood that Mia had moved on.

Macy pulled a napkin from the glove compartment and wiped away her lipstick. She felt foolish as she looked down at her cropped sweater and silk pajama pants.

'Maybe it's better this way.'

She turned up her radio and flicked the last inch of her cigarette onto the pavement. Macy cranked up her window and pulled away.

Chapter XI

Ellie inched a box from the top shelf.

Crash.

The box's tape, brittle with age, gave way and an array of photo albums spilled onto the floor. Ellie shrieked and hopped back just in time to avoid her toes being crushed by the box's contents. She breathed a sigh of relief, then went to her car to obtain a sturdy plastic tub to store Les and Valerie's scrapbooks.

Since her children's departure, Ellie had kept herself busy by sifting through her late parent's home. Ellie's siblings had given her the job of deciding what to sell and what to keep.

Ellie knew that it was only a matter of time before the right offer would be placed on Les and Valerie's house. The evidence of her parent's lives would be reduced to their business, boxes, and the memories held by their family. The task of reducing their belongings was time consuming, but Ellie was equipped to handle it. She had a natural inclination to overindulge in nostalgia and, as she cleared out the final items, Ellie took frequent pauses to relive the unearthed memories.

She reverted to the uncomplicated mindset of her youth every time she unlocked Les and Valerie's front door. Objects Ellie had forgotten about sat in every corner of the house. Stiff, dusty band posters that had rotated through King's were rolled up in the attic. In the living room, stacks of Les' favorite albums sat right where he had left them. Valerie's sunburst clock still hung above the kitchen sink.

Since Ellie and Jon's return from 1997, the days had grown shorter and the to-do list longer. Through late summer and autumn, before they visited Mia, Ellie took an unhealthy amount of refuge in rummaging through Les and Valerie's house. It was like stepping back into a life not yet impacted by the permanent loss of her son, Cooper. Ellie used the escape as a crutch, and it was apparent in her and Jon's relationship.

The task started as a great distraction, but as she emptied her parent's house, the space shifted from a getaway to a reminder of Les and Valerie's cessation.

Ellie came back inside with two tubs. Rather than fill the containers, she sat down on Les' recliner for a break. She was contemplating how much more of her night to spend there when her cell phone rang.

"Hi love," she answered.

"Hey baby, on my way home. Are you about done at Les and V's?"

"Yes, I think I am."

"Give yourself a rest tonight. I think we both need some down time," Jon said. "Now that the end of the season is in sight, maybe we can make plans for the winter."

"I'd like that," Ellie responded.

They hung up and Ellie started toward her parent's entryway. She heaved another box from the floor to add to the growing stack in her and Jon's basement. Ellie took one last look at the vacant living room.

The home's former glory was no longer reflected by the cold, empty space. Les and Valerie's gathering place, sacred in her family's eyes, was once filled with life. Now, it had become a shell. Ellie could still picture the holidays of her upbringing: running around with her siblings and cousins, the adults gathered at the dining room table for euchre, trays of meat and cheese set out across the kitchen countertop.

Ellie's family had gathered in Les and Valerie's home just days before, hoping to revive their Christmases of old. They decorated the house with Valerie's vintage flair and followed her recipes to a tee. They played Les' personal holiday record collection and exchanged gifts, but it wasn't right without Les and Valerie's presence. The adults proceeded to indulge in too many spirits and concluded to hold next years' family Christmas elsewhere.

Ellie switched off the light and trudged into the cold. As she drove, Ellie remembered a conversation she'd had with Jon, just weeks before.

"What will I do next, Jon?" Ellie asked him after a day of sorting through her parent's house. "King's and the Court will take my time throughout the holidays, but what will I do when winter comes? When I'm done cleaning out the house and things slow down? Should we try to visit the kids again?"

"Let's worry about that once busy season is over," Jon suggested. "And we don't always have to go somewhere or do something. What happened to just being together?"

Ellie sighed, "I'm sorry. You're right. We'll get through the holidays then go from there."

Though they were greatly enticed by the prospect of Time Travel, after their visit to the nineties, Jon and Ellie didn't have the time nor the energy to go through the process again anytime soon. They were needed in the current era. The Court was booked with holiday parties, and they knew being absent for another acclimation period would take away from their bottom line.

Not only was the venue in constant need of event preparation, but their record store was abuzz with holiday gift-seekers in search of the perfect record for their loved ones. Jon and Ellie spent long days in the same room but had little time to truly connect.

As Ellie pulled into the driveway, she noticed smoke coming from the chimney and wondered what Jon was up to inside. She parked in the garage, turned off her engine, and stacked more tubs in the garage's corner.

Ellie opened the garage door which led to their kitchen and stomped her boots on the entryway doormat. The sound of familiar holiday tunes floated from the living room and the sting of cold began to diminish. Ellie pulled off her stocking cap.

Jon approached his wife and put his hands on her shoulders.

"Welcome home, baby," Jon said and drew in Ellie for an embrace. "Need help with anything?"

"I've got everything stacked in the garage." Ellie said.

"Can it stay out there overnight?" Jon asked.

Ellie nodded and Jon helped her out of her coat.

"Close your eyes," he said and guided Ellie into the living room. "Okay now, open!"

Ellie's eyes lit up. Standing before her was a majestic, blue spruce. She spotted the box of ornaments next to the tree; it was ready to decorate.

"I didn't think we were doing a tree this year," Ellie said.

"I know this year's been *crazy*," Jon stated, "but I couldn't help myself. It's obviously different without the kids and without your folks, but *we're* still here. I know you were disappointed by the family Christmas at Les and Valerie's. It wasn't like the ones

276

you remember," he tucked a stray hair behind Ellie's ear. "I want you to understand how much I'm looking forward to all of the memories there still are to be made."

"Thank you, Jon," Ellie said.

"You know, some of my favorite Christmases were just you and me. Remember when we got snowed into our first apartment and couldn't make it to your parents'?" Jon asked.

Ellie laughed.

"I thought Mom was going to make us snowshoe over to her and Dad's. She lived for our family Christmas. I can hear her now, 'The roads really aren't that bad if you just take it slow.'"

"They always cared for us so much," Jon said.

Though losing Les and Valerie had strongly affected his wife, Jon was glad that Ellie had maintained a close relationship with her parents through their final days and saw them off into their eternal rest.

Jon hadn't been so fortunate. His abusive, addiction-plagued dad was fatally injured in a car accident when Jon was twelve. Jon's mother constantly hustled to keep a roof over their head. Even before her husband's death, she put in the work of a single parent. Jon's mother cleaned houses during the day and served as a cocktail waitress in the evening.

Throughout Jon's childhood and teenage years, he spent most of his time with his grandparents. Their house was clean and warm and in the evenings, it was always filled with music. When Jon was young, he poked fun at his grandparent's stacks of records, but as he aged, he grew to appreciate vinyl's distinct qualities. He adored the crackle, the artists' orchestrated experience, and the album covers.

As records regained popularity, Jon fervently expanded his collection. He thought he'd stumbled into heaven upon his first visit to King's Records. King's selection captivated him, then Jon's gaze was drawn to the young lady who priced the records. Ellie, the owner's daughter.

Jon placed the needle on a circle of red vinyl. The festive album was a housewarming gift from Jon's grandparents. It was given to Jon and Ellie for Christmas in their first apartment. Playing the album had become a ritual every year while they decorated.

"Thanks for doing all this tonight," Ellie said.

"You deserve a night off. There are no shows tonight, everything's taken care of at King's, why not kick up our feet?"

"There's just always so much to do," Ellie responded. "I've become used to being busy. I'm worried for the time when we're not busy, once things slow down after the holidays. I'm beginning to pack some of the very last things from Mom and Dad's. Soon, there will be no more secrets of the house to discover, no more surprises to learn about their lives. I will have seen all the pictures and read all the letters. I'll dole out the remaining heirlooms to each of my siblings, then we'll sell the house and that will be it. The ending of a chapter."

"We'll still get together with the family," Jon assured, "you know that."

"Today, I just thought of all the holidays we spent in *that* house. All of us kids playing," she reminisced. "I remember telling Mom and Dad I was pregnant with Derek and," a lump rose to her throat, "Cooper."

The unexpected tragedy of Cooper's overdose was a wound that always ran the risk of breaking open. The silence of winter magnified the silence in their home and Jon noticed that the record had come to a halt. Jon dabbed Ellie's dampened face with a tissue. He mustered a small smile, determined to make the most of the holidays, even without the kids.

"Let's enjoy the time we have, shall we?" He asked.

Ellie nodded. She walked over to the record player, lifted the needle, and flipped the album to Side B, just as she did all day at King's.

"We've got the lights, the ornaments," Ellie evaluated the living room. "What about the hand-made ornaments?"

"I'm on it."

Jon went to the basement to fetch the box which held an assortment of ornaments made by their family. Ellie didn't have the heart to get rid of the weathered pieces, however tacky they were. Jon came back upstairs and set the box near the tree.

Ellie opened the flaps and pulled five wooden snowflake ornaments from the box. Les had handcrafted the snowflakes and each was strung with a red ribbon. There was one for each member of their family. Ellie and Jon positioned the snowflakes on the tree, ensuring that one of the crafted ornaments could be seen from every angle of the room.

The children's kindergarten ornaments were next. Derek and Cooper's had been made to look like mini chalkboards. Their signatures from when they were five years old were scribbled across a construction paper blackboard. Ellie smiled at the memory of the twins fighting over whose handwriting was better. Mia's ornament was a tiny frame encrusted with glimmering sequins and a beaded border. In the center was Mia's kindergarten photo, complete with her wide grin.

Jon saw his wife cheering up and his heart warmed. He couldn't resist the surprise any longer.

279

"I'm going to pop a bottle of wine," Jon said and disappeared into the kitchen.

He uncorked a bottle of Chardonnay, a shelf above the ones he usually selected, and pulled two glasses from the cabinet. Jon reached into the cabinet where he'd stored Ellie's gift before she got home. He sauntered back into the living room with the gift in his pocket.

"I have something for you," Jon said and placed the wine glasses on their coffee table.

Ellie picked up her glass and took a sip.

"Mmm," she smiled, "Just what I needed."

"It's not just the wine."

Jon revealed the parcel. "For you," he stated and presented the box.

Ellie beamed at the elegant wrapping.

"Jon, I thought we weren't doing gifts this year," Ellie stated. "I thought we were going to save up to visit Derek after the holidays."

"We'll do both," Jon said. "Sometimes, you forget how well the business is doing. I couldn't resist. Go on," he gestured to the present, "open it."

Ellie peeled back the wrapping paper and opened the box inside. She pulled out a glimmering ballerina ornament. Ellie ran her fingers along the tutu's stiff fabric and the dancer's crystal-studded bodice.

The ornament roused Ellie's memory of viewing the Nutcracker every Christmas with Mia, fast asleep on her lap.

Jon pulled an envelope from his pocket.

"Part two," he said.

Ellie shook her head, "Now I feel even worse for not getting you anything!"

"Go on," Jon instructed.

Ellie opened the envelope.

"Two tickets to see 'The Nutcracker?" She clapped her hands together. "In New York City?"

A date was printed on the edge of the tickets.

December 24.

"No, in two days? For Christmas Eve?" Ellie shrieked and wrapped her arms around Jon.

"I thought we could try out a new tradition this year," Jon said. "'The Nutcracker' in the city. We can stay in that hotel by the theater, get dinner at that place you've been wanting to try, we can celebrate Christmas in style."

Ellie bubbled with excitement. Though their tree was beautiful, embellishments were scattered throughout the town, and their customers were in the holiday spirit, Ellie had yet to find her own excitement for the season.

She knew the emotions that would hit her on Christmas Day. No amount of holiday adornments, sugar cookies, or cozying up to the fire would make the house feel less hollow. Jon had come up with the perfect antidote for the dread Ellie was working hard to avoid.

"Oh my, Jon. I can't wait to pack! I'm going to bring everything I've been saving for the right time to wear."

Jon put his arm around Ellie.

"I'm surprised you're excited to pack after months of boxing Les and Valerie's entire life," he said and refilled Ellie's glass of wine. "We could have gone to the sixties or back to the nineties for Christmas. It would have been hard, but we could have made it happen. We could have hosted dinner for your brothers and sisters and their kids, but none of those ideas seemed right. This year, I wanted you to myself. A night to put Kings and the Court out of our mind, to lay our worries about the kids to rest," Jon smirked. "A night to reconnect."

"To the best husband there is," Ellie toasted and clinked her glass with Jon's. "Accompanying me to the ballet and all," she said. "Not every husband would do that."

As the spirits kicked in, Jon and Ellie danced through the living room to their festive favorites.

"Let's spend Christmas Day in our hotel robes!" Ellie declared.

"And let's spend some of that hard earned money on a spa day," Jon said.

Ellie stepped away to get another bottle of wine and as she walked away, she saw Jon in a different light. She got the same feeling as when he pursued her at the record store, years ago. Ellie felt herself being pulled out of the past few years of tragedy, and back into the zest of life. They lounged on the couch and lost track of time.

Eventually, Jon looked at the clock.

12:15AM.

Jon scanned the room and was satisfied with the evidence of their evening. Two empty bottles of wine sat on the coffee table. Stray bits of tinsel glinted from the floor.

Their house was filled with joy for the moment. Jon imagined putting on a suit, going out on the town, getting champagne sent to their room, evading all expectations of past holiday seasons. He finished his final sip of wine and the lights of the tree reflected off his glass.

Ellie grew quiet as she fell asleep against Jon's worn flannel with the most peace of mind she'd had in years.

Derek turned the lock.

He flipped the sign from 'Open' to 'Closed'. Derek peered out from *En Blum's* window and noticed flickers of white beginning to scatter about. A moon further enhanced the seemingly idyllic scene. Derek realized that he looked upon a virgin full moon, her lunar surface not yet disturbed by human steps. The silver orchestrator of the tides glowed in the night, brighter by the hour.

Just as he was about to step outside, Derek heard the back door open.

"Hello?" Derek called through the empty boutique.

Derek heard Renee patting objects, trying to feel for the light bulb's string. The moonlight allowed Derek to navigate the boutique's floor and he snuck up on Renee.

Renee finally pulled down on the string.

"Boo!"

Renee gasped, then began to laugh once she saw it was Derek.

"You're too easy!" Derek teased

"You wanker!" Renee smacked his arm.

"It *is* a full moon," Derek stated and raised his eyebrows. "Never know what could happen tonight. What are you up to for the holidays?"

"Well, Grant, Angelene, Germain, and I have been invited to spend the holidays with '*ma tante*.'"

"Your what?"

"Oh sorry, I forget Americans' inability to understand anything but English," Renee smirked. "My auntie," she said with an exaggerated twang. "Her house is in the most wonderful French village, the place my grandparents called home before moving to England," Renee explained.

"Ah, man," Derek said, "I hoped to hang out with Germain over the holidays."

"He cannot miss this trip. His father would not allow it. You'll have Grant and Angelene though. They barely got out of the trip. Convincing Marcel over the phone that he wasn't fit to go," Renee shook her head, "poor, sweet Grant."

"Poor guy is right," Derek said and changed the subject. "Someday I'll understand the web of your family."

"It's a long story. I haven't the energy to explain, but Germain's and my family go way back."

Derek raised his eyebrows, hoping for more of an explanation.

"Long story short, our grandparents settled here in England together. We've known one another," Renee shrugged, "since before we were born. Angelene and Grant came into the picture when we were kids."

Derek noticed Renee's exhaustion as she spoke.

"Tell me another time," Derek said. "I'll be here."

"Ugh, to rest on this holiday will be a dream," she stated.

Half circles of purple were painted beneath Renee's eyes. Her smooth skin looked blotchy, and her frame undernourished. For the entire month of December, Renee went to one holiday happening after another, all hosted by various A-listers.

Quietness fell upon Derek and Renee, and they looked into each other's eyes. Renee walked to Derek and placed her hand on his cheek. He took Renee in his arms. She dropped her head onto his chest and Derek stroked her snowflake-studded hair.

What was once a lusty relationship had evolved into a connection of comfort. Renee would always be a dear friend to Derek no matter how high she was shot by fame. Derek rested his chin atop her head.

"Safe travels," he said and kissed her soft cheek.

Renee stepped back from their embrace.

"Happy Christmas, my dear Derek."

She slid the bag, which she had come to retrieve, from her desk. Renee faced Derek one more time, blew him a kiss, and stepped out the back door.

Derek finished closing and went out onto the street. As he walked toward his apartment, a plethora of thoughts came rushing in. Derek wondered how he was still without an Aid. The device, which had been created to reduce worry, caused Derek more stress since his knowledge of its existence. He felt left behind and was disappointed that Vaughn had yet to follow through on his promise. Derek wondered if he'd been duped by his friend, just as Grant had been fooled by his friend in California. Both "friends" were carrying out a mission, their intentions unclear.

Not only was Derek deserted by his friend from OT, but he was now left behind by his new friends. He'd hoped that Renee would extend an invitation to join their family holiday, but the lack of welcoming to the event hit Derek with the reality of his ranking in Renee's life.

To delay the night spent alone in his apartment, Derek decided to linger outside his nearest TRN hub and see if new Travelers emerged. Many nights, Derek had been tempted to go inside the hub for a consultation, to see if his acclimator was still in the area, but he held back, apprehensive to leave the best parts of the era, and unwilling to admit that his issues weren't fixed by a new location.

The snowflakes grew larger, and Derek thought back to the holidays with his family. He remembered his grandparent's home and the memories never to be relived. Derek shuffled away from the TRN hub and sat on a curb. He watched glittery flakes fall to the ground. He gazed at the Christmas lights, lining the buildings; a contrast to his melancholy.

Just months before, Derek had it all: a goddess for his lover, a reset mind, a solid group of friends. As he sat in the snow, Derek felt defeated. Though ending things with Renee had loomed for months, their interaction that night left him with a real sense of romantic closure.

Derek heard footsteps crunch through the thickening layer of snow. A bundled-up figure walked his way. He turned his head in the direction of the sound.

As the steps grew closer, a familiar face emerged from the night. She was wrapped in a thick, wool duster, her curls twirling in the wind.

"Angelene?" Derek asked.

"Is that Mr. Derek Hayes?"

Angelene and Derek's time together had dwindled with the holiday season. She and Derek ran into each other only a handful of times and exchanged formalities when checking in on Grant.

Grant's emotional state was slowly improving, but the mystery of the lost autumn night still weighed on all their consciences.

"What are you up to?" Derek asked.

"I'm on my way to a jazz joint. Grant and I hung back from the crew's trip to France," she explained. "I would hate for Grant to go off the rails around such precious next-of-kin."

"Can you explain how you all know one another?" Derek asked. A sharp gust of wind hit Derek and took his breath away. "Maybe not here," he added. "Are you meeting anyone tonight?"

"Just going on my own," Angelene replied. She hung her head. "Grant usually comes with me to the club around the holidays. Our mother used to work there. So did Germain's father and grandfather. They're all getting on the train tonight though, and Grant is finally sleeping so here I am, alone in our annual tradition."

She looked around to see if Derek had company and realized he was by himself.

"Are you waiting for someone?" Angelene asked.

He laughed, embarrassed.

"I wish I could say yes. I wasn't ready to go home yet," Derek admitted.

"Care to accompany me?"

Derek beamed.

"I would love to."

They walked for what felt like much longer than it was, when Angelene slowed her pace.

"Here we are. It's down the stairs," Angelene said.

Derek realized he had passed by their destination several times but never noticed the place. A set of stairs led from the street down to the club. Derek and Angelene descended the slick, narrow stairs, clutching the railing.

Angelene opened the door and Derek followed her inside. Garland lined the windowsills. The ambiance was an instant reprieve from the sharp breeze which continued to strengthen outside. A small audience exuded warmth which was reverberated by the club's low ceiling. At each round table were two chairs.

Derek and Angelene seated themselves. A single tealight danced in the center of their table. The wall sconces were draped with holly. A bartender softly chatted with his rotation of guests.

The crack of a drumstick followed by an occasional splash swept the tempo along. Derek bobbed his head to the stand-up bass' strum. The rhythm sauntered to meet a bright piano melody.

"Thank you," Derek said and reached across the table.

Angelene placed her hands in his.

A whimsical flute and provocative saxophone joined in at different points throughout the marathon of tunes. Derek and Angelene didn't speak of the ups and downs of the past few months. Though Derek's journey to the sixties was proving to be a wild ride, only the good times were articulated at that moment.

Bar close came and the club opened its doors to the winter. The wind pummeled Derek and Angelene, their liquor-warmed bodies shocked by the frigidity.

"Bloody hell!"

Angelene tugged her coat collar snug to her neck.

"You're welcome to come to my place," Derek suggested. "It's much closer."

"I don't know, Grant fell asleep on my couch. I should go home to check on him."

"Just come over to thaw out," Derek said.

"Did you plan this all along?" Angelene teased.

"Yes, I cast a spell to invoke this squall," Derek said. "No really," he reiterated, "You don't have to stay, we just need to get inside before you chatter your teeth down to nubs!"

Angelene tensed with a chilling gust.

"Oh alright," she agreed. "But don't get any funny ideas, you have a girlfriend."

Derek was about to explain that Angelene was mistaken but was interrupted by the biggest blast of wind yet. He put his arm around Angelene, and they hurried to his flat, their haste restricted by the icy pavement.

When they arrived in front of Derek's building, Derek already had his key in hand. Angelene swayed impatiently as he failed to fit the key into the lock.

"Come on!" She shouted.

Finally, Derek controlled his hands enough for the key to slide into its slot. Derek barreled the door open, and they leapt inside.

"Ahh," Angelene sighed.

Derek led the way upstairs to his unit. He unlocked his front door and gestured for Angelene to come inside. She took a seat on the sofa and exhaled. Her shoulders relaxed.

"Thank you for inviting me over," she said. "You were right, your place is a much closer walk than mine."

Angelene peered into Derek's kitchen and spotted a bottle of spirits.

Derek followed her gaze, "Care for a glass? That will warm you right up!"

"Well, I don't want to drink alone," Angelene smirked.

Derek made his way to the kitchen and set two glasses on the countertop. He poured a hefty serving into each.

"Don't have to tell me twice," Derek said.

"A bit heavy-handed, are we?" Angelene remarked. "I guess we started pretty strong at the club," she shrugged, "might as well keep our momentum."

Derek opened the balcony curtains to reveal a whiteout. He pulled two blankets from his couch and wrapped one around his shoulders. He offered the other to Angelene. Her golden, wind-blown ringlets appeared soft and cloud-like.

With every sip of the amber libation, their cold-induced rigidity eased.

"Going there was worth nearly freezing for," he stated. "Where I'm from, there are few places like that. I can't believe I've passed those stairs so many times without venturing down. I didn't realize where they led."

"I fancy that club more than anywhere else in the city," Angelene stated.

Her mouth formed a hint of a smile as she gazed off into the distance. Angelene's thoughts drifted to the memories of her music-filled childhood. Derek watched as she went somewhere else in her mind.

"What are you thinking about?" he asked.

"Being young. This time of year causes one to think about the past, doesn't it? Mum used to tote us all around the city to these jazz joints," Angelene started. "She was a performer. She danced, sang, waitressed, she really did it all. Mum was always so busy with the holiday soirées, the late nights. She did her best, she really did. And seeing her on that stage, the way she lit people up, it must have been exhausting, but exhilarating." Angelene pointed in the direction of the club, "That's how Germain entered our lives.

Nearly every night, Grant and I went to mum's work. I mean, what was she to do as a single mother of two young children? Leave us home alone?" Angelene paused. "No, she brought us along with her. That's how we came to know Marcel,

Germain's father. They were both important members of the area's jazz circuit and they were both sole parents."

"What happened to your father?" Derek asked.

"We don't know," Angelene sighed. "One of the downsides of mum's lifestyle. It was always just the three of us; me, Grant, and Mum."

"And Germain's mother?"

"She died years ago," Angelene replied. "Germain was just a baby."

"I'm sorry," Derek said.

"Bloody shame for Germain and Marcel. Word has it that her voice brought grown men to tears," Angelene paused to collect herself. "Right, so Germain was always around. He was a music kid like me and Grant. We ran around backstage together, got ourselves into trouble as we got older, we became like family. Mum and Marcel's relationship wasn't romantic," she hesitated, "not that I know of at least, but Marcel was always there to support us. If we were short on rent or food, Marcel always had a few extra pounds and a warm meal. That's how Grant and Germain became so close, we grew up together.

And Germain and Renee, they go back even further," Angelene continued. "Their grandfathers fought together in World War One. They remained friends and neighbors and lived together in the French countryside. When World War Two began to heat up, they got the hell out of France and moved to England together. From there, they settled in this very neighborhood," Angelene stated.

She took another swig from her glass.

"Music. It's how they all met, all our ancestors. Germain and Renee's grandparents met at a concert. Germain's grandfather's troop brought jazz over here from America you know, all the way across the ocean. It really is the single most unifying thing there is, music," Angelene shook her head, "I think it's the one thread holding this wild world together."

Only a thin layer of liquid remained in the bottom of their glasses.

"Thank you for tonight," Derek said.

"I was glad for the company," Angelene confessed. "Thanks for appreciating the club with me; not everybody would like it. I like to think I'm unbound from ways of the past, but jazz makes me question that impression of myself. It's just...timeless."

"Do you think the art being created right now will still be appreciated in the future?" He questioned, wondering if people from the past knew what they had.

"I hope our art will remain important," Angelene replied. "But I, a poet, a dying breed of artist, cannot answer that question. You'd have to ask a frontman or perhaps your darling model Renee."

"She is darling, but she is not mine," Derek replied. "And I'm learning that prestige is not as glamorous as it looks from the outside."

"It's a tough lesson to learn. Reminds me of when mum became so busy, she didn't have time to tuck us in at night. I don't mind the lack of fame so long as I make rent and have enough to eat. I'd rather stay in my little cafes than have the world think I owe them every bit of my life."

"What I've noticed is that the artists I love the most are the ones I discovered for myself. Not the ones I'm force-fed by the radio," Derek said. "I prefer the artists in the little cafes."

Angelene blushed.

"The radio's not so bad, I like to hear music overpowering the ads. Everything's changing. The stations are playing *our* music. Magazines are now filled with *our* artists, *our* photographers' view.

For me, those who will endure keep their essence once everyone knows their name. They've outgrown the small venue's capacities, yet somehow, they're still who they were when the crowd was small. Even though they're now for *everyone,* they're still for *themselves.*

Those whose artistic origin takes root in being *for everyone* will fizzle out like the end of a candle's wick and they'll be deserted by their once-large crowd when the hype dies down. They will evaporate into thin air with no legacy, and no one will have heard of them.

The artists whose work will remain relevant, their disregard for the idea of appealing to everyone is, ironically, just what everyone has been searching for. Their fire lies in the magnetic pull of their calling." Angelene continued. "There also lies their devotion, divinity, anguish, and reward; a crowd just happened to stumble upon their flame. I think there are many flames in our world right now. We're living in a fiery crossroads," Angelene stated and finished her drink.

"Crashes occur at intersections. We're living through a transition between the old way and the new," Angelene chuckled, "But I suppose we're not the first society to believe that. Either way, it seems the world is ignited. That it all will burn up into nothing, but from this fire who knows, perhaps we can forge untouchable works of art, their potency remaining strong for years to come."

"So, what do we do?" Derek asked.

"Rather than sit and watch the world burn, I want to be at a desk with a pen and paper. I want to extract the *truth* from what is happening and spill it on the page. I want to offer human perception, to record the world in poetry, rather than report cold journalism for those reading about this time down the road, a road that, perhaps, smooths out miles ahead from where we are."

Chapter XII

Winter fell upon Birchmont.

Noisy streets softened with the students' dispersion. Campus grew vacant as the youthful crowds thinned. The vastness left by the collegiates' absence was enhanced by the snow-covered ground. For those who remained, a sense of wonder lit the college town.

A new tenant, a young Time Traveler, jumped at the chance to occupy Mia's old apartment before the new year. After convincing the landlord to let them into their new place early, Macy and Mia had moved everything but the heavy furniture into their shared apartment. They resorted to sleeping on a mattress in the living room until EJ and Jaq had the chance to help move their beds. Mia was thrilled for consistent company.

"What a relief! I was so done with the rando roomies," Macy stated on their first day in the apartment.

"I don't know how you did it," Mia said.

"You're lucky you missed the dorms freshman year. It was fun, but man, I don't miss living with strangers."

Even after their steamy history, Mia and Macy still found great comfort in each another's company. Once they moved in, Mia was grateful that Macy acted like nothing had happened. The halt of action had been a blessing in disguise.

Macy came home the day after her last final with grocery bags looped around her arms.

"It's Christmas time," Macy sang. She pulled a bottle of spirits from a brown bag, "Thank you, EJ."

That night, Mia and Macy bordered their patio and living room with multicolored lights. They bought a small tree and adorned it with strands of popcorn and cranberries. The cheerful décor was fueled by a cheap bottle of White Zinfandel, holiday movies, and pricked fingers.

The Tuesdaze were booked to play for the Loop's holiday bash on December twenty-third, and it was all they could think about. Every year, the Loop's event was highly anticipated by those staying in Birchmont for break. It would be the last time the Tuesdaze got together before each of them, except for Mia, spent a stretch of time with their families.

When the Tuesdaze asked about Mia's holiday plans and why she wasn't going home, she grasped for an excuse.

"Plane tickets are too expensive," Mia bluffed. "I can't afford it, and my parents just visited this fall. Plus, the weather out east isn't looking so good, and I don't want to spend Christmas in an airport."

To Mia's relief, the Tuesdaze asked minimal questions to avoid emphasizing her holiday alone.

"Well, I will be here until we *have* to go," Tiffany had responded. "I can't spend my entire break with family anymore. I learned that lesson after going home for nearly a month last year."

"Same here," Macy agreed. "These days, I don't even talk to people back home."

Tiffany's family lived just an hour away. Rather than go home and come back for the show, she stayed in Birchmont at Macy and Mia's apartment.

EJ and his brother left for home right after their last class of the semester, an entire week before the concert. Mia was envious of their early completion of Finals. The Jaquez brothers came back the night before the gig. Mr. and Mrs. Jaquez accompanied their sons.

After a final practice for the show, Mia and Macy gave the Jaquez brothers a tour of their new apartment. The brothers arrived with tinfoil covered trays, sent by Mrs. Jaquez. Mia struggled to find a place in the kitchen for the food.

"It's still coming together," Mia said as she looked around at the half-empty boxes and displaced appliances. "We're going to invite everyone over once we're settled in!"

"No doubt," Macy agreed. "And tell Mrs. Jaquez we need her to make our party food! These tamales are off the chain!"

EJ laughed.

"In our living room, we have our band poster from that Lakehouse gig," EJ explained. "Ma saw it and told me to 'bring those pretty girls some treats.' Vaughn might not be so quick to leave if Ma keeps bringing us grub. I think he ate more than me and my brother combined."

Mia did her best to downplay her emotions surrounding Vaughn's dwindling time. His offer to join TRN's team had been unexpected, but the more Mia considered the proposition, the more scenarios played out in her head. Scenarios where she took him up on the offer. The places she could visit throughout history.

Every night, Mia asked her magic eight ball what to do but no final decision ever stuck. Mia had everything she'd hoped to gain from Travel: the band, the friends, and the discovery of her genuine identity. On the contrary, she daydreamed of the experiences there were to collect in other years. Mia told herself she was lucky to have options, but her optimism had yet to lead to an answer.

Vaughn was instructed to leave by the dawn of 1998. Whether he liked it or not, he was bound to his contract with the Time Regulatory Network, and they would notify him when they had an open hub to which he could report. The consequences of breaking his contract were something he couldn't even consider. Vaughn put his efforts toward convincing himself that he was ready to go.

When he accepted the task of monitoring the Hayes, Vaughn knew he was blurring the line between his personal and professional life. Rather than deny Jon and Ellie's investment in their children's wellbeing, Vaughn took on the task with confidence. Now, weeks away from his departure, he was disappointed that he'd allowed himself to get tied up with Mia. He broke his own rule of keeping everyone at an arm's length. Vaughn told himself that someday, the time would be right to make a home.

Meanwhile, the clock ticked down to the Loop's holiday bash. Vaughn made sure he had all his belongings for the night out. In his pocket, he felt the gift he intended to give Mia after the show.

Vaughn set off for the Loop. The twenty-third of December had always been one of Vaughn's favorite nights of the year. The pressure of Christmas had yet to set in, and the melancholy of the post-holiday comedown wasn't on people's minds yet. Vacation officially commenced, no matter what era he was in.

Trees glistened in the streetlights. The insulated sounds of the college town were only broken by the snow crunching beneath Vaughn's feet. He took advantage of the moment of solitude before the raging concert on the other side of the Loop's entrance.

The Loop housed a tight crowd for the show. Festive movie posters were hung on the Loop's walls. Tinsel lined the doorways and lights flashed behind the bar.

Lars sat at a high top and tipped back his shot glass, swigging down the potent spirit. He scowled as he watched Vaughn enter and shake hands with one of the Loop's co-owners, Marty's second-in-command. Lars wondered how Vaughn had made connections so quickly when it had taken Lars years to earn the venue owners' trust.

'*And he's leaving so soon,*' Lars thought to himself.

Before Vaughn came to Birchmont, owners and organizers had only looked to Lars to scout bands and connect with artists. Vaughn had begun to take over Lars' role and, even worse in Lars' eyes, was Vaughn's lack of investment in Birchmont. Vaughn was transferring after the first of the year. *Leaving.*

Vaughn had mentioned something about an ailing parent on the west coast, but Lars sensed there was more to the story. Lars sat alone and realized he had been placed on the bench of his own circle of friends. He went to the bar and ordered another shot. Lars concluded that it was to be the last night Vaughn held any of the cards.

"Give it up for the Tuesdaze!"

The crowd cheered as the owner handed the microphone to Macy. The Tuesdaze opened with a fast-paced version of a Christmas classic, revving the audience.

Vaughn smiled and remembered his own college experience as he took in the Loop's scene. He lived on his own terms throughout his adolescence, finally able to stay put rather than be led by his family's commitment to the country. College was the sweet spot between Vaughn's role as a high school misfit and the expectations imposed by adulthood.

Vaughn caught a glimpse of Lars through the crowd and pointed him out to Jaq.

"Check it out, he's blitzed," Vaughn said.

Jaq shook his head.

"Hopefully we don't have to deal with him later," Jaq responded. "Gotta go, I'm up next."

Jaq, an ex-trumpet player for Birchmont's marching band, came in for the upbeat brass bars of the Tuesdaze ska covers. Mrs. Jaquez whistled, and the sound pierced through the crowd. EJ chuckled from behind the drums. Macy worked the growing audience and by the time Mia struck the last chord of their first set, the fans needed a break.

"*Ow oww!*" Macy exclaimed into the mic. "Stick around, we'll be back soon!"

Macy blew a kiss to the crowd and the Tuesdaze exited the stage. They stepped down from the three-foot-tall platform and began their short walk to the Loop's back-alley door.

"Let's get some air," Tiffany said and fanned her face.

The Tuesdaze exited the venue and Marty, the owner, flipped on the music system for intermission. He braced himself for the surge of drink refills. To honor the staff's holiday vacation time, Marty and just two other staff members had absorbed more work than they could handle. Vaughn watched as the Loop's skeleton staff was overwhelmed. He slapped his hand on the sticky bar top to get Marty's attention.

Vaughn cupped his hands around his mouth and shouted, "Need a hand?"

"You got any experience?" Marty asked. "Otherwise, you'll just be in the way."

Vaughn shrugged, "I bartended in college." His offer was met with a look of relief, and Marty waved Vaughn behind the bar.

"Your expertise never ceases to surprise me," the weathered bartender patted Vaughn's back. "Great call on this band! They're almost *too* good! I've never seen the crowd eat a group up like this! Last minute, Lars tried to talk us out of booking them but man, I'm glad we went with our gut."

Lars overheard the compliment and rolled his eyes. He stood up and walked out the front door without paying.

"Asshole," Vaughn said and shook his head.

Once their heads were above water, Vaughn scanned the Loop to locate the Tuesdaze. They were nowhere to be found. Another wave of drink orders were demanded before the second half of the show, and Vaughn threw himself into the task at hand.

In the Loop's back alleyway, the Tuesdaze were refreshed by the cold air. The Cav was parked out back, and the Tuesdaze gathered around the car. Though EJ and his brother were of age, the rest of them had to drink discreetly.

"We're going back in for a drink before the second set. Pop the trunk, then the cork," EJ winked. "There's a bottle of bubbly for you in the back. We will go inside and see how the 'rents are holding up. Keep an eye out," EJ warned, "the fuzz is a little more harsh over the holidays."

EJ and Jaq tried to pull open the Loop's back door, but it was locked. They beat on the door and were let inside. The girls piled into the backseat without starting the engine.

"Can we at least turn it on for a few minutes?" Macy asked. "Why am I even asking? It's my car," she said and reached into her pocket for her keys.

"You heard EJ, the cops are out! We can't draw attention to ourselves. It has to appear as though the Cav is empty. Do you want to tell your parents that you got caught drinking?" Tiffany fretted.

Macy sighed, "You're right. Pop that champagne. It'll warm us up."

Mia unscrewed the wire and bubbles fizzed over. Before a drop of champagne could be wasted on Macy's backseat, Macy snatched the bottle and put her mouth over the opening to consume the foam. The three of them cheered.

"That first set was bitchin'!" Tiffany cheered. "Let's do this forever." She took a more serious tone. "Is it just me or does anyone else have a tough time caring about class when we could make money as musicians?"

"Ugh, I've been thinking about that too," Macy agreed. "Why would I give a shit about calculus when we could just play? If I spent half as much time practicing as I do on studying..." she trailed off.

Macy tipped back the champagne, then offered the bottle to Tiffany and Mia. Mia took the bottle and downed a few long gulps. She passed the champagne to Tiffany.

"Someone's drinking their feelings," Tiffany teased. "What's up?"

Macy and Tiffany looked to Mia for an explanation.

"Nothing!" Mia said. "Macy, you crushed that set, and Tiffany, that bass line was perfect. It's like you said Tiff, I never want to be done playing for the Tuesdaze. There's got to be a way we can do this forever."

"What makes you think we can't?" Macy asked.

"You've just got me thinking with the college talk and making money playing," Mia explained. "Why can't we just do life our own way? Why do we have to follow this… format?"

"Alright, it's time to annihilate this bottle before we all drop out," Macy declared.

They each took another long glug and emptied the champagne. Tiffany and Mia slipped out the side doors and Macy scooted herself from the middle of the backseat. Macy tossed the bottle into a nearby dumpster.

"Stars of the show, and here we are, drinking in an alley," Tiffany laughed. "I can't wait 'til we're twenty-one."

Macy knocked on the Loop's back door. Mia fumbled with her charm bracelet and felt for the Aid. It was gone. She panicked and surveyed the snow-covered ground around her. Mia remembered what had happened the last time she was mindless with the device. Then, she thought of Vaughn. Once he went on without Mia, the Aid would be her only method of communication with him.

Someone opened the Loop's back door and Tiffany turned to face Mia.

"Hey slowpoke, hurry up, it's cold!"

"I, uh," Mia stuttered, "I left, or dropped," she paused to come up with an excuse, "my keys! They're somewhere in the snow." Mia crouched and patted the ground, feigning an urgent search. "Close the door, its fine," Mia assured. "I'll knock when I find them."

"Okay," Tiffany agreed, "but we go back on in five, make it quick," Tiffany snapped her fingers at Mia. "I don't want the manager getting after us."

Mia gave Tiffany a thumbs up and Tiffany closed the door. Mia felt foolish at her own desperation to find the Aid. The action reminded her of people in Original Time who had a toxic relationship with technology; attached to their phones, documenting every moment of their lives for the world's validation. Rather than enjoying the time at hand, they put a screen between themselves and life.

The time in ninety-seven had taught Mia that living in the moment wasn't just a cliche. She saw why Vaughn was so enthused with the lessons offered by each era.

Mia pulled open the Cav's unlocked backdoor as the remaining minutes of their break flew by. She got on her hands and knees after switching on the dome light to assist in her search for the Aid. Mia's ears perked up and she snapped her head back; footsteps clomped through the snow in her direction.

"I like this view," a familiar voice said behind her.

Lars.

He rested his hands on the car's roof, blocking Mia's exit from the backseat. Adrenaline circulated through her body. Mia's focus flipped from finding the Aid to obtaining a weapon. Her gaze darted around the Cav's interior.

"You babes did great in there you know," Lars moved closer to her. She was overwhelmed by the smell of menthols and cologne.

He rested his knees on the edge of the backseat, blocking Mia in.

Lars went on, "You think you're on the way to the big time, don't you? Do you really think you would have gotten on stage tonight without my legwork?"

"Easy Lars, step back," Mia warned, "we have a set to finish, they'll come looking for me in a few minutes," she stated, trying to sound brave.

Mia found her weapon, an ice scraper laying on the floor of the backseat. She wrapped her fingers around the handle. Lars did not heed Mia's warning. He slinked closer to her.

Mustering her strength, Mia slashed his shoulder with the ice scraper. She heard the fabric of his jacket tear. Lars wailed and held the site of Mia's strike. He crippled onto the backseat floor.

Mia made her escape out the opposite side of the vehicle and ran toward the Loop's back door. She scanned the snow for the Aid along the way. Mia made it up the wooden stairs to the door and banged hard. Lars hobbled across the parking lot and grabbed one of Mia's ankles. She lost her balance on the icy stairs, slipped to her knees and Lars dragged her toward him. She extended her fist and rapped on the backdoor as hard as possible.

Lars pulled himself to his feet, blood seeping through his jacket. He stood Mia up against the side of the building and gripped the back of her hair.

"Why are you fighting so hard?" Lars growled. "I'm not that bad! I've given you everything you wanted! Why isn't it enough?"

"In what world do you think this is what I want?!" Mia shouted.

Tiffany whipped open the backdoor. Rage ignited her eyes. Lars' fingers were still entangled in the hair of Mia's nape. Mia's terror subsided.

With expressions of shock, the onlookers surrounding the back door gasped at Lars' behavior. He eased his lock on Mia's hair.

Looks of disdain bore into him. Lars held his hands in the air. Mia kicked her boot into his groin and Lars' knees buckled.

He collapsed onto the slushy floor and curled into a ball. Mia was shaky but empowered by the small bit of justice served.

"Someone get him out of here!" Tiffany pointed at Lars, still crumpled on the floor.

"They're ready for us," Tiffany said and led Mia toward the stage.

On the way, Tiffany explained the situation to Marty and made him ensure an end to Lars' night. They took their spots and, without missing a beat, the Tuesdaze started in on their second set. Lars was left cold in the alley with the door locked behind him.

During a short water break, Vaughn rushed to Mia's side of the stage.

"You okay?" He asked. "I just heard what happened."

Mia nodded.

"I'm fine. This is our night, not his," Mia said.

Vaughn grinned and watched the Tuesdaze make the most of their last show of the year.

The Tuesdaze packed their gear into the Jaquez's van. Inside the Loop, Vaughn was still wrapping up his impromptu shift with their fading audience.

"Ladies, go get some rest," EJ said. "Me and Jaq will unpack tonight."

Mia, Tiffany, and Macy wished the Jaquez family a Merry Christmas and prepared to go their separate ways.

The three girls slept at Macy and Mia's new apartment on their makeshift bed, a mattress on the living room floor. Mia lay awake, wishing she could have caught up with Vaughn after the show. She thought about sneaking out but didn't know if she could pull it off. She also feared that Lars would be lurking on the streets. Mia heard Macy tossing and turning while Tiffany snored.

Between Christmas and the new year, Macy's parents were set to leave for their first seasonal stay in Arizona. Her father would pass his business onto his associate for the winter, and her mother managed to take the season off work; her years spent at the hospital were finally paying off. Though Macy dreaded the days ahead of her family's passive criticism surrounding Macy's lifestyle, she caved into her family's request to come home for Christmas before they left.

Macy's pre-med sister, who had the heart of an angel, was bringing home a new boyfriend to meet the family that year, widening the sibling's contrast to each other.

"Are *you* seeing anyone, Macy?" Macy could hear her mother ask.

Despite the downsides, going home for Christmas was not an option for Macy, but an expectation. Morning came and Macy prepared her bags. She pulled on a set of black sweats and didn't bother to wash off the previous night's makeup. Macy packed a stack of the Tuesdaze's new t-shirts as gifts for her family.

"It won't be so bad, Macy," Mia said, missing her own parents.

Tiffany finally woke up but lay in bed until Macy was fully packed.

"You must have been tired," Mia said to Tiffany.

"Yeah, you were snoring all night!" Macy laughed.

"Knowing that Lars may be sterile after Mia's kick gives me great comfort," Tiffany stated and pushed herself up from the mattress. She went to the kitchen and poured herself a glass of water.

"Mia, are you sure you don't want to come home with me?" Tiffany asked. "I could really use someone to relieve me of kid-time."

"How old are your step-siblings again?" Mia asked.

"Eight and ten. They fluctuate between being little angels and spawns of Satan."

"I couldn't just join your family Christmas," Mia said. "Plus, I've seen your little sisters, they're adorable! You'll be fine."

"If you say so," Tiffany said and hugged Mia goodbye.

"I'd better be off too," Macy sighed. She heaved her duffle bag from the floor. "Already looking forward to New Year's Eve in the city," Macy said.

Tiffany gathered her purse and put on her coat.

"Merry Christmas, Mia," Macy embraced Mia and exited the apartment with Tiffany.

Mia was left with just garlands, lights, and a mini fiber optic tree to celebrate the holiday by herself. Mia laid back down and clicked on the TV. She landed on an old holiday comedy, a Hayes family favorite. Mia could have left with either of her friends, but she knew why she stayed and couldn't let him go without bidding him farewell.

As she watched the film, Mia remembered the decorated tree, standing in her family's living room. She got lost in the daydream and could almost smell the coniferous aroma. Mia recalled her and the twins placing each ornament on its own branch.

Every year, the Hayes siblings alternated choosing the Christmas tree. A smile crept onto Mia's face as she thought of the tree she had selected as a little girl, flocked with gold and red sparkles. Derek always chose the trees with long needles. While the soft needles were beautiful, the ornaments always slipped off its flimsy protrusions.

Cooper had chosen the best trees. Mia's heart ached whenever she remembered that there would be no more Christmases with Cooper. She stood up, steadying herself on the mattress, and went to the kitchen. Mia heated a cup of water in the microwave. Just as Mia stirred the last powdery bits of instant cocoa, her phone rang. She rushed to the phone and hit the big red talk button.

"Hello?"

"Merry Christmas Eve," Vaughn said.

"And to you," Mia replied.

"Would you like some company? The Jaquez family is great, but I feel a bit awkward, the temporary roommate and all," Vaughn admitted. "And the prices of plane tickets to California are astronomical, there's no way I can afford to go see Mom before the holidays," Vaughn chuckled.

"Ah yes, the ailing mother out west. Very compelling."

"I'll head over there right now. I meant to catch up with you last night, but things got so crazy. Are you okay?"

"Yeah," Mia said. "I'm trying to forget it happened."

"You guys really lit up that place. I've got something for you. I want you to have it soon," Vaughn said.

"Please tell me you found my Aid out back," Mia said.

Vaughn replied, "N-not exactly."

"I've got something for you too," Mia lied and smacked her hand to her forehead. "I need to shower and do some unpacking," she stated, hoping to stall Vaughn so she could rummage for a gift.

"Alright, is a half hour good?"

"Yeah, that's fine."

"See you soon," Vaughn replied and hung up.

Mia rifled through her boxes for something formidable. In the process of her search, Mia absorbed the disastrous state of her and Macy's new apartment. The previous night's stage-outfit candidates were scattered across the floor. Mia collected the colorful tops, skirts, and tights and shoved them back into boxes. Her quick, careless actions caused her grandma's bracelet to snag on a fishnet. Mia shrieked; she'd already lost one important charm in the last twenty-four hours. She looked down and saw that the silver jump ring, which bound the eight-ball charm to her bracelet, was caught.

To free the precious heirloom from the stockings, Mia spun the tiny, metal loop. Despite her delicate efforts, the jump ring bent open, and the charm fell off.

Mia halted her gift search. She held the tiny figure in her palm and admired the eight ball, the omen of chance. Mia knew just what to give to Vaughn for Christmas.

She looked for the hemp string she and Macy had used to craft jewelry months before. Mia found the string taped onto the front of one of Macy's autumn magazine issues.

Mia slid the string through the eight-ball charm's small loop, then held the bracelet-in-progress around her own wrist. Mia gave the bracelet more slack to fit on Vaughn's wrist and cut the end of the string. The gift was complete.

Mia went on to tidy the apartment while playing a hypothetical conversation in her head. She mustered the strength to let Vaughn down and did her best to gather the right words. Mia told herself that the decision would serve both of their best interests.

A knock at the door caused Mia to jump. She was edgy from the lack of sleep and her heart raced. Mia passed by her reflection

310

in a mirror. She scowled at her plaid flannel pants and frumpy sweatshirt.

'*Too late to do much now.*'

She let her hair down from its silk scrunchy and attempted a playful tousle. Mia applied her cherry lip gloss. She shoved the remainder of the living room's clutter into a closet. Mia looked through the peephole. Vaughn awaited on the other side, and she unlocked the door.

"Ooh," he said as he looked around her apartment. "So festive," he smiled at Mia and rested his hands on her hips.

Vaughn pulled her in for a long kiss. Under the multicolored lights, his skin glowed magenta, green, and gold. Though she told herself to start pulling back from him, now that she was in front of Vaughn, Mia couldn't resist him. Cracks began to form in her once concrete decision.

"Cocoa?" Mia offered and started toward the kitchen.

"Yes please," Vaughn said. "Actually, want me to run to the corner store and grab some peppermint schnapps?"

"That sounds fantastic," Mia replied.

"Be right back."

The door closed behind Vaughn, and Mia resolved to harness the extra time alone. She needed to collect her thoughts. A pep talk was in order if she was to adhere to her plan and remain in the nineties. The more time that she spent with Vaughn, the less clear her choice became.

The inability to shake Lars also tempted her to reconsider leaving.

Mia focused her efforts on Vaughn's gift which needed wrapped. Mia remembered the stack of magazines in Macy's bedroom and decided to use one of the pages to conceal Vaughn's bracelet. She began to sift through the collection.

'Macy won't miss one page of one issue.'

Mia scanned the publications' bindings for the most outdated magazine.

'October 1997, December 1997,' Mia read, *'September 1997!'* She slid the old issue from the pile.

A wave of emotion hit Mia; September was when she first began to play with the Tuesdaze. The magazine was instantly more special, but her heart dropped when she saw the cover.

Smiling back at Mia was the lost princess.

Mia traced her finger along the glossy image. She was told about the incredible mourning period following the royal loss but didn't fully understand until that moment. As she flipped through the pages, her heart ached. The reality of the past set in.

Mia heard Vaughn's footsteps approaching the front door. He knocked and Mia hugged the magazine to her chest to show him. She tucked the unwrapped bracelet into her pocket and went to open the door.

Vaughn made his way back into the apartment with a brown paper bag in hand. He kissed her and his cold nose brushed against Mia's cheek.

"No hot cocoa?" He asked.

In the rush to wrap his present, Mia had forgotten to heat the water.

"Sorry, I found this," she showed him the magazine from Macy's room. "Look at the cover. The losses, the things that people go through in these times you visit," Mia started, "this all means so much to them. This time is all they *have.*"

Vaughn was stung by Mia's statement. He often questioned the advantage of being a visitor rather than a resident. Guilt began to pour in.

"Here," Vaughn walked to the kitchen. He opened a cupboard and pulled out a mug. "I will make the cocoa; you go find a good movie."

A lump rose in Mia's throat. She was frustrated, not with Vaughn, but with his contracted commitment to detachment. Mia clicked through the channels, paying little attention to what flicked across the screen.

Vaughn made his way back into the living room with two peppermint-spiked hot chocolates. He handed Mia her mug and carefully lowered himself onto the mattress. Mia didn't know what to say, so she continued to channel surf.

"Stop," Vaughn said.

Mia thought Vaughn was about to call out her spiteful response to his predicament, until she realized she'd landed on her holiday favorite, 'the Nutcracker.' It wasn't just any Nutcracker movie; it was *the* Nutcracker famously choreographed by the unmatched Baryshnikov.

"I remember Derek saying how he hated watching this every year," Vaughn scooted next to Mia and playfully elbowed her. "He said you and your mom fell asleep to it every Christmas Eve."

Mia smiled at the memory.

"I miss them," Mia said. "Think it's possible for me to take a last-minute trip home for the holidays?"

Vaughn sighed and shook his head.

"Not this year," he said. "I work for TRN, and *I* can't even get home 'til after the holidays."

Rather than dwell on the distance between themselves and their families, they watched the magical ballet. For the next hour and twenty minutes, Mia was swept away by the timeless Suite. She laid her head on Vaughn's shoulder.

On the screen, young Clara peered out the foggy window to watch the falling snow. Mia could imagine how the ballerina's character felt. Both had been living in a dream world, and a break in the fantasy arrived. Vaughn approached the end of his allotted time. Mia reminded herself that Vaughn didn't depart by his own choice, he had an obligation to fulfill, and Mia knew her affection wasn't making it any easier for him to leave.

The triumphant credits rolled, and Vaughn pulled a small box from his pocket.

"For you," he stated, "and for me."

Mia took the gift from Vaughn and ran her fingers over the shiny paper. She tore back the wrapping and opened the box. Inside was something that looked like the Aid, but slightly different. It was larger and more oblong. After losing her Aid outside of the Loop, Mia didn't know when she would obtain another one of the gadgets.

"Is this some other version of the Aid?" Mia asked.

"It's the UpgrAid," Vaughn explained. "You can see, it's a different shape, but there are updated features with this new model. I can't believe it, but the hub here in Birchmont got a small batch of them. A Christmas miracle!" He chuckled. "The device is like the Aid, but we can communicate more effectively. It's not just for emergencies. I'm making sure Derek gets one of these after the new year too. Production is finally back on track. We can really keep in touch through this. It's like texting, we can actually have a conversation."

Vaughn fished a device from his pocket, identical to the gadget he gave Mia. He slid it open, and Mia saw that there was a small screen once the device was extended.

"You can call me any time, even just to catch up," he said.

Mia's answer to his offer was written all over her face. Vaughn attempted to make peace with her decision.

"I've loved being here with you," Vaughn said. "But my time is up, and I've got to keep moving. I don't want this to be good-bye, but I know you've got more here that you want to fulfill."

Mia pressed her lips together to keep the lump in her throat in check.

"I'm really going to miss you," Mia uttered. A tear streaked down her cheek. "But you're right. I can't go, not now. Not while we've got a chance as a band." Mia prayed that she wouldn't regret the decision.

Vaughn was about to remind her of the dangers fame posed to Time Travelers, but Mia interrupted.

"Close your eyes."

Mia sat tall and pulled the bracelet from her pocket. She laid Vaughn's forearm across her lap and tied the bracelet around his wrist.

"Okay, open."

Vaughn grinned at the token.

"One of Valerie's charms? Mia, I can't take this."

He thought back to the night he asked Mia to come with him and remembered her magic eight-ball. He pulled Mia in and wrapped his arms around her.

"Thank you, Mia, for everything," Vaughn said. "A piece of you will always be with me now," he held up the bracelet. "If the eight-ball ever gives you another answer, I'll come back for you somehow. I promise."

Snow covered the sidewalks and swirled through the air, adding even more whimsy to their holiday in the city. The

315

flurries which had ushered Jon and Ellie into the theater had grown into a sparkling blanket after the ballet concluded.

Ellie buried her chin in the fur coat she had donned to the theater. The aroma of their pre-show dinner hung in the fabric.

Their hotel was within walking distance of the theater, and she and Jon shuffled through the snow, laughing like children. They halted at the crosswalk for a red light. Ellie paced, excited to get back to their room and change into their robes for the night.

"It's so cold! Maybe we should consider going somewhere warmer next year," Ellie said.

Finally, the light turned green. Jon took Ellie by the hand, and they scurried across the street. He looked at his wife's beautiful face. Her skin was illuminated, and Jon saw her eyes widen. He followed her gaze, and, within an instant, Jon saw the brightness of an oncoming car. Then nothing.

Chapter XIII

Dr. Lowell heard footsteps outside his office. Every action he had made since starting with the Time Regulatory Network moved to the forefront of his mind. For the first time in months, he thought of the first clinical tests he did with Psilopram and his stomach turned. Dr. Lowell opened his desk drawer and reached for his bottle of pills. He popped open the lid and dry-swallowed a capsule. He wondered if he should take another for the pending conversation with TRN's Chief Operations Officer, Adrian Glass.

The door handle turned, and Adrian walked into Dr. Lowell's office.

Adrian looked at Dr. Lowell with his usual, unreadable expression. Dr. Lowell felt foolish for anticipating any warmth during Mr. Glass's personal visit to his workplace.

"Make yourself comfortable, Mr. Glass. I don't know what this meeting is about, but I know how busy it's been around here, and I thank you for taking time to meet with me," Dr. Lowell said. "There must be a pressing issue."

"Busy is an understatement," Adrian scoffed. "But yes, I believe the matter which I'd like to discuss is worthy of our time. We must come up with a solution and word of your," Adrian hesitated, "unconventional thought process has circulated throughout the North Wing."

"Well, hopefully I can live up to the expectation. Thank you for meeting in my office. I could have come over to meet you in the North Wing. Perhaps I could meet some of your colleagues who promised my thoughts on the matter," Dr. Lowell replied.

"I fear we would have risked too many cooks in the kitchen," Adrian said. "I wanted to discuss this situation with you alone. It's hard to get anything done over there. Lots of red tape, you know. Plus, this area seems quiet tonight."

Dr. Lowell shrugged.

"Funny you say that," Dr. Lowell responded. "People must finally be clearing out. It is the holiday season. For the last couple of months, there's been someone here at all hours."

"Might there be listening ears?"

"I doubt it. You know the walls are very insulated. You oversaw TRN's move-in to this building. Plus, it's the day before Christmas Eve," Dr. Lowell assured, "many of this wing's staff are working with Travelers face to face; monitoring or styling. The staff has been incredibly busy. Not that the North Wing isn't equally as chaotic," Dr. Lowell backtracked. He wiped the beading sweat from his forehead. "What is it you wanted to discuss?"

Adrian sighed.

"Let's cut to the chase. You and I both know we don't have time for this dance. TRN is in trouble. When Travel started, everyone was in. It was deemed safe. People were leaving our current era and we were beginning to make strides in our planet's recovery. Now, they're returning. They're running home scared. That damn Aid," Adrian gritted his teeth. He slammed his fist on Dr. Lowell's desk causing Dr. Lowell to jump. "I had a feeling it was a bad idea. All the sudden, ensuring TRN hubs in every year since 1910 with a facility every hundred miles is considered insufficient. Now we must have a safety device at their fingertips."

"I'm sorry," Dr. Lowell said. "I didn't realize the device was such a topic of stress. I knew about the halt in this last round of distribution, but I didn't know there was so much hesitancy surrounding the device's release."

"There was hesitancy alright. And we should have listened to our instincts. Yes, it's handy for those in sticky situations, but since the Aid was distributed, hundreds of Travelers have returned home. They signal yellow for every questionable situation, and we don't have enough staff to support them. Though I will say, less staff to take my time has led me to a possible... solution for all this. A solution I can control with less input from those working on Aid distribution."

"The Aid *was* distributed to keep Travelers safe," Dr. Lowell stated. "And you're-you're *okay* with the shortage?"

The look in Adrian Glass' eyes made Dr. Lowell regret his words. Dr. Lowell broke eye contact. He wished he would have taken more pills.

"The Travelers are getting reckless and, with the Aid's help, now our government knows that there are inevitable..." Adrian pursed his lips, "oversights at TRN. They're shifting funding away from Travel. Some states are looking at pulling *all* their funding from TRN. They're considering calling Travelers to come home."

Dr. Lowell shook his head.

"Look, the point is this," Adrian continued. "We need to do two things and it's going to take every department's effort. First, we need to restructure our staff. Stylists, researchers, they need to become monitors. Maybe even adjustors. We've got to cut the fluff. Travelers can figure out style on their own. Second, I need your lead on something, an urgent project we have in the works."

Dr. Lowell's skin prickled.

"What do you need me to do?" He asked.

"Travelers, they trust you. So do your colleagues and staff. They all see you as this…" Adrian paused, "guru. Like a leader for their spiritual quest. Our problem is that Travelers are returning. It's killing our plan to restore the earth's resources.

We've interviewed those who have returned, and many aren't coming back because they didn't like their chosen era, but because they have commitments here. They must come back and see family, carry out their job, maybe they just come back because it's familiar, but we don't know for certain. That's what I want you to research. I want you to find out their reason for returning. I want specifics: family members they're returning for, jobs they've come back to fulfill, we need to know the cords that are keeping them here. While many are without the Aid, we'll figure out how to sever their cords with OT."

"What?" Dr. Lowell asked. "This seems unnecessary. You said it brilliantly yourself, in your last press conference. You said the technology was advancing so efficiently that Travelers can go back and forth as they please," Dr. Lowell stalled. He understood. "That wasn't true, was it?"

"They can go back and forth, but our original projection of the influx was way off, and the funding has *got* to be there for daily operations to continue. Of anyone, Dr. Lowell, I figured you would understand how dire this is. In the end, Travelers' absence from our current era is what propels our planet forward.

While they're living on another plane, we can recover. And that's why you invested your time and knowledge into Psilopram, right? Recovery. If they all come back now, if they stay attached to what's familiar, the hope to stabilize our planet is toast. You've forgotten that all of this is for the greater good."

Dr. Lowell sighed.

"Can't we just focus on getting more private investors? You have no shortage of connections."

Adrian shook his head.

"Aside from my contributions, many of the other investors have pulled their investment in Travel. They're in another era, retired in their forties, making the most of the Travelers' rate of exchange. The investors are the Travelers I'd welcome back with open arms, but they don't care about this era now that they're settled back into their glory days. I'm holding this whole operation on my shoulders."

Adrian leaned forward.

"If we don't do something soon, if we don't restructure or act on ways to keep people in the past, the capability of Travel will fizzle out. There will be a mass exodus away from past eras back to Original Time. The system will fail, especially if we can't supply the technology to return to OT. We're walking a tightrope. If we don't get them to stay, just long enough for our current era's recovery, our finances will slip and people will be stranded in the past, not by choice. Even worse, those benefiting from Psilopram…" Adrian gave Dr. Lowell a once-over, "will no longer have their supply. How will we keep up the drug's production without funding?"

Dr. Lowell rubbed his hands down his cheeks.

"Did you really have to drop this on me around the holidays?"

"It's the best time to figure out why people are coming back," Adrian answered. "Let's call it a night. We'll talk more tomorrow. First thing."

After taking more pills, Dr. Lowell wandered around the halls of the hub. He couldn't return to his empty house with so many thoughts in his head. Dr. Lowell resolved to remain at TRN until the Psilopram kicked in, then, he would lock himself in his office to process. He heard activity coming from the styling area. Laughter. A welcome sound to lift the weight of TRN's predicament.

Dr. Lowell stepped out of his office and rounded the corner toward the styling area. Francis Platt and her stylist were the only two left in the South Wing. Francis was startled when she saw Dr. Lowell out of the corner of her eye, then realized it was him and began to laugh.

"Sounds like this is the place to be tonight!" Dr. Lowell stated.

"You scared me! I thought it was just me and Rae."

"There's always someone around," Dr. Lowell said. "You'd know if you stayed past five every once in a while," he teased.

Rae, the stylist, rested her hands on Francis' shoulders.

"What do you think of her new look?" Rae asked.

Francis couldn't stop looking at herself in the mirror. Rae had transformed her outdated hairstyle into something fresh and modern. Francis felt younger, lighter.

Dr. Lowell smiled.

"Looks wonderful, Mrs. Platt," he said.

Rae looked at the clock.

"Did you need a trim?" She asked.

"No," Dr. Lowell responded. "I best be getting back to my office. Some things came up."

Francis sighed. "I'm guessing you came in here for help?"

Dr. Lowell hesitated. The burden of knowing Adrian's perspective on TRN's future was all-consuming. Dr. Lowell wondered if Francis, a lawyer, and an original TRN employee like himself, would have an innovative approach to the growing problem.

"I don't know, maybe," Dr. Lowell said. "Not many people know about it yet."

Rae got the cue. She cleaned her station and began to pack her equipment for the night.

"Be ready for full books," Francis said to Rae. "All the nineties' kids are yours."

Francis ran her fingers through her hair one more time and started down the hallway with Dr. Lowell. Their offices were

323

right next to each other in the South Wing which served as the Time Traveler-facing division of TRN. She noticed Dr. Lowell's forehead was shiny with perspiration.

"What's going on?" Francis asked.

Dr. Lowell ushered her into his office and shut the door behind them. Dr. Lowell collapsed on his leather sofa and Francis sat in a chair to face him.

"Adrian Glass met with me tonight. I'm sorry to put this on you, but there's a lot of change about to be put in motion. I don't want you to be blindsided and," Dr. Lowell rubbed his eyes, "you were right. I need your help."

"Whatever it is, I'm not sure I want to know right now," Francis said. "Can it wait until after the holidays?"

"Yeah, go home. I'm sorry to trouble you," Dr. Lowell replied.

Francis noticed that his desk drawer was open.

'Psilopram.'

"Are you meeting anyone tonight doctor?" She asked. "Or will you be alone?"

Dr. Lowell replied, "I'm staying here. Hopefully figuring out how to deal with this."

"Looks like you've had a little help dealing with it," Francis said and gestured to the desk drawer. "How much did you take?"

"Go," Dr. Lowell instructed, "before I spill the beans."

Francis sighed and made her way to the door. As she turned the knob, she gave into her curiosity.

"Tell me but make it quick. And know that I'm not *doing* anything about it until after Christmas. My daughter and son-in-law are coming back tomorrow, and I've got a lot to do before they arrive. I'm not spending the night here."

"Adrian said TRN's about to go through serious restructuring. Stylists will be asked to go through training to become monitors and adjustors. He thinks we need more staff sprinkled throughout the eras to compensate for the Aid's distribution error. It's like he's planning to clear out our hub.

He's worried about funding too. He thinks that the progress being made with the dispersed population will be offset by returning Travelers. He thinks the government's initial support will wane," Dr. Lowell leaned into his couch. "He wants me to figure out why Travelers aren't staying in their chosen era and report back to him with data."

"What's his plan once he knows why they're coming back?" Francis asked. "Banish them to the past? We can't do that."

"I know. I've been asking myself the same thing since he assigned me this task. What evil is this data going to support? But then, I think to myself, what if we *do* lose funding and Travelers are left with no connection to Original Time? We can get ahead of it now, or we can wait for everything to unravel."

Francis took a moment to process the information.

"You're right." Francis said.

They sat in silence for a few minutes. Dr. Lowell closed his eyes and Francis wondered if his Psilopram had kicked in. A knock at the door startled Francis. She smacked her forehead as she noticed she'd left the door open a crack. Francis peeked her head out to see who still lingered.

"Hello?" Francis said into the hallway.

"Sorry to interrupt." Rae handed over Francis' car keys. "These must have fallen out of your purse."

"I'll be needing those soon. Thank you for bringing them all the way down here."

"Of course," Rae muttered. "I'd better be going."

"Want me to walk out with you?" Francis offered. She wondered how much Rae heard.

"No, that's okay. I got a good spot this morning. Got here early. You know, the holiday season," Rae said. "Living on coffee and the occasional cookie."

"Here, I'll walk you out," Francis closed the door before Rae could see Dr. Lowell on the sofa, dropped into his trance. "What have you got planned for the holidays?" Francis asked.

"I'm finally Traveling for my own enjoyment," Rae said. "A friend of mine, Eva, is meeting me in the nineties. We booked the trip last summer. She and I went to cosmetology school together and have stayed friends ever since."

"How fun! How long are you staying?" Francis asked.

"Hopefully a couple of weeks," Rae answered. "I guess it depends on how long they'll give me."

"Thanks for walking me all the way out here," Rae said.

"It's the least I could do for this new look. I feel wonderful right now," Francis smiled. "I can't wait to pass another mirror. I didn't know how much I needed this change."

"Thank you for the referrals. I'd better enjoy this vacation. Sounds like it might be the last one I take for a while."

Francis' stomach turned.

326

"What did you hear?" She asked.

Rae shook her head.

"I can't believe they're restructuring. I've finally started to get busy as a stylist. Now, they're going to pull me in another direction?"

"We don't know for certain yet," Francis responded. "We've known that the returns to Original Time are problematic for the grand scheme of things, but you're right. They can't take people from their calling just to monitor and adjust. I'll see if I can do something about it."

Rae nodded.

"Thanks, Francis. Now get home, show that husband of yours the new you."

Francis gave Rae a half-hearted smile.

"See ya in the new year, kid."

Rae's hands shook as she dialed up the volume.

"Hello?" Eva answered.

"The whispers are true," Rae said. "I heard it tonight. They're pulling staff from our wing to monitor and adjust."

Eva was silent.

"Yeah, I didn't know what to say either. I overheard Dr. Lowell and Francis talking about it."

"They're just speaking about it in the open? Like it means nothing?" Eva asked.

"No, we're not that lowly to them yet. That, or they don't respect us enough to give us a heads up. Francis forgot her keys in my chair after her appointment and I saw her heading toward

Dr. Lowell's office. I still wonder if there's something going on there."

"With the way Mr. Platt treats her, I wouldn't blame Francis for stepping out," Eva said.

"Me either. Anyway, it sounds like Glass is making moves. We should try to bump up our trip. Or at least get to the nineties and have some fun before they make us work on our vacation."

"It's gonna take me a minute to process this. We *just* got busy in the salon."

"That's exactly what I said to Francis. She said she'll try to help. I believe her, but I don't know about Dr. Lowell. He's too spineless," Rae stated. "I think he'll do whatever Glass wants."

"He does what he's gotta do. We all do. And you and I both know we'll both continue doing it."

"I know," Rae admitted. "But it's so unfair. The whole world has discounted our industry and now TRN, the ones who were supposed to fix everything are yanking us around with complete disregard for our craft?"

"You started out too hopeful at that place," Eva said.

"I'm figuring that out more and more."

As Rae spoke with Eva, she suspected that TRN had access to their conversation through the UpgrAid but didn't care. Beginning that holiday season, the South Wing employees were required to bring the UpgrAid home with them. Stylists were on call to accommodate Travelers who opted to invest in a last-minute session. Physicians, legal representatives, scientists, and support staff were also on call for the busier-than-anticipated season.

"Well, thanks for the heads up," Eva said. "Let's meet for lunch tomorrow to get our trip in motion."

"Sounds good, see you then," Rae said and hung up.

Light grew visible on the eastern horizon. Dr. Lowell approached the employee entrance and scanned himself inside the TRN hub. He looked at the entryway clock.

7:30.

Thirty minutes until Adrian Glass was due to visit his office. Dr. Lowell turned the knob to his office door and hurried to his desk to collect his thoughts before the meeting. After starting a fire to add as much warmth as possible into the space, Dr. Lowell furrowed his brow at a legal pad which he didn't remember setting on his desk. The top sheet was blank. As he flipped through the pages, he saw that the entire pad was blank.

Then, what had happened in his Psilopram haze the night before came back to Dr. Lowell. He pulled the decryption glass from his pocket and began to read Francis' letter.

"He's arrogant and dangerous," Francis had said as she drove Dr. Lowell home. "He's got everyone under his spell with the cool decryption glass, and the Aid, and the newsletter, but his façade doesn't work on me."

"Francis, keep it down," Dr. Lowell replied, paranoid. "We don't know when they might choose to listen in through our devices."

"I don't care what they can hear. I want to meet with Glass and speak to him myself. We have committed to advocating for the Travelers and we must remain a united front."

"Francis, I respect your care for our clients, but Glass is right. Either we maintain the improvements made since Travel was opened to the public or we backslide, and we're all screwed. We were too generous. Too shortsighted in our offerings. TRN promised the Travelers, *we* promised, that they could go back and forth as they please. Then we gave them the Aid in case they fucked up and couldn't deal with the consequences. Now, they're using the device as a crutch. They're demanding even more with the UpgrAid and skipping eras without telling us to go see friends and family.

The projections for cleaning up the planet show notable promise. If we can just get people to stay where they are for a while, to be responsible and not lean so heavily on the support of the Aid, we can fix up this place for their return," Dr. Lowell rambled.

Francis was quiet for the next few blocks. She pulled up to Dr. Lowell's darkened home. She shifted the vehicle into park and the doors unlocked.

"Good night, Dr. Lowell."

Dr. Lowell turned to face Francis. Her freshly lightened hair glowed in the streetlights. Despite Dr. Lowell's panicked state of mind, he was comforted by Francis' presence.

"Go inside," she said.

Dr. Lowell looked at his front steps. The stairs looked slick and forlorn, almost as unappealing as the lonely interior of his home. He stepped outside and closed the door. Rather than climb his stairs, he walked around to the driver's side and tapped on Francis' window.

She laughed to herself and lowered the glass.

"Care to join me for a drink? Perhaps you can shed light on how I should best approach this conversation tomorrow."

Francis smirked and nudged Dr. Lowell toward the door.

"Join you for a drink, huh?"

"And keep me company," Dr. Lowell admitted. "I could use a distraction from all this."

"Dr. Lowell, you've already decided your course of action. Now, let me have the night to decide if I'm going to comply with this new demand. I'll let you know my stance by tomorrow. Use this," Francis pulled her decryption glass from her pocket.

"Why are you giving me this? What if you need it?" Dr. Lowell said and handed the glass back to her.

"Do you still have yours?" Francis asked.

Dr. Lowell scratched his head. He couldn't remember the last time he used the decryption glass, let alone where he'd left it.

"That's what I thought. They're pointless. A glass made by Glass. How thoughtful of him," Francis said. "Tell him I don't need it."

"What about your Glass pen? They only gave those to the Notaries. You only want to write, not to read?" Dr. Lowell teased.

"If I ever need that piece of glass again, I'll know where to find one."

Before Dr. Lowell could ask Francis to elaborate, she rolled up her window and drove away.

Dr. Lowell set Francis' decryption glass on the legal pad. He wondered when she'd snuck into his office. Dr. Lowell's heart rate accelerated as he hurried to read the letter before Glass arrived.

'Dr. Lowell,

I'm writing this letter to you in confidence, hoping that we've established some level of trust with one another. Keep Glass in check today. Though he'll say you're simply collecting data to evaluate specific reasons for Travelers' return, remember what he may do with that data. I will not be in the office today as I am meeting with a somewhat exclusive group we've formed here in the South Wing.

We are discussing an idea which I think will be of interest to you. If you would like to know more, join us this afternoon at 3:00 at the address below. Hope to see you there.

Destroy this letter.

Francis'

Eva and her boyfriend, Josh, were the first to ring Rae's doorbell.

Rae unlocked her door and invited her friends inside.

"Eva, Josh, come in. Get us started," Rae said.

Josh sat down and pulled a device from his pocket. It was the same size and shape as the rectangular UpgrAid but served the opposite purpose. Josh snapped the device onto the UpgrAid.

"You sure I shouldn't wait for Francis?" Josh asked.

"She's running late. We'll show her when she gets here. If it works, that is," Rae answered.

Eva grinned.

"Here we go."

"TRN," Eva said. "TRN, TRN, TRN. Time Regulatory Network. Green, Yellow, Red. Original Time. Current Era. Acclimate. Adrian Glass. Dr. Lowell. Francis Platt. Dr. Chandra. The stylists. Time Travel."

Eva went on to spout as many Time Travel associated keywords as she could, including some of her clients' names. After the outburst, they sat in silence. Five minutes dragged by. The three of them jumped up when Josh's phone rang. He switched on his speakerphone.

"What's the word?" He asked.

The voice on the other end replied.

"Nothing. The block works."

"If we are forced to monitor," Rae grinned, "we're doing it without TRN in the room."

Dr. Lowell ripped Francis' letter into pieces and tossed it into his fireplace. He watched the shreds blacken until they were decimated by the flame. He wished he could do the same with the obligation to which he was about to comply. To shred it up and make it disappear. But he knew from his past that nothing disappeared, it was always somewhere within the ethos, whether it resided in the mind, body, soul, or generational karma, things couldn't disappear, they could only be transmuted.

Dr. Lowell was determined to transmute TRN's chokehold approach on their troublesome situation into a gentler method. Adrian Glass' swift knock at the door snapped Dr. Lowell back into the situation. Francis' warning weighed on his heart.

"Come in," Dr. Lowell said.

Adrian walked into the room. His outfit was crisp, and his eyes were clear.

"Take a seat," Dr. Lowell gestured to an empty chair.

"Before I sit down, I must know, are you in or not?" Adrian asked.

Dr. Lowell broke eye contact and nodded slowly.

"Yes!" Adrian said. "Thank you for coming to a decision so quickly. I knew you were a smart man. You've taken all the right opportunities here, Dr. Lowell. Don't think it's gone unnoticed."

"I can't say I'm as well-rested as you appear," Dr. Lowell stated. "You've asked me to collect data. And I will do that. But I am concerned with what you will do with it. I must say, my mind goes to dark places when I put the pieces together. I will only be involved with what is best for the greater good if it doesn't affect the lives of those we serve."

"We serve all of our planet, Dr. Lowell. Do we not?" Adrian asked.

Dr. Lowell craved Francis' adherence to ethics as Adrian grew more convincing. He couldn't argue his superior's point.

Adrian continued, "Look, I remember you telling me that, in the past, that you've been unable to continue in your previous line of work because of your connection to the patients. And I understand, you're a human, not a robot. However, there are sacrifices to be made for the success of the grand scheme.

None of this is about *you*. Rather than weaving *yourself* into this situation, just get us the data. We'll take care of it from there. And when food is again naturally abundant, when trash doesn't flood city streets, when the seasons have regulated and become what we remember from our childhood, you can say you had something to do with it."

Dr. Lowell gazed at his crackling fire, took a deep breath, and extended his hand to Adrian Glass.

About the Author

Hallie Baur, historical fiction novelist and poet, has put ink to paper since early childhood. She views the world through a nostalgic window and uses her fascination with the past to transplant readers into the story's setting.

Baur lives in Des Moines, Iowa with her husband. When she's not writing, she can be found in her studio, making her way to the front row of a concert, and exploring new places.